D0456251

INTO
THE
BLUE

INTO THE BLUE

pene henson

interlude press • new york

interlude ✦ press • new york

*For Cameron and Misha—clear-eyed critics,
exceptional humans and generous friends.*

*"Those who live by the sea can hardly form a single
thought of which the sea would not be part."*
—Hermann Broch

PROLOGUE

IT'S ONE OF THOSE BRIGHT evenings. The ocean breathes under their boards and rolls itself into perfect, heavy barrels. Tai runs a hand over his face. The saltwater stings his eyes. Beside him, Ollie squints into the sun. They've been out for hours now. Same as yesterday; same as the day before. Long enough that the sun's settled down and the water's nearly black beneath them. When the waves curl up and over, light breaks through and turns the water glassy green and turquoise and gold.

Most of the kids their age have already gone home. But Pipeline's turning sweetly. There's always time to chase one more wave.

"Top five breaks," Tai says in a pause between sets.

"Based on what?" Ollie asks, his gaze on the incoming surf. "Consistency? Whether it barrels? Height? I don't know, the epic wave we'll still talk about when we're fifty?"

"Based on what you want to ride, Ollie," Tai laughs. "Five breaks. Anywhere in the world."

"Okay." They let another set slide under them. There's nothing worth catching in it. "I'd start with this one," Ollie says. "Obviously."

"Obviously." Tai grins. They agreed years ago that Pipeline was in all of their top fives.

Ollie points out a wave with his chin. "Incoming."

Tai's already turning toward shore. He drops flat and paddles. They might still be the kids out here, but they catch almost everything they go after. The wave picks him up easily. Tai stands and flies toward shore. The deck of his board is steady; the water surges beneath his feet. He tumbles off and turns his board to head back out. There's no point wasting the last light.

Another wave rolls in. Even in silhouette, Tai recognizes the surfer on the lip, making perfect turns. No one rides a wave like Ollie. Water fans from the tail of his board and catches the golden light. Tai waits so they can make their way out together. Ollie's eyes are bright with the exhilaration of a ride. Tai and Ollie paddle in unison. "Okay. Five breaks. Here you go. Pipeline, J-Bay, Teahupo'o in Tahiti, one of the big breaks in Australia, and... that island you read about in Indonesia."

"Mentawai." Tai thinks about it. "That's a good list. Maybe I'll come along."

"Of course you will," Ollie says. That's never been a question.

The surf's dropping. The sun dips lower. They need to be home before it's too dark to see.

"I'm gonna head," Tai says. "Come to my place for dinner. Momma's cooking so there's plenty for you."

Ollie scrunches up his face. "I wish. I'm starving. But Mom's at work late, so Jaime's home alone."

"That's easily fixed. Bring him along."

They catch the next wave side by side, weaving all the way to shore. One day, Ollie will be famous. In the meantime, everything's perfect. They live in Hawaii, where it's always summer. They have the surf and their boards and the greatest friendship in the world.

CHAPTER ONE

EVEN IN THE EVENING, WITH summer long gone, the air's bright and heavy. It tastes familiar—like salt and iodine and kelp, like sunscreen and the ocean, like all the things that have soaked into Ollie Birkstrom's skin over twenty-two years.

The sun's low on the horizon. Light slants across the sky to meet the deck of the bungalow. The Blue House, the locals call it, though it's more aqua than blue, and the deck is unpainted wood, faded brown. But the early evening makes the rough boards golden and pretty and hides how much the whole place needs help. A renovation. Maybe someone to knock it down and start fresh.

Ollie leans on the deck's railing and watches the ocean as it breaks over and over. A car drives past, music turned up too high for its tinny speakers. The beat vibrates in the soles of Ollie's bare feet. He tries not to feel as if he's waiting for something.

Out there, past the cars and some windswept palms, is Banzai Pipeline. Ollie hasn't been to many places, but he knows surf. This is the best reef break on the entire planet. He keeps his eyes on the waves and runs his fingers over the warm, cracked surface of the railing. In his head, he counts peak after trough after peak after trough, watches the line along which each wave spills, and works out the space between sets. It's a good, pretty consistent left break. He should be out on it with his board.

But it's okay. It's rare enough to get all the Blue House kids home at once. There are five of them: Ollie and Tai, Sunny, Hannah, and Ollie's kid brother, Jaime. This is their little household, the family they've held together for more than four years, through a move, through SATs, through bad jobs and worse jobs and job hunts, through fights about the dishes and who clogged the toilet this time and if there should be a curfew on ukulele and whether they can afford to eat this week.

Usually when they're all here, they have a friend or two sharing the worn couch and the view of the ocean. Today it's just them. Ollie knows how much Tai values any time they all have together at home. So Ollie won't leave while they're hanging out on the deck of their house. Not even to surf.

Tai's at the top of the stairs that lead down from the deck. His head is bent over his phone. His shoulders are edged with gold in the sunlight. They're broad and dark, with an intricate sleeve tattoo down one arm; its Samoan ocean and sky symbolism is as familiar to Ollie as his own skin. Sand clings to Tai's back. He's near enough to Ollie that Ollie considers reaching out a hand to brush it off.

Tai turns his head and meets Ollie's gaze. He gives a flash of a smile, then goes back to his phone. The muscles in his back shift as he bows his head. Ollie peers over his shoulder at the tiny screen, but from where he is he can't read what any of it says. He exhales. It'll be okay. Tai's got this. He'll tell Ollie if he reads anything that matters.

"Guys," Sunny says to everyone and to no one in particular. She looks up from the book in her lap, squints into the sun, and shakes her hair from her eyes. She's bleached it and dyed its usual black a coppery sea green. It's weird: choppy and rough. But Sunny cut it herself, and she's proud of it. She tends to know what she wants. "Mom and Samuel are desperate to get us over to their place for lunch this weekend. I'm pretty sure Mom's spent the entire week making lumpia and building a fire pit for some poor pig. They're under the impression that we need feeding." Sunny leans back against the wall of the house. Her legs are splayed out on the warm wood. They stretch brown and curved and comfortable in front of her.

Ollie keeps counting the waves in their long, almost parallel sets, but he considers what she's said. Sunny's mom, Mrs. Castillo, is right. The Blue House fridge is mostly filled up with soda. The last time he opened the cupboard they had ramen noodles, rice crackers, and some mac and cheese in boxes. Even Tai and Hannah can't make a decent meal out of that.

"I like the stuff we eat," says Jaime from the swing seat on the deck. He perches cross-legged as the seat rocks back and forth. Hannah's beside him on the swing, with Hannah's guitar between them.

"Of course you do, James baby," says Sunny, no-nonsense. She grins at him to take out the sting. "You've got no taste. No teenager does, especially if they've been half brought up by this bunch of savages." She waves to indicate the rest of them. "But seriously, you can't tell me you don't like what my mom cooks more than anything we have in the house. Don't you remember the feast she pulled together when you turned sixteen?"

"Yeah, okay." Jaime says with a shrug and a nod. "You've got a point." He pulls his phone from his pocket and glances at it. Ollie has no idea what he's reading. Messages from friends? Some new girlfriend Ollie hasn't heard about yet? Ollie bites his lip and frowns. He's pretty sure it's one of his jobs as older brother to know the people Jaime's talking to. Tai probably knows all about it.

Hannah speaks up in her low voice. "Your mama's food's amazing, Sun. If she wants visitors, tell her yes from me, any day." She leans back in the chair. It rocks back and forth. She's probably imagining the perfect meal.

Not for the first time, Ollie wonders whether Hannah feels left out of their shared childhood. Ollie, Jaime and Tai spent years pushing their dripping, sandy way into Sunny's kitchen at the right time of day so they could devour Mrs. Castillo's chicken and rice or beef mechado. Not that Mrs. Castillo minded. She seemed to know when they'd be there. Something was always simmering on the stove and almost ready, "If you wait five minutes, sweeties."

Hannah wasn't part of that. Her parents split and her mother moved from the Big Island during Hannah's senior year, after the rest of them had spent a couple of years growing up while chasing the perfect meal and the perfect wave.

The four of them were already housemates then, in a hole of an apartment back behind the gas station—Tai slept on a pull-out bed in the living room, Sunny squeezed into the sunroom, and Ollie and Jaime irritably shared the only real bedroom. When Hannah started at their school, she was drawn in among them—Samoan like Tai, connected to them all by her surfboard and her guitar. She spent that first year sharing chili in their living room or spread out on the floor with Sunny, chatting about books and TV shows and surfboards. She was always there; she started smiling more often. So that then, when the Blue House came up for rent, run-down, but with four and a half bedrooms and a living room that opened right up onto the beach, Hannah moved in too. She fit as if she'd been there the whole time.

Hannah pushes the swing seat back. It swings, but creaks in protest. Sunny turns back to her book.

An SUV pulls up onto the grass outside, surfboards tied fast to the roof racks. The driver leans out his window. "Good evening, Blue House," he calls up to them. He's part of the older crew, a Japanese guy, an ex-banker or lawyer or money person. He's one of the guys who gave up the rat race back home, bought his North Shore dream house and now spends all his time out on the surf or talking over a beer or shaved ice with the locals.

Ollie raises a hand in acknowledgment.

Tai leans out. "I'll have that board for you to look at tomorrow, Tadashi," he says. "It's a good one, man. You'll be happy."

Ollie agrees. He's seen Tai's latest board. It is beautiful. Ollie rides a similar short one Tai made for him a year or two back. It carves through even whitewater like butter and pivots neatly under his feet. It's almost magic.

"Thanks, Tai," Tadashi says from the car. "I'm certain I will be. I'll come by in the afternoon, yes?"

"Sure thing. I'm on at the café, so make it any time after about three."

The guy waves as he accelerates out of the parking lot and away from the beach.

"That board's a piece of art, Tai." Ollie worries his thumbnail with his teeth. "I hope this guy appreciates it."

"He does. He does." Tai nods. "Don't get stressed about Tadashi. He's one of the good ones."

Ollie's still dubious. After all, Tai's nice about everyone. His boards are special. They should be taken seriously. Ollie's ridden them ever since Tai first shaped one. Even the earliest boards were pretty decent. Now they're amazing. Each one is unique. They all have their own individual style, some with more drive, some glassy smooth on the waves, but every single one is sweet and amazingly responsive. They do precisely what Ollie's body tells them to do. Ollie could never blame his board for a single one of his failures in the surf.

On the swing seat, Jaime wraps one slim arm around Hannah's guitar. He plays a tuneless rhythm, which doesn't fit with either the crash of the waves or the regular, irritating, un-oiled squeal of the swing as it moves back and forth. He's awful. He strums enthusiastically and messes up a chord entirely. Hannah laughs, low and mostly kind, and shows him the chord again.

Ollie can't laugh it off, though. He's already tense, and the noise grates on him. He tries to count the waves, but it's hard to focus on their rhythm when Jaime's like this. The noise is painful.

"Hey. Can you cut that out?" Ollie says at last. His voice comes out pinched. He always sounds peeved when it comes to Jaime. He goes on, "I'm pretty sure that guitar hates you. Along with any living thing within a mile radius."

Whatever, it's his job to be annoyed. Jaime's his little brother. The kid has no focus; he messes around and chats endlessly. He's nothing like Ollie, really, and everyone loves him. If it weren't for the pale, freckled skin and white-blond hair he and Ollie shared with their mother, they might both have found a way to deny the relationship years ago.

"I'm getting way better," says Jaime. "If you got your head out of your sandy asshole for a second, you'd know that." He takes a breath and winds up to say more. "Now that you're surfing again, I thought your filthy mood might improve. Guess I was thinking of someone else's brother."

He plays more loudly, misses a chord again, and thumps the heel of his hand against the guitar body.

"Oh, come on," says Ollie through his teeth. He's stung, but he keeps his voice pretty firmly under control.

"Fuck off, Ollie." Jaime's chin is thrust forward.

"Jaime," Ollie tries again, as though this time the kid might listen, which is increasingly hard to imagine. It hasn't happened in five years, not since their mother died.

"Guys, cool it," says Tai. He doesn't move to look at them. He never misses much, especially when Ollie's involved. "Ollie, whatever you say about the guitar, the kid's still better with it than you are."

"Hey," Ollie protests. But he's going through the motions. It's not as if Tai's wrong. "Whatever, dude. At least I don't force everyone to listen to me make that kind of noise."

"That's just 'cause you avoid doing anything you're not immediately best in the world at," Tai says. Ollie frowns and looks away. Being known so well is both a blessing and a curse.

Tai turns back to his phone. He reads, then freezes. Ollie leans closer and eyes Tai. "Take a look at your email." Tai keeps his voice low, but tension and anticipation struggle in it. He looks up at Ollie. "Seems like the surf league's sent out the wildcard invites."

Their eyes meet for a quick, electric moment. Ollie breaks the glance. They hope for too much.

"Okay," he murmurs. He pulls his phone from his pocket with slightly shaking hands. He breathes steadily and ignores the quick thud-thud thud-thud of his heart. Tai is still, watching.

And there it is in his inbox: a new message from the World Surf League. Ollie's eyes skim over it.

"Greetings from the North Shore of Oahu, where the sun is shining and the pipe is turning. Oliver Birkstrom, you're invited to compete in the Banzai Pipe Masters wildcard trial round which will occur in the week starting..."

Ollie leans against the rail and exhales shakily. He's in. Well, he's got a chance to be in. He's one of sixteen Hawaiian surfers invited to compete for the two wildcard spaces in the Pipe Masters this year. He's made it this first step.

Two years ago, he wouldn't have had to fight for this spot. At nineteen and twenty, Ollie was one of the golden boys of the surfing world. He had two Junior Surf Masters titles. *Freesurf* and *Stab Magazine* had done profiles on him. He had an agent named Paul and was talking sponsorship with a couple of the surfboard companies.

Back then he'd have been in this competition automatically, all on his own merits.

But after the injury and a year and a half of poor showings, things were different. Tai spent hours on the phone, telling various World Surf League bureaucrats that Ollie deserved another shot, was good to go, was in the zone, was going to show. He said they had nothing to worry about, that his ankle injury was a thing of the past, that Ollie Birkstrom, the surfer they all remembered from two years ago, was back.

Listening to Tai talk on his behalf was humbling. Ollie paced. He couldn't watch. He chewed his lips and came close to telling Tai to hang up and let the whole thing go. But he didn't. Because beneath the humiliation of it all, Ollie still desperately wanted this second chance.

A month ago, he and Tai were out on the water. It was one of those gray evenings with just the two of them, a few of the old guys, and the waves; the tourists had headed back to their bars and hotels and beds.

It was a good night. Somehow every wave came easily when he was alone with Tai.

Ollie took a ride on Backdoor. He swam back out to reach Tai, then sat up and straddled the board. Another heavy wave moved under them, too flat and full of water to catch anywhere.

When Tai looked over at Ollie, his eyes were deep and dark against the gray sky. Ollie could see each individual drop of saltwater on his face and in his hair.

Tai said, "So I need to ask, Ollie. Do you really want this? To surf pro? Do you want to try again?" He turned his board into an oncoming wave but kept his gaze on Ollie.

Ollie pressed his lips together and tasted salt. He'd never want anything more than the breathless, patient, vast joy of surfing. But surfing pro could mean more than that to all of them. It'd mean Ollie wouldn't come home to find no hot water, or no lights; maybe he wouldn't stress out while they scraped together the rent, late as always. Sunny wouldn't have to choose between their electricity bills or grocery money. Ollie could help Jaime pay for Hawaii Pacific University or some other school. He could stop worrying about the stupid stuff, for a few years anyway. All he'd have to contemplate was when the next wave was coming and how it would rise under him.

When he met Tai's gaze, Ollie was already nodding. "Yeah. Absolutely. Absolutely I want this. Believe me, Tai."

It was easier to say it out on the ocean; it was easier to be brave and push down the paralyzing fear that he'd left the comeback too long. He was afraid he couldn't get in, of course he was, after so much time and so many failures. He was afraid maybe the whole thing was a stupid kid's dream, and he should have dumped it long ago and gotten serious about his life.

He hadn't said any of that to anyone. But the way he saw it, he had one more shot at this thing he'd wanted all his life. This shot. And then he was going to accept his lot, toss it all in and take a business course, or something in hospitality, or maybe bookkeeping; he was pretty good with numbers.

Tai looked him in the eye and nodded. "Okay. Then I've gotta tell you, now's the time. You look great on the water. You're riding waves as well as you ever have. At least as well as any of the pros. You can wait and see, give the qualifiers another go. But honestly, if you're not in Pipe Masters this time around, I can't see anything happening for at least another year. And the longer it's been since the last time you competed, the harder it's going to be for you to get back. Now's the time, Ollie."

Ollie took a breath. This whole conversation scared the shit out of him, but Tai was right. He swallowed. "Okay," he said.

"Okay," echoed Tai. "So, you want this. Then, Ollie, let's go and fucking get it." He grinned, intent and bright.

"I'll get right on it," Ollie said with confidence that was mostly genuine. For that moment, he believed it could be that easy. He could wish himself back into the world circuit.

Almost in reply, the water turned glassy beneath them, a sweet spot. A set of three was coming in to the left with a perfect wave at the back, its tip curling over.

The two of them didn't need to look at one another. Ollie gave way to Tai and Tai gave way to Ollie. Tai laughed, loud and happy, as both of them caught the wave, flying fast. They carved around one another toward shore. It was impossible to think beyond the rush and the instinctive joy. No one worries while they're right there on the front of a perfect wave.

Now, on the Blue House deck, Tai and the girls watch Ollie closely. Even Jaime pays attention with his hands poised on the guitar strings. Ollie takes a breath and reads the email again. Okay. Okay.

"I got it," Ollie says. He looks at Tai for a bright, terrified second, then around at everyone. "I'm in. I got a spot in the wildcard trials." He can't hold back a grin, even as he readies himself for the hugs he knows will come.

Tai's there almost before Ollie can think. He pauses to check Ollie's face, then wraps Ollie in his arms and squeezes. Behind him, Sunny whoops and Jaime stands. Jaime almost drops the guitar as he leaps forward to join in the hug. Hannah steadies the guitar as she stands to her full height. She reaches around Jaime to grab Ollie's hand. Sunny scrambles to her feet, claps her hands and grins at him, then bowls in to hug them too. Ollie's surrounded.

Unexpectedly, it's okay. Ollie prefers to have his space. But this is his family. These are the only people in the world who can grab onto him like this, wrap him up, and leave him comfortable.

When they step back, Jaime and Sunny are bouncing. Hannah's smile is proud, and her eyes are wet. Tai beams. His hand is a steady, calming weight on Ollie's shoulder. Tai's so certain of everything.

Ollie tilts his head. "You guys are aware that I still have to win," he says. He holds his lips together around a bubble of nervous laughter. "It's a trial. There are sixteen surfers. After these past two years, they're not about to just let me in to surf in Pipe Masters."

"You'll win," says Jaime, his eyes bright. "I know it. You'll get through."

Ollie reaches to brush Jaime's cheek in an old familiar gesture, then pulls his hand back and shakes his head. "I need to be in the top two. All the other locals will be competing too. I've seen some amazing talent."

"You're the best of all of them," Sunny says. "You always have been."

"Not anymore," says Ollie, almost to himself. But he smiles. Their enthusiasm and confidence buoy him up despite his humming nerves.

"We'll get on the water first thing in the morning, Ollie," says Tai. "This is awesome. But if we're gonna do this, we'll need to double up on training. Maybe we should make ourselves a schedule."

Ollie nods. He knows it's true, though between training and work, and sometimes needing to eat and sleep, he can't imagine how they'll fit in a single other thing.

Hannah's watching him. "I can take one of your shifts at work," she offers. "And we can do all the cooking for a bit, right, Sun?"

"Hey. I know how to cook too," says Jaime. "I'll help." It's a sign of the others' support for Ollie that no one disagrees.

"Thanks, guys." Ollie looks around at them, then back out at the surf. He's thrilled. He really is. It's all so close, right at his fingertips. But behind the thrill, he hears the waves beating, over and over. "Last chance, last chance, last chance."

"We need to celebrate," says Hannah. "I'll make tacos." They're Ollie's favorite.

"Do we have any sour cream?" asks Sunny. She follows Hannah into the house.

"Nah, but there are beans and cheese, and I found a random few dollars in the pocket of my shorts. We could get an avocado if the mini-mart is open," Hannah says. "Anyone got beer money?"

Ollie smiles and lets himself be hustled and high-fived into the house.

CHAPTER TWO

IT'S EARLY. THE SUN ISN'T up yet. Tai Talagi stretches out on his bed. The mattress is solid; it has one broken spring, which is both out of place and oddly comforting. He lets his body wake up, stretching his muscles and tendons with his eyes still closed.

He listens as the surf rolls and thuds against the sand, past the scrub and palms that grow between the Blue House and the beach. He doesn't need to look outside. He knows the wind's from the northwest. He can hear the heavy swell.

Aside from the sound of the ocean, the house is silent. Tai's always lived in places full of noise and family and surfboards and everyone's flip-flops lined up at the back door, including some that don't have an owner and the ones Aunt Jeanette will never come back for. But this place, this stitched-together little family, this is home. However frustrated he sometimes becomes with the everyday details of making sure they all survive intact, he always wakes up happy and proud to be here.

He cracks his eyes open, blinks. The pale light of the sky is creeping around the bed sheet they pinned to the window frame when they first moved in. Tai rubs his eyes, then swings his body around so he can drop his feet to the floor. He leaves the lights off as he pads over the wooden floorboards into the narrow hall. He knows this house deep in his bones.

Hannah's door is closed. Sunny's too. Tai can hear their breathing. The streetlamp lights Jaime, who's asleep in his closet-sized room with his arms flung up above his head like a kid who passed out hours ago and hasn't woken up enough to move. His walls are covered with drawings in pencil and ink: comic book characters, superheroes he's invented and spent years perfecting, wizards and shape-changers and dragons. More recently, he painted a fantasy scene over one wall: lightning and storm clouds and oceans, giant waves and a castle in the air.

Ollie's room is at the other end of the hall. Tai knocks on the light wood, then opens the door.

Ollie's asleep. He's tangled in the sheets; his thigh is lit by a patch of early morning almost-light. He's clutching a pillow with one long, faintly freckled arm and one long, faintly freckled leg flung across it. He's gorgeous—lovely on the surface and underneath, in the heart of him. His face is still and soft in a way it never is when he's awake.

Tai doesn't let himself look too long. Some itches are way too sensitive to ever, ever let himself scratch.

"Pipe's breaking left." He keeps his voice low.

Ollie moans sleepily. "Seriously, Tai? What are you doing? The sun's not up. It's basically still nighttime."

It's been three weeks since Ollie got the invitation to the wildcard round. They've had this same conversation every morning. A pile of clothes sits on the chair near the door. Tai balls up a T-shirt and tosses it at Ollie's head, then turns away without bothering to answer. In the kitchen, he grabs some toaster pastries and a huge glass of juice. A minute later, Ollie joins him, yawning dramatically. He's still rumpled and all kinds of adorable. It makes Tai cranky.

"Stop complaining," Tai mutters. He pops the pastries into the toaster with a practiced flick and leans against the unsteady kitchen table. "It's almost five, Ollie; I have to work at seven fifteen. And if you want to get through and into the Masters, you need to keep training." Tai turns away from Ollie. "Des is out most days. Whitey, too. Sure, you can beat those guys in a heat, no problem, as long as you pick your waves right, but there are other guys we don't know coming from Maui and Honolulu. However much we run the beach or swim the hotel pool, training on the actual break, knowing exactly what will look good on those waves—that's the best thing we've got. It's what'll get you ahead of the others in the end." He takes a breath, but he's on a roll. "If you don't want this, then let me know. I'd love to sleep in. I honestly don't have time to waste on someone who doesn't care."

He doesn't mean to lecture Ollie. But it makes things easier if he focuses on that weird balance between them. They're so many different things to one another: old friends, surf brothers, housemates, and family. And now also trainer and surfer. It's simplest if Tai keeps each thread separate.

"Okay, okay," mutters Ollie. "I do want it. One hundred percent. You know that."

Tai does know. He hands Ollie a pastry. It's warm from the toaster and leaves Tai's fingers slightly sticky. Brown sugar. Ollie's favorite.

"Thanks, Mom." Ollie takes a bite. It's half apology, half attitude. Tai ignores him.

In minutes, they're splashing through the narrow section of shallows with their boards. They dive over the wash and into the vast Pacific. The board is a reassuring weight in Tai's hands. All of his irritation is swept away in the water.

Pipe is curling into perfect tubes, so even this early a few surfers are on the lineup. Some of the locals shift aside for Ollie; others seem to get in the way on purpose. They all know him, of course. He's a local celebrity and hard to miss, covered as always in a dark, long-sleeved rash guard, with his shock of white-blond hair and that undeniable talent.

Everyone reckons that surfing Pipe is different from surfing anywhere else. Here, the locals ferociously defend a pecking order; no visitors sit out deeper than they do. Tai's in with the local kids, of course, but he still keeps an eye on who's sitting where.

He watches as Ollie waits for the right wave, positions himself carefully, and then shoots into the blue and white tube. He holds his breath until Ollie's spat out the other side. Ollie bends his body to turn the board and carve into the messy wash. When the wave collapses into shallower water, Ollie heads back into the deep, shaking his head like a shaggy white dog. The water droplets catch the yellow light and glitter around him.

Tai sighs. He knows the best and the worst of Ollie, but he will never think he's anything less than remarkable. He rolls his eyes at himself and sets up to catch the next wave in. He gets up, centers himself, and bends his knees into it. The surface of the board is waxy under his toes. The ocean surges beneath him and lifts him effortlessly. He leans into the wave and catches sight of Ollie's laughing grin as he flies past.

"You should compete in this thing too," Ollie says as Tai paddles out to reach the cluster of surfers in the lineup again. "That was a nice ride." But it's not true. That hasn't been an option for years. Tai's good, sure. He understands the ocean and he knows his body and the board beneath him. But Ollie's great, and Tai's mostly okay with that.

When they were kids, the two of them came up with a whole future together. They met out on the surf, both of them thirteen with saltwater in their veins, both of them good enough surfers that they had nothing to prove. Tai had friends, and a family spread out over the whole of the Pacific. But from that meeting on, all his big dreams included Ollie. Late at night, when the other kids had headed for home, they'd lie on their backs on the sand and look up at the stars, listen to the waves, and talk about their future. They were going to practice on big swells and small, in rain and sunshine. They were going to go all over the world and be the greats.

They'd stay out on the beach until Jaime or Tai's big sisters were sent to yell up the street for them. They knew one another for a week, then a month, then two months, and two years. Even after that time, Ollie still seemed new. Tai still wanted to hear every single thing Ollie ever said and see every single thing Ollie ever did.

The sun's up now, warm against Tai's skin. There's time for another wave if he's lucky, and then he has to get to work.

"You don't need to come in yet," he says to Ollie when they're close enough to speak above the noise of the water and the people. "Aren't you on a nine a.m. shift with Hannah?"

"Yeah, I know, but I need to drag fucking Jaime out of bed. It takes him a year to get dressed and get his hair perfect. And he's been late for school two days in a row. A third late this week will have protective services on my ass for sure."

Protective services has bigger things to worry about than a healthy sixteen-year-old getting to school ten minutes late, but the possibility that they'll take Jaime terrifies Ollie. It has from the beginning. Jaime's the baby. He's special. He's their responsibility.

Two years ago, fourteen-year-old Jaime was picked up drunk by a couple of local cops. The cops knew the Blue House kids. They were reasonable about it, but Ollie went white as they talked about "other relatives" and "better alternatives."

"I've fucked up with Jaime," Ollie said that night. His hands shook.

"You haven't fucked up," Tai said. "Jaime's a good kid; he was messing around, trying stuff out. We can work it out."

Ollie's glance was withering and unconvinced.

"They're not about to take him from you. From us," Tai said. "Promise."

After that, Jaime was subdued. Ollie swung between avoiding him and watching him like a hawk. And in all that self-blame and fear, along with an unexpected competition loss, a minor injury, something got stuck and his confidence on the surf crashed and burned.

For now, out on the ocean, Tai says, "We're stuck with him, Ollie. You know we've got this." Between Ollie and Sunny and Hannah and Tai, things with Jaime have been okay for two years. Tai lifts his chin. "There's a good set incoming."

Ten minutes later, back on the sand, Tai dries off with a worn towel and pulls on a T-shirt. He and Ollie grab their boards and walk across the beach with their shoulders bumping against one another.

Tai relaxes. Ollie's never minded this kind of weary, accidental contact. Times like this it's all so easy. Ollie was strong on the waves. His old ankle injury isn't bothering him. They head across the parking lot and up their sand and gravel drive to toss the boards into the laundry room under the deck.

"See you tonight." Ollie heads into the quiet house.

Tai doesn't need to go in. He walks to work, jogging the last couple of streets. His flip-flops slap against the ground. It's not far. The café is named Nalu Kua Loloa, which means "really long wave." They call it Nalu.

Tai opens up most mornings. A second cousin of Tai's mother's neighbors in Samoa owns the place. The owner's name is Maile Alekamo, and she's been family for as long as Tai's been alive. She's also pregnant, and these days spends most mornings in some combination of exhaustion and nausea. So she's not at the café this early.

Tai's happy opening the place. He's got a system. He turns on the coffee machine first and listens to it burble as it warms up. Then he flings open the wide windows and breathes the beach air, puts up the umbrellas, moves the tables, and lifts the sign out onto the street. After that he starts morning food prep: slices cheese and vegetables and big spiky pineapples. Maile arrives as Tai is finishing. Sometimes the prep work is restful, but today his wrists ache from chopping. He flexes them and wrinkles his nose at her.

"Oh, no. Sorry I'm late, cuz," she says.

"Nah. You're good. I'm not mad at you. How's the baby?" He gestures at her belly.

"She's great. Kicking like a whole team of Samoan rugby players. She told me she'll be even better if you have time for a back rub, later."

"Tell her that her momma shouldn't lie about her." Tai smiles, and goes on. "You know I'll do it if you ask."

"Okay then."

He waits.

"Will you give me a massage, Tai?"

He raises his eyebrows.

"Please?" she adds.

"Of course." Tai flexes his fingers. "But not till after I'm done with the prep."

Maile sighs. "Thank you." She comes near to survey the little galley kitchen and then peers at him. "Your hair's still got sand in it," she says. She reaches to brush it out.

Tai shakes her away. "Stop that. You don't want it in the food. I was surfing." Of course she knows that.

"Something new for you. How's Ollie doing?" She's the same height as Tai is, so she meets his eyes easily.

"Good. Pretty good."

"Is he going to put on a decent show next week?"

It sounds so much sooner when she says it. Tai takes a long breath. "I don't know, Mai. He always surfs great when it's not a competition, so we'll see. He doesn't seem nervous though. He's, you know, focused. A bit distant and intent."

"For a change." Maile laughs. She likes Ollie, but she doesn't get him, not really. She likes him for Tai's sake and because she defaults to liking people she spends time with.

Tai takes the cut vegetables and cheese to the walk-in fridge in the back room. "Whatever happens with Ollie at Pipe, it won't be for lack of training," he says. "We've been out every day, even when it's flat."

"I know," she says. "Aunty Bee reckons she saw him out on the beach at five on a flat day, dragging a huge tire around."

"Yeah. Resistance training."

"You've got him in hand."

Tai blushes. He's proud of the work they're doing, but he doesn't need everyone to comment. "It's important. We want him to be really strong in the water. He needs endurance. If he gets through to the finals he could be surfing three or four heats in a row. That's a lot of paddling, even for Ollie."

"Sounds good. Let's hope he gets through." She perches on a stool to open the register. Her distended belly is in the way of the cash drawer as it slides open, and she sighs and shifts backward.

"He will." Tai's said it over and over. He'll make it true if he can.

The café door swings open, and Maile smiles warmly. "What can I get you, Mario? The usual?" She's always sweet to customers. Most of the time her sweetness is genuine, which is why they come back. It keeps the café open and keeps Tai in a job he needs.

Tai pulls a pan down to make Mario's eggs. "Scrambled, a little bit of butter and maybe throw in some ham," he hears. Tai knows what that means. He lets the pan heat to the perfect temperature, then lobs in a huge knob of butter and slices a generous amount of ham.

"You want cheese, too?" he asks.

Mario grins. "Why not, kid. Everyone needs to live a little."

The eggs sizzle in the pan. Tai flips them and grabs the cheese.

"Mario, you don't live a little. You live a hundred times more than most people I know," he says, and the old guy laughs at him.

"You're a charmer, kid. That's for sure. What you doing hanging around here making old guys their eggs?"

CHAPTER THREE

"TIME TO GET UP, JAIME," says Ollie through Jaime's open bedroom door. The room is tiny and still mostly dark, but he can see Jaime in bed with his arms spread out wide like the kid he still is sometimes.

"On it," mumbles Jaime. He curls up, turns toward the wall.

"I'll grab you some breakfast." It's easy to be magnanimous after the perfect surf.

Hannah comes out to the kitchen, stumbles over a skateboard—her own—and blinks at Ollie. Her hair is a tangled mess around her head, with one thick braid dropping over her shoulder.

"Juice?" Ollie asks and carefully hands her a glass.

"Thanks, babe." She stares at the pantry door for a while and takes a gulp, still waking up. Sunny steps in, dressed in a swirly white dress, her hair pinned up. She's neater than usual, though still beachy pretty, dressed for work at the resort shop.

"Need a ride, Sun?" Ollie asks.

"Nah, I'm good. I'm gonna walk on the beach and get some shells before I head over there at eleven." She collects shells, piles of shells and tiny stones. Then she puts together little strings of them along with beads and tiny pieces of greenstone and pearl to make jewelry.

Ollie has one of her pieces pinned to the windowsill in his room. He knows its dark spiral shell and tiny coral pieces by touch. Tai wears one tied around his wrist. He never takes it off. It's rough, now, after a year or so going in and out of the ocean. It's not the first one she gave him; that one fell apart five years ago. This is the third.

Ten minutes later there's no sign of Jaime, no sound or movement from his room.

Ollie heads up the hall to Jaime's room. He has to get ready for work. He doesn't have time for this. "J, we need to leave by quarter after eight. It's almost seven thirty. You said you need to shower, and I know how long it takes you to make yourself pretty."

When Jaime doesn't answer, Ollie flicks on the light. Jaime groans and pulls the covers over his head.

"I can walk to school," he says to his pillow.

"Not anymore," snaps Ollie. "One more tardy and they'll call me, and if that keeps happening they'll involve protective services, and what am I gonna do then? You want to move to the group home at Pearl City and waste the rest of your life sniffing glue?"

Jaime groans again. "That's not about to happen, Ollie. You're completely overreacting." But he rolls over. Ollie watches from the doorway as he slides out of bed.

"Have you done your homework?" Ollie asks.

"Yeah," Jaime manages. Ollie narrows his eyes. Jaime snaps, "I've done it. Sunny helped. Fuck off." He stalks into the bathroom and bangs the door.

At a quarter past eight, Ollie tosses Jaime's backpack onto the back seat of their 1999 Escort wagon and climbs into the driver's seat. Hannah climbs in next to him and ineffectually combs her hair with the fingers of one hand. She's already had one breakfast, but holds a huge bowl of granola and milk, which she tries to balance on her lap. Ollie starts the car. It's a relief when the engine turns over right away. He resists the urge to lean on the horn. The neighbors would hate it.

After several infuriating minutes Jaime appears and clambers into the back seat. He's dressed in tight turquoise pants rolled above his ankles and a red striped shirt with flamingoes on it. His hair flops artfully over his eyes. The kid looks ridiculous, but the outfit probably took half an hour to plan. Ollie manages to hold his tongue as they drive the few minutes to Jaime's high school.

"Bye, Han," says Jaime. He's making a point of not speaking to Ollie, but Hannah smiles and mumbles "Bye" around her breakfast cereal. There's a pause.

"Bye, Jaime," says Ollie.

Jaime looks at Ollie for the first time since Ollie switched on his bedroom light. "Bye."

"I'll see you tonight," says Ollie. Then before he can stop himself, "You've got a test tomorrow, so head straight home after school, okay."

Jaime rolls his eyes. He vanishes through the school gate and into a huge swarm of kids.

At the resort, Ollie parks between two palms in the staff parking lot. He and Hannah walk past one of the pools and go in through the service entrance. The guys' locker room has a concrete floor. It's tidy this early in the day and smells pleasantly of hibiscus and less pleasantly of humans. Ollie changes into his uniform with practiced speed. The lightweight floral shirt buttons tight about his chest. He might need a new one.

He and Hannah are both on the front desk this morning. They handle changeover with the night staff with a good minute and a half to spare. By the time their manager, Maribel, walks through, Hannah's already on the phone with someone who wants more towels.

"Morning, Ollie. Did you get the room upgrades?" Maribel asks as she lines up the tourism brochures in their stand. They were fine before. Maribel's always polite, she takes her job seriously, but she checks on the staff more often than is necessary. Ollie understands it, but it still winds him up.

"Yep, I'm about to check them against the available rooms." He keeps his voice even and pretty cheerful.

"Good. Good work. Let me know if there are any issues." As if he'd do anything else. It's not rocket science. He's been doing this for a year.

Maribel pauses. She smiles as she leans over the desk and pats Ollie's shoulder. Ollie startles. He moves away a little. He's known Maribel for three years and likes her as much as he likes most people, but the familiarity raises the hairs on his skin.

She draws her hand back. "I heard about the wildcard trial thing, Ollie. Congratulations." She meets his eyes. "You must be excited."

"Thanks. I am." Ollie's never sure how much Maribel knows about surfing, let alone how much she cares. But it's a small community. Everyone is up in everyone else's business, and here surfing is everyone's business.

"I'd like you to help out at concierge today," Maribel says, all business. "Head over there at eleven, when Jenny arrives. Michael's out 'cause his oldest is sick, and with the surf league delegates in town I need my best guy." She twinkles at him. "That's you. In case you wondered. It'll help with that training course we've been talking about."

"No problem." Ollie glances at Hannah, who's on another call. He hasn't mentioned the hospitality course to the other Blue House kids. It's not important. It'd only be a certificate. Anyway, nothing might come of it, but Maribel and the other manager are confident it's the only way up in the resort. And Ollie might need that kind of long-term plan.

As she turns to go, Ollie takes a breath. "Hey, Maribel." She turns back. "I was hoping I could switch my shifts for next week." She looks at him blankly. "I need to keep myself open for the wildcard comp on Wednesday." He draws breath and runs on under her gaze. "I've checked the offshore swell charts, and it's likely we'll get in the water then. It's a significant competition for me, and I'd like to take off the Tuesday as well as the days I've already organized."

"And you want Hannah to fill in for you?" Maribel says, frowning.

"No she's already got an early shift that day. But I've talked to Brandi and she could cover for me at the desk. If—"

Maribel takes a breath. Her eyes are worried, and Ollie knows this isn't going down well. "I don't think so, Ollie. I get it, really. But

Tuesday's a critical day for the delegates. There's a private function here with ninety guests. I need to know we'll have good cover. You can take Wednesday of course. But I need you Tuesday for the long shift."

Ollie says, "I just—" He has a good read on when a battle's already lost, but this is important. He can't not ask again. "The thing is, this isn't a little local competition or something. It's the Pipe Masters. And Brandi's getting really good. Or I can ask someone else. If I work late Tuesday, it means I won't have any prep time at all before the comp."

Maribel's smile is tight. "I'm genuinely sorry, Ollie. It's not that I don't sympathize. But what we're doing here matters, too. It matters to Hawaii. Tourism is all we have in the state, and I can't let people leave the resort in the lurch because their board is calling and the tide is right."

Ollie can't bring himself to say anything, but he nods and swallows around the disappointment. His head feels tight. He needs this job. Not only for now, but in the long-term he could play a more significant role here. There aren't many places he can work. He's only got a high school education. So he needs to act as though the work here matters as much as the waves do. He has Jaime to consider, and rent and food. If everything goes badly at Pipe—even if it goes well—he needs to keep working.

A call comes through. Maribel grimaces. "Sorry," she mouths at him as he answers the phone.

"Reception desk, this is Oliver. How can I help you this morning?" He's relieved that she walks away.

Half an hour later, reception is quiet. Hannah sits in a chair. Ollie props himself against the desk. He's managed to be pleasant while speaking with the guests, but he's still furious. "Is this what you want, Han? Working here. For good?"

Hannah folds her hands behind her head and leans back.

"I don't know about 'for good.' But what else am I gonna do, Ollie? There's not much on offer on the North Shore."

"So you just accept it? That's not gonna make you happy."

"I don't see why not. Anyway, I need the cash. It's not as if I have some secret stash of gold hidden somewhere. And you and Sunny are here. I go home to a house on the beach. It's a good life, better than most. There doesn't seem much point in getting mad at it."

Ollie half envies her attitude. The other half wants everything to change. He's still angry.

TAI LIFTS THE CORD OF his sander to one side and puts Tadashi's finished board onto the stand. He leans down to look across its surface, then turns it to examine the underside. It's as close to perfect as he'll get. He grabs a cloth for a final wipe down.

The board's solid, thick but not too heavy, long enough to have that longboard feel, and short enough to take on waves with energy. It has come out exactly as Tai first saw it, when he was faced with the blank and Tadashi's adult, flowing style of surfing. It's beautiful.

He's patterned it with rolling waves in a woodblock print style that Jaime helped him research. It's reminiscent of Japan, and of the North Shore too. The waves roll under a glass-smooth gloss that Tai's carefully wet-sanded and polished. With Ollie's boards and his own, Tai leaves the sanded surface without polish. The boards don't last as long, but they're lighter that way and quicker in the water. This board's different. The gloss will lift the color and make the board both beautiful and durable.

Tai's shaped boards since his early teens. But when Ollie started losing in the comps he ramped it up. He couldn't fix things for Ollie, couldn't get him out of that rut with words or reassurance. He couldn't make Ollie win. He could, however, shape boards. He wanted to make something magical that would solve everything. He spent hours in his shed, feeling out surfaces and profiles. He refined board after board, changed nose shape and fin position and thickness. He didn't find that one magic board, but he made some Ollie loved. Every time one was near enough to perfect he'd hand it to Ollie.

"Test this one out for me?" he'd ask, as though it was a favor.

Ollie would narrow his eyes, but he'd take it out the next time he surfed, and Tai would watch him hopefully. Maybe this board would be a new beginning, unlike all the boards before.

Tadashi knocks on the doorframe of the shed while Tai is rubbing a last soft shine onto his board. They study it together. Tadashi's hands are careful on the surface. He's always handled Tai's boards with a reverence that makes Tai trust him.

"It's perfect, Tai," says Tadashi. "Thank you."

"No problem. I'm glad you like it." Tai's more comfortable with Tadashi every time they talk. The guy can be a bit formal, but he's pretty old, in his forties, so that makes sense. He's also sincere, thoughtful about boards, and generous.

Tadashi leans forward to trace the board's pattern with a finger. His hair falls past his shoulders and he pushes it back impatiently, more like a local than Tai's seen him look before.

Tai laughs. "You need a haircut, dude. You're starting to look like every old guy on the North Shore."

Tadashi considers him. "The hair's too much?" he asks.

"Nah. No, I was teasing. It's cool. It's awesome." Tai holds his hands out peaceably.

"Okay," says Tadashi. He's so pleasant and so serious that Tai sometimes finds himself tongue-tied. It's unusual for Tai. Tadashi says, "To be clear, I am not that old."

"Yeah, gotcha."

"I am really impressed by this board."

Tai looks at his feet. "Thank you, man. Thank you."

"I don't want to be every other old dude living out his surfer dreams on the North Shore," says Tadashi.

"Nah, man, that's not what I meant."

"Of course it's not." Tadashi examines the board again. The edges of his eyes crinkle up. "I'm looking forward to taking her for a ride. The forecast's good for tomorrow; will I see you out on Pipe?"

"Only if you're up early," says Tai. "I'll be heading to the café at seven."

"I'll be there," says Tadashi. "You can watch how this beauty goes on the water with an old man riding it." He turns the board over carefully and leaves it on the stand while he pulls out his wallet. "What are you going to do now, Tai?"

"I don't know." Tai runs a hand over his face. He's starting to realize there's a future beyond the café, but it's just a glimmer of a thought. "Keep on looking for the next magic board, I guess."

As Tadashi hands over the payment, he bows. Tai pockets the money and bows back. Tadashi lifts the board under his arm. Tai follows him out.

"Want a hand?" Tai asks.

Tadashi shakes his head. "Thank you, I have it."

Tai turns back to step into his shed. He grabs the pencil still tucked behind his ear and lifts a new blank onto the shaping stand. As he runs his hands over it, the board's already shaping itself.

It's after eight on the evening before the wildcard round, and Ollie's only now getting home. He pulls off the street into the driveway.

He's had the windows wound down for the trip home, so he can lean one arm out and let his hand move in the rushing air, at least get a feel of the salt wind. His skin is tight. He's not sure his muscles haven't forgotten something important. Like how to surf.

The house smells of Tai's beef stew. There's a huge pot of it, warm, on the stovetop. Ollie smiles to himself and blinks a little at the unasked-for kindness. It's better than family, what they have. He takes a plate of stew and a big glass of water and goes out to Tai's shed. The lights are still on. Tai lifts his head as Ollie walks in. He's wearing a respirator, which he pushes back onto his head. His hair is full of pale foam dust.

"You had a long day," he says. He wipes his face with the back of his hand. "It doesn't seem fair."

Ollie nods as he hoists himself onto one of the benches and lets his legs dangle. He balances his plate on his knees.

"I'll be okay."

Tai goes back to his board, pulling on a tape measure and jotting down dimensions in pencil on the surface of the blank. He tucks the pencil behind his ear, tips his head close to the board and views it from an angle, then re-measures and crosses something out. Ollie doesn't interrupt, just takes a few mouthfuls while Tai works. After a few minutes, Tai looks up at him through the mask.

"The stew's good," Ollie says. "Thank you."

Tai lifts the mask. "Thought you could use a feed." He settles one hip against the bench and considers Ollie in silence.

Ollie lets himself breathe. It's restful in the small room he knows so well, filled with pictures of surf and boards, tins of resin and epoxy, tools and blanks and stacks of sandpaper. From outside comes the regular pounding of surf and the far-off voices of a crew setting up stands and equipment at the other end of the beach. Tai stays still for a while, watching but not watching, letting Ollie be, then goes back to his work. Ollie relaxes.

Ollie finishes the bowl of stew. Tai runs his palms over a curved edge of the board, then packs his gear away. He wipes his hands on a cleaning rag, which he tucks into his back pocket.

They walk up to the house together. By unspoken agreement, they pause on the deck. It's low tide, so the surf sounds far away. The crew must have finished with the stands for tomorrow's comp; it's almost silent. For one moment, the sky is bright with layer upon layer of stars all crowded together and dazzling. But then the clouds that swoop in every night are right there, covering it all.

Tai rests a careful hand on Ollie's back. It's welcome, and Ollie leans into it.

"Don't be a hero, tomorrow," Tai says. "The surf's gonna be pumping. All you need to do is ride clean. You don't have to try anything special."

Ollie turns and grins at him. "You know, I was planning on trying to land a 540. It'd give me something to do."

"Asshole." Tai hits him with the cleaning rag. "I'm gonna take a shower." At the door he says, "Ollie, you can win this thing." Ollie meets Tai's eyes. Maybe he can.

Ollie rinses his plate in the kitchen sink. It's nine thirty. Late enough for bed, given the early start he has tomorrow. He sticks his head in the living room to say goodnight. Hannah and Sunny are piled on the couch together playing video games. The light from the screen is greenish on their faces.

"No, but Han, you have to shoot that bunny thing," says Sunny.

"You're a hard woman, Sunny Castillo. I can't do it," smiles Hannah, "look at the little tail on it. It's too cute." She's toying with Sunny. Her eyes are bright.

Sunny groans and kicks her. "If you don't kill it, it eats everything."

Ollie interrupts. "G'night, guys." He pauses. The shower's running. He glances down the hall. Jaime's bedroom door is closed. It's usually open when he's in there.

"That's Tai in the shower?"

"Yeah," says Sunny.

"What's Jaime up to?"

"No idea, babe," says Hannah. "I don't think he's home yet."

"Well, where is he then?" asks Ollie, more sharply than he intends. Sunny lifts her head. "Sorry, I don't know." Hannah shrugs.

"Where did he say he was going?" Ollie asks.

Sunny frowns; her dark eyes watch Ollie. "We haven't seen him."

Ollie dials Jaime's number. Jaime doesn't answer. He tries again.

Sunny says, "Ollie, he's sixteen. I'm sure he's okay. He's out somewhere. Same as we all were. Where were you at sixteen?"

"I was surfing," Ollie snaps. "Not 'out somewhere.' Anyway it's not about that. I told him to be home. It's a big day tomorrow. And just 'cause he's not going to school in the morning doesn't mean he can skip doing his homework."

Sunny uncrosses her legs and sits forward on the couch. "He does his homework, Ollie, pretty much every day. He's a good student. The way I remember it, he's better than you and Tai were."

Ollie ignores her and presses his ear to his phone. "He's not answering," he says after it rings out for the second time.

"Ollie." She pauses the game and scrutinizes him, then shrugs and shifts gears. "Okay. Okay. Give me a second and I'll call around to a couple of people." She turns to Hannah. "I'll try Lena first?" Hannah nods agreement.

Ollie chews his thumbnail and resists pushing Sunny aside as she hunts for her phone among the couch cushions. She pulls it out and calls.

"Hey, girl, you seen Jaime tonight? …Okay, no problem, no, nothing's wrong, we're just wanting to get a hold of him. Any parties or whatever on over this side?" She laughs. "Right. I'll give one of that crew a call. Mahalo."

Ollie refrains from pacing the floor. It's not that he thinks anything's happened to Jaime, not really. But tonight everything needs to be right and under control, and Jaime doesn't even have the sense and thoughtfulness to be here.

Tai walks in with a towel wrapped around his waist. He rests a hand on Ollie's shoulder. "What's up?"

"Jaime's not here."

Tai says, "He—yeah. It's okay. I know he's not." Ollie swings about to face him and shrugs off his hand. "He went to Tex's party with a couple of the kids from his class."

"I specifically told him to be here," says Ollie, his voice low.

"That might be why he's not."

"What?" Ollie says sharply.

Tai holds his gaze. "He came to me earlier and mentioned the party. It sounded okay. Anyway, it wasn't as though he was asking. He has to let us know; but he hasn't needed to ask where he can go since he turned sixteen."

"Fuck. Maybe he should ask," says Ollie, though that's unfair. They had all talked this through at the time. "He's just a kid and he's an idiot."

Tai looks as if he's about to say something, but Sunny gets off the phone. Her face is bright. "Found him. He's up at Tex's place. There's a party on."

"We got that," says Ollie. "Turns out Tai told him he could go."

"Okay..." Sunny hesitates. "So we know he's all right. Then it's all good?"

"No." Everything inside Ollie is tangled and anxious and infuriated. "Fuck it, Sunny, it's not all good. You guys lie around playing fucking—"

Hannah interrupts. "Leave it be, Ollie." She holds up a hand.

"How about I drive over and get him," Tai says. "The girls'll come, right? We'll handle it, Ol. You need to get some rest for tomorrow."

"You know I won't sleep," Ollie says shortly. Tai's supposed to know everything without Ollie needing to say it. "The girls can stay here and play. I'll come with you."

Tai eyes him for a steady moment.

Ollie falters. "Jaime can't do this—I can't afford to waste tonight worrying about him. So I go with you, we find him, then things can calm down."

"Fair enough." Tai nods. He grabs the keys from the kitchen bench and slips into his flip-flops at the door. As they walk to the car, he says, "Ollie. I'm sorry about this. I wanted to give the kid some freedom."

Ollie's tired of being the bad guy. "From what? From me?"

"No. Of course not." Tai frowns as he gets into the car. "That's not what I meant."

Ollie gets in beside him. "He shouldn't have talked to you at all. He knew I wanted him home. I told him. He's so—" Ollie doesn't have the time to think about all of this. He stops talking.

Tai starts the car in silence.

They're quiet for most of the trip. They watch the headlights sweep out across the black road. Tex's place is around the headland and up the hill, away from the beach.

"He's a good kid." Tai turns into the street. "He needs—"

"Not now. Don't tell me he's a good kid. I know that. He's my brother." Tai lets it go.

Tex's party is pumping for a Tuesday. The music is loud, and kids in the front yard spill onto the street, laughing and talking, arms flung over one another's shoulders. Ollie climbs out of the car. He holds himself carefully. This kind of party has always felt claustrophobic to him.

Tai scans the yard, then strolls through the front door, at ease. He shakes hands with one guy, hugs another tight. The guy gives Ollie a hug too. Ollie's skin prickles.

Eventually they find Tex. He's a tall, skinny, Filipino guy, recognizable by his cowboy hat.

"Tex, man. Hey. We're looking for the kid, Jaime."

Tex crunches up his face, confused. Ollie wants to smack him. That's not going to help. He steps back.

"You'd know him. Scrawny white kid, white hair. Looks kinda like this one only better dressed," Tai waves a hand at Ollie, behind him.

Tex grins recognition. "Aw yeah, that kid? Yeah, man, he's out back."

They push through the people in the front room and head down the hall and into another room. The place smells of beer and sweat. Ollie steps over someone's legs splayed across the floor. In front of him, Tai smiles at one girl, hugs another. People Ollie has never seen pat Tai on the back or yell to him down the hall, calling him "bro." Ollie takes a breath and follows in his wake.

They find Jaime in a back room lit by a couple of standing lamps with pretty blue and green light bulbs. He's on a girl's lap, looking happy and at home. He has a plastic cup in one hand and is waxing poetic about something. His other hand circles in the air. Ollie can tell that the kid is drunk. Again. It makes Ollie sick to his stomach. The last time Jaime was drunk, it sent them all off course. Ollie had held it together after their mom died. But just over two years later he was faced with the fact that he was failing his unpredictable baby brother, who wasn't a baby anymore.

From then on, Ollie crashed out on too many waves, was held under too long on a couple of nasty sets. He caught his foot pushing up from a stony bottom. Up seemed like down, and as the swell pulled him he twisted his ankle. He came up terrified, his ankle screwed up, his eyes aching and lungs burning. He couldn't ignore the saltwater in his veins, but the ocean wasn't a friend anymore.

He hates how little his relationship with Jaime has changed since then. They're lucky to have the house, to have Sunny and Hannah and Tai. But the kid needs direction. That's pretty obvious.

Jaime lifts his head and catches sight of them. He smiles brightly. "Ollie! Bro!" he says. "Tai! You came!" Then he blinks and seems to realize the trouble he's about to be in. "Hey. You can't just come in here and—"

Ollie speaks low and fast. "We can just come in here and whatever we like, Jaime. You're an idiot. You're sixteen and you're my responsibility and you're a fucking stupid idiot." He's shaking.

"Hey, man," one of the big white guys stands up from the couch. "No need for that." He steps forward.

Tai speaks to the guy. "Leave it be, Russ. They're brothers, you know how it is." Russ nods slowly. Tai stands his ground. He turns to Jaime. "We want to get you home, kid. Ollie was—we were all worried about you. And it's getting pretty late. We've got an early morning." Jaime stays sitting and fixes Tai with his eyes.

"I only came for a second," he says.

"Yeah," says the girl whose lap he's occupying. "Plus, he's a super cute little thing." She eyes Ollie. "So you're the big brother, then." Ollie turns away to roll his eyes.

"I'm not little," Jaime says. "And leave my brother out of it." He turns back to Tai. "I haven't been here long. He doesn't need to—he's not my mother."

Ollie tenses. He wants to grab Jaime by his skinny arms and drag him out of here. But Tai reaches back and touches Ollie's hand without looking at him. He speaks gently. "He's not your mother, Jaime, we all know that. But we do have to look after you."

After a pause, Jaime stands up. He stumbles a little and blushes, but his eyes flash when Tai reaches to steady him. "I don't need help," he says.

"Um… yeah you do," Tai says, his tone soft and fond. When he grins, his eyes are bright. Somehow, as Ollie watches, Jaime's anger washes clean away. It's exactly the sort of thing that comes easily to Tai. Ollie aches with how impossible this seems for him and Jaime. He also aches with gratitude.

When they get home, Jaime climbs unsteadily out of the back seat. The house is lit up behind him. Ollie pauses beside the car.

"I didn't mean to scare you," Jaime says to Ollie. His eyes are pale like Ollie's and earnest blue in the half dark. "I'm always careful, Ollie. I promise. I don't want you to get scared. If you don't worry about me, then it'll all be okay. Yeah?"

Ollie holds his tongue. It's not okay; he can't leave Jaime to work it all out himself. But Ollie nods, not trusting himself to speak without yelling. He really does not have time for that tonight. Jaime hugs him clumsily, his wiry body squeezing Ollie, then lets go. When he steps away, the night air is cool against Ollie's chest.

"Okay. Get to bed," says Tai, hugging Jaime himself. "We can sort all this out in a few days. No rush." Jaime's face is teary and grateful. He turns away and walks inside. Ollie goes in behind Tai.

In the shadowed kitchen Tai says, "I made a bad call with that. I'm sorry."

Ollie's on edge, but his immediate frustration deflates with the apology. He sighs, tired and past anger. "Yeah. I don't know. It wasn't all your fault. And you sorted it out, too. So thank you."

Tai frowns at him. He pauses, then says, "Ollie, I don't need you to thank me. Jaime's my family too." He keeps his tone light, though his voice rings. It's important to him.

Ollie nods. Sometimes it's as if Tai's the one who holds it all together while Ollie makes everyone miserable—especially when it comes to Jaime. If it had been just him and Jaime, Ollie's not sure where either of them would be. Probably not talking or surfing at all. Ollie can't escape the fact that he has a lot to thank Tai for.

But he gets it. Tai doesn't look after Jaime simply for Ollie's sake.

"Well that's a relief, bro. I'm awful at being grateful."

Tai smiles in the dim light. "You really are." He props himself against a bench. "Hey." He takes a breath, and Ollie knows what's coming. "Are you okay?"

"I'm fine." Ollie tries to make his return smile convincing.

Tai settles his weight, leaving Ollie space. "Okay. I know. You've got this." He glances up the hall toward Jaime's room. "Jaime's okay, Ollie."

"I don't want to talk about it now," says Ollie without heat. "I need to focus on the comp for the next couple of days."

Tai meets Ollie's eyes. "Okay. Not a problem."

"And after that you can tell me all you want about how Jaime's fine. I'm heading for bed. See you in the morning." He stops at the door. He's safe with Tai, even when they don't agree. "I do mean thank you, though. Not for helping Jaime, tonight. For helping me."

Tai meets his gaze. "You're welcome. Sleep well, Ollie."

Ollie closes his eyes and tries to sleep. He's nervous. He's worried about Jaime. Beyond that, he's prickly and uncomfortable after touching all those people this evening.

He's always needed to hold himself slightly apart from the rest of the world, especially when he's competing. So many of the things that come easily to Tai and Sunny and even quiet Hannah are complicated to him. Touching other people is painful, visceral and immediate. It makes him flinch, sometimes, and then he's awkward about it, as if he's doing it wrong and thinking too hard. He's too sensitive.

He rolls onto his back and lets the regular beat of the waves slow everything down until he sleeps.

CHAPTER FOUR

It's early. Ollie's out on the grass putting a final coat of wax on his board. Tai watches through the window before he steps outside.

"You eaten?" Tai asks once Ollie's finished.

Ollie looks up and shakes his head. Tai holds out a smoothie. Ollie takes it.

"What's this?"

"It's a smoothie, dude. Jaime wanted to make it for you."

Ollie raises his eyebrows.

"I told him he could make it next time. I made this."

Ollie grins and downs half of the smoothie. "Thanks." He runs a hand over the board. Tai watches, trying to get a handle on Ollie's mental state. He looks okay.

Soon after six, they all crunch across the sand toward the stands that have been put up on the southwest end of the beach. It's comforting—the familiar view, the coarse sand, the Blue House kids on either side. Hannah's carrying a mug of coffee and a piece of toast and blinking into the sun; Sunny wears a striped sundress that matches the pom-poms she's holding.

When she came out, everyone had glanced at Ollie with trepidation, but Ollie laughed. "Whatever, Sun, you can't embarrass me. I can pretend not to know you," he said.

"O. L. L. I. E.," Sunny chanted, waving the pom-poms in his face. She's never been a cheerleader. Ollie laughed again.

Now, beside Tai, Jaime still seems a little foggy and subdued, but he's determinedly cheerful. Tai's grateful for his maturity.

Ollie has his favorite board tucked under his arm. Tai's carrying his second favorite.

A growing number of people—officials, reporters and spectators, walkers and runners—have stopped to see the wildcards battle it out. The invitational might be a preview for the main Pipe Masters event, but it's still a big deal.

Tai turns to Ollie, who's gazing out to sea, his mind on the waves. Ollie's chest rises and falls. Jaime gives Ollie a tiny smile and a quick squeeze, then steps over to the girls and flops down in the sand where a couple of local kids have set up camp.

Of one accord, Tai and Ollie walk to the edge of the water. The water rushes up to their ankles, then rushes away as their feet sink into the wet sand. Pipeline has two good breaks. Today they're both running, so every wave breaks from a single peak and travels in two directions, to the right in Backdoor and to the left in Pipe.

"Pipe's splitting," says Tai. It's not as though Ollie hasn't already noticed. They both heard it as soon as they woke up.

But Ollie answers him anyway. "Yeah. Backdoor looks good."

Tai nods. "It'll give you more options."

He keeps his voice steady, but the closer they get to the start of competition, the more nervous he is. His heart pounds. It's not as if he hasn't watched Ollie in a comp before. But back then it seemed as though Ollie would win everything. Ollie was Ollie, brilliant, risk-taking, uncomfortable with sympathy. A loss was never the end of the world. There was always another comp to win. But now Ollie hasn't won anything, not a single heat, in more than eighteen months. This comp may be his only chance.

Tai shakes his head to clear away the negativity. Beside him, Ollie doesn't move. His jaw shifts.

"You've got this. You can wait for the right wave," Tai says. "There'll be lots of sets, and you have time."

Ollie nods.

"You've got this, Ollie," Tai says again. "You know this break better than anyone I know. You've killed it here a million times."

He strains to make out Ollie's voice over the sound of the surf. "I've messed it up about as many."

Tai takes a breath. He wants to say the perfect thing, the thing that will make Ollie win.

There's a crackle over the loudspeaker, and the competitors are called to the stands.

"I'll see you after." Ollie flicks a glance at Tai.

Tai thumps him on the shoulder. "I'll be right here."

Tai sits in the sand next to Sunny. As Ollie paddles out with the other two surfers in the heat, Tai toys with the string of shells tied around his wrist. Watching Ollie surf is always amazing, but now Tai's tense.

Hannah leans forward from Sunny's other side. "Bro, nothing you can do now."

"Except freak out."

"Nah, Ollie's okay. But you're taking years off your life."

"He looks good," says Jaime quietly. He's asking for reassurance, but he's also right.

"He really does," says Hannah.

Sunny says, "Our boy's got this."

They watch in silence. From the first, Ollie's positioning in the lineup is good. He waits through the first set of waves. One of the other surfers takes a wave in the second set, leaving two surfers in the deep. Ollie watches, then turns and paddles onto the final wave of a large, breaking set. He carves one turn, then two more before his wave curls into a tube. Ollie's floating through it. They lose sight of him, hidden inside the green room. On the beach, the supporters are buzzing with excitement. Tai gets to his feet. Ollie shoots from the tube as the crowd erupts in a huge roar. He finishes cleanly with a tidy snapback. Tai swells with pride.

The wave nets Ollie a huge 10 out of 10 from the judges. Even from a distance, Tai can see the brightness in his face. Not long after that he has priority again and propels himself onto another beautiful tube, executing three swift turns before bending over the board and letting the barrel swallow him. The judges award him an 8.5, which will add to the 10 for his final score. The other surfers never catch up.

They don't talk before the second heat. Tai stays where he is. Ollie hops up and down at the water's edge before he heads out.

He's up against a guy none of them know, Cal something. The crowd is getting behind Ollie, the local boy. Tai watches closely.

The first wave Ollie takes seems perfect, but then out of nowhere he tumbles over the back in a whirlwind of limbs. The judges give him a 2.0. After that Cal takes his time before taking a nice 7.0 wave. The pressure's on. Ollie looks stuck, unable to commit to taking anything for what seems like hours. It's only about five minutes. Still, five minutes matter when you're in a thirty-minute heat.

Finally Ollie takes another wave, and Tai holds his breath. Sunny clasps his hand. But Ollie's form is only mid-range. Cal takes another low-range wave. Time ticks by. Tai glances at Jaime and the girls. They're all intent on the ocean. Just at the end of the heat, a sweet wave starts to curl into a tube. It looks too tight to ride, especially for someone Ollie's height, but it's probably one of the last waves of the heat.

"Take it," Jaime mutters. "Take it."

Ollie takes it, gets right down over his board as the pipe starts to collapse. It's far from Ollie's best ride, but it's both daring and tidy. The judges award him a 7.5 and he scrapes through in front. Tai breathes again.

Ollie paddles to shore. His strokes are weary.

"He'll wanna talk to you," says Sunny to Tai.

Tai makes his way to stand in the area where Ollie will land. Ollie comes out of the water and plants his board in the sand. He flops down beside Tai's feet.

"I can't do this." He looks up at Tai. His shoulders drop as though he's already lost.

Tai sits beside him. He stretches his legs in the sand. A tiny part of him longs to tell Ollie not to worry about it. The semis will put him up against Matteo Christoph, who was ranked twenty on the world circuit only two years ago. Matteo's in great and consistent form. His first heat was incredible to watch. The truth is, Ollie's probably going to lose. It's a competition. This isn't just about the joy of the ocean. Tai bites his lip. That tiny part of him wants to say, "Let's go home." He's watched Ollie lose before. Winning matters more now.

But, of course, this is the world circuit. It's been Ollie's dream since long before they met. And beneath Ollie's exhaustion and nerves is a steely, competitive core.

Tai says, "Hey, so you know, back when we were kids, there were a couple of years when there wasn't much between us on the water. Sometimes I'd get the better run, sometimes you would. And we both wanted to be pros. But I watched you get better and better, and even though I improved, it wasn't the same."

Ollie frowns. "What?" But he waits for Tai to go on.

Tai grins. "You were so fucking annoying, Ollie, always getting that last perfect piece of air off the back of wave. You'd fit in five turns on a wave when I'd barely scrape four. I didn't have a chance. But I didn't stop coming out with you. Even when it made me sick and jealous to watch. The first time you got called up for a comp and I was left out? It burned. But it was you, so I was thrilled too.

"What I'm saying is this. It'd be unfair to sad little teenaged me and all those waves I watched you catch over the years if you decided you couldn't take on this guy. You're amazing, Ollie, and this is it. This round will get you into the finals, and that's all it takes to go to Pipeline this year." He looks Ollie in the eye. "Don't give up now."

Ollie blinks. He nods. After a moment he pushes Tai over into the sand. Tai lets himself topple.

"I wasn't about to give up," Ollie says. But his shoulders lift. Tai sits up and brushes sand out of his hair. "Thanks," Ollie adds.

"Anytime."

When they stand, Ollie's body bumps against Tai's. He hoists his board under one arm and faces the ocean. His limbs don't shake.

Tai stays near the water, a little away from the others, to watch the semifinals. Ollie's upright on his board, tense in a way that Tai never associates with Ollie on the water. He's being careful for most of the heat, and is awkward. But Tai holds out hope. Ollie knows these waves.

Tai sees the perfect wave at the same time Ollie's eyes fix on it. Ollie carves into it, lets it curl above him. He's silhouetted in the tube, then shoots out perfectly before the wave folds over itself. He's framed by the blue and white of the ocean. He's so beautiful that Tai doesn't want to blink.

Tai holds his breath as the scores come in. Ollie makes it through.

Tai leaps into the air. A surge of pride and relief washes over him. Ollie's in the top two, which means that whatever happens now, his Ollie is going to the Pipeline Masters next month, as they've hoped for months and, really, for years. Forever.

There's almost no time before the final. Jaime and Sunny and Hannah run to the water's edge and stand with Tai to watch Ollie. He's already into the Masters, but this performance still matters. The surfing world will notice.

Beside Tai, Jaime and Sunny are almost squeaking. "I knew he'd get through," says Jaime, thudding his whole body into Tai's and grinning at him.

"Me too," says Tai giving him a squeeze. "Your brother is awesome."

Sunny and Hannah hold hands and watch.

Out on the waves, it's as if all the nerves have gone and Ollie's himself again. He's perfect. He's bold and precise and everything Tai has ever hoped for him. It's as if Tai's there with Ollie, riding the waves alongside Ollie's calm and skill. When the buzzer sounds, Ollie looks right at his family before hopping up onto his board to take another wave into the beach.

As he steps out of the water, Ollie's surrounded by photographers and reporters, and cheering spectators, too. Tai watches with some concern. Ollie's shoulders begin to tense. But then Ollie looks over all the people, says a couple of words, and runs toward his family. No one can stop grinning.

"We're going to Pipe Masters," yells Jaime. "Told you so." He's glowing. Ollie bends to kiss his hair, then beams at Tai over the top of his head.

"Thank you," he mouths.

Tai shakes his head, embarrassed and proud and thrilled.

A COUPLE OF DAYS LATER, Ollie's in the living room. Jaime and Hannah are there too, watching YouTube videos of stenciling onto T-shirts.

"How about we write 'Ohana' in a different font," says Jaime. "Something like this."

Jaime and Hannah are in tune in a way that's so quiet Ollie sometimes forgets it's there. They all need this family, but Jaime and Hannah need it the most.

Ollie's phone chirps. He reads the invitation on the screen. There'll be a formal dinner at the resort—a big deal. It's in the ballroom. Everyone associated with Pipe Masters is invited: the surfers, the surf league and officials, coaches and agents and sponsors and media. Ollie has no interest in going, but even he can tell it's not an optional extra.

Tai flexes his hands as he steps into the living room. He's been in the shed with his boards. He smells of foam dust.

"You have to come with me, Tai," Ollie says.

"Come where, now?" Tai stretches his shoulders and back. Ollie taps on his phone's screen and turns it toward Tai, though Tai can't possibly read it from where he's standing across the room. "Next week for the surf league dinner. I got an invitation. It says plus one."

"I don't think they mean me."

Ollie shrugs. "Who else would I take?" He wrinkles his face.

Tai eyes him. "You're supposed to take a date, Ol." There's a challenge in the words that Ollie can't figure out.

"Whatever. It doesn't say I have to be dating the person I bring. You helped get me here, Tai. You deserve to eat the lobster or whatever. Anyway, you know I'll only have fun if you're there."

"Why didn't you ask me to go with you?" says Jaime from the couch.

Ollie frowns and is about to speak, but Tai says quickly, "Because I'm the one who's suffered through weeks of five a.m. starts and your brother's grumpy ass before breakfast. I get to take advantage of a fancy dinner."

Jaime glares at them, but relents. "Yeah, yeah. Okay."

Tai sits on the couch. Ollie hands his phone over. Tai thumbs in the code. He raises his eyebrows as he reads the invitation, then tosses the phone back.

Later, when Jaime's in the shower, Tai says, "You get to stay the night at the resort after the reception thing."

"You bet we do. Brandi'll put us in one of the good rooms."

Tai frowns. "You sure you don't want to take Jaime?"

"You're the one who got me here." The logic is self-evident.

"Nah. Pretty sure you're the one who got you here, Ollie." Tai stretches out his legs in front of the couch.

"Anyway, Jaime's always saying I kick if we share a bed."

"You do kick."

"Careful, bro, I bet Sunny would like to come along."

Tai reflects Ollie's grin back at him. "Not a chance. You asked me; you're stuck with me. What's a plus one need to wear?"

CHAPTER FIVE

IN THE BACK OF HIS wardrobe, Ollie finds the dark gray suit he wore for his mom's funeral. It's weird to get it out again. The suit was a little big four years ago. Now it fits him. It's slim through the hips, and they have to beg Sunny's mom to let the cuffs down. She even irons his pale green shirt, though Ollie could have done that himself, probably. He dresses in his room. He puts product in his hair and turns this way and that to inspect himself in the narrow mirror. He feels a little like someone else, but he looks okay.

They don't dress up often, there's never reason to, so the others are treating this like a bit of an event, hanging out in the living room to watch the show. When Ollie comes in, Hannah gives him a smiling thumbs-up.

"Ooh," says Sunny. "Hello, handsome."

Everyone sits around while Tai gets dressed. He doesn't have any formal clothes. But Maile's offered a suit her husband, Isaiah, has from when he was hoping to get a "real" job as an accountant in Honolulu. It's a little big on Tai's compact form, but Sunny's mom loosely hems the pants and sleeves and puts in a stitch or two to nip in the waist. "It'll hold for tonight," she promises.

"Thanks, Mrs. C." Tai pulls the suit on over a plum shirt he's borrowed from Jaime. The color glows against his skin. He adjusts the jacket in the mirror.

Sunny gives a decisive nod. "Hot." She moves to stand behind him and settles the jacket about his shirt collar. Her hands smooth over his shoulders. They're relaxed with one another. The ease and sweetness of it makes Ollie's lungs feel tight.

"Do I need a tie with this?" Tai asks. "Before you answer you should know I don't have one."

Jaime tips his head. "I've got ties in my room, but I'm pretty sure on you a tie would make it less cool."

Tai lets his shoulders drop as he stands tall. "Okay?" he asks Ollie. "At least you won't be ashamed of me."

"No," says Ollie. "No, I won't."

He doesn't turn away. The suit fits. Ollie has seen Tai scarf down a whole packet of chocolate pretzels and pee off the side of a boat. The Tai here in the living room seems nothing like that kid. He looks a little awkward, but distractingly great.

"You do need shoes, though, sweetie," says Mrs. Castillo. "No flip-flops."

Tai sits to put them on. Ollie blinks. He grabs his wallet and keys.

They've climbed into the car together a hundred times before, but it's something new to do it all dressed up for an important night, not just wearing their slightly better boardshorts and newer T-shirts.

Tai drives. Around the headland, the sun is gold behind them. Ollie's attention shifts between the streaked sky and Tai's hands on the steering wheel, lit by the sun.

Generally, Ollie finds things easy with Tai and the others. They know him, so they leave him room; but he doesn't mind when they hug him, not so much. He doesn't need to worry about protecting himself.

It's different tonight. Tonight they're alone. Tonight that matters. Ollie's skin tingles with Tai's proximity. He leans against the passenger door to keep the space between them.

It's strange to park in the same lot as the hotel guests. They walk across the lot and up the stairs to the entry hall. Photographers and reporters hover near the entrance to the ballroom, but they're focused on the comp's big names, the champions and superstars among the veterans, so Ollie and Tai make their way easily through the crowd.

Tai snags two champagnes near the doorway. "Thanks, Tierra. Hi, Polly," he says to the waitstaff.

He hands one glass to Ollie who sips from it. It's dry.

The mass of humans makes Ollie motion sick, but Tai's free hand is a familiar, anchoring pressure, low against his back. Of course, Tai knows half the people in the room. But they make their steady way past everyone to the bar, where they can lean and watch.

"Hey, Ju," Ollie says to the bartender. Juliana's not in their inner circle, but she's known Ollie and Tai since long before they could legally drink alcohol. Ollie hands over his champagne and asks for two rum and cokes instead. He gives one to Tai. As he's putting a tip in the martini-glass tip jar, he hears his name.

"Ollie Birkstrom."

Ollie turns. He knows that voice. "Paul."

Paul Dalziel holds out a hand, and Ollie shakes it. He was Ollie's agent until a couple of years ago. "Good to see you back in shape, man," says Paul. "You should give me a call if you need anything. Honestly. I'd like to hear from you." He hands over a card and turns to shake another person's hand and is taken up into the crowd. Ollie glances at the card, then pops it into the martini glass with his tip. The glass is full of red-dyed water. It soaks into the card.

Ollie turns to beam at Tai, who'll get the joke, but Tai is frowning. "I don't know, Ollie, you might be able to use an agent."

"You reckon?" Tai should know better.

Tai shrugs. "Yeah, yeah. I guess not Paul, though."

A woman leans against the bar. She's dark-eyed and dark-haired. Probably Hawaiian. She's not as young as Ollie and Tai, and with those broad shoulders, in this crowd, she's probably a surfer.

"He's the biggest surf agent in the business, you know," she says. She nods after Paul. She seems earnest, as though she's under obligation to tell Ollie this.

"I know," says Ollie. He's not about to be mesmerized by Paul's famous name and fancy car again.

"You don't like agents?"

"No, no. They're fine," says Ollie. "They handle all the stupid stuff I hate."

"He means the stuff he's terrible at," says Tai. "Like people." Ollie directs a glare at him but Tai ignores it.

The woman frowns. "Then why get rid of his card?"

Tai smiles toothily while Ollie takes a sip of his drink, "You can ignore Ollie. He's an idiot is why."

"That's not fair," Ollie says. He wants to explain. "The guy was my agent for a while. A couple of years back."

"And?" Her attention is focused on him. "You didn't get along?"

"No. It was cool. I was just a kid. I was easy to impress." Ollie thinks. "Look, the truth is he dumped me, in the end. Maybe I'm still bitter. But it wasn't only that. I didn't feel like he really heard anything I said, you know, about my goals and—I get that it's his job to help me get exposure and all that, but I started to feel like he wanted me to sell everything I was." He half laughs at himself. "That sounds dramatic."

He stops talking. Tai's presence is solid beside him. Ollie usually tries not to think about all he could have had, back then. If he hadn't fucked it up.

The woman nods. "Interesting. What kind of goals didn't he listen to?"

Ollie shrugs. He's not as clear on that as he once was. "I was nineteen. I wanted to be able to make my own choices. About what to wear and stuff. Sponsorship comes with so much baggage. I wanted—it was important to me to stay Hawaiian. I didn't want to be owned by some mainland brand name that decided when I wore which hat and what I said when I talked to grommets on the street. Anyway—" He stops. He's embarrassed. "It wasn't a great time, but Paul's good at his job. I probably should fish that card out." He looks through the glass at it. It's soaking wet and crimson.

"Or you could take mine." She reaches into her handbag but doesn't hand over the card right away. "I'm Carise. I think we could work together."

"You're an agent?" Ollie's shocked. "You don't seem like an agent." All the agents Ollie's met are perfectly polished, excessively extroverted guys from California.

"I'll take that as a compliment and not think you're basing it on the fact I'm a woman."

Ollie winces. "I thought you were a surfer."

"I was." She nods. She smiles, but her eyes go a little distant. "A long time ago. But I tore my shoulder in a Jet Ski accident in the middle of my rookie year. It never recovered. I tried again a couple of times but it kept tearing. So I can't compete anymore. But as it turns out, I can't stay away from surfing either."

Ollie understands that. "You're based in Honolulu?" he asks, glancing at the card.

"I am. I believe in this state. You should call me. I can at least promise I'll listen to you."

She hands over her card. It has a photo of Sunset Beach on the back. Ollie nods and pockets it. "Okay."

"You can put it in the tip jar once I've gone," she adds.

After she leaves Tai says, "She seems nice."

"Yeah," says Ollie carefully. He doesn't throw her card away.

"Anyone you want to talk to here?" Tai asks. He glances around. "Damn, too late."

"Ollie!" says a bright voice Ollie doesn't recognize.

He turns. "Hi."

"It's Alex. From *Freesurf* magazine."

Ollie nods. The guy is pretty polished.

"You must have snuck in here," says Alex. "I was waiting for your arrival. I want to get something from you for a story."

"Oh, right." Ollie definitely doesn't want to encourage this.

"What do you need?" asks Tai, close beside him.

"Just some comments from your boy here. I want to work the comeback angle, you know, talk about what happened to you, and how incredible it is to be here again."

"Oh. Nope," says Ollie. Tai's a calming presence at his elbow.

"You want to get sponsorship," says Alex, "you'll need more than just surfing skills. You need a story. And this'll be a great one. Your fall from surfer grace. Trying again after you crashed and burned."

Ollie shudders. He hates publicity. And that kind of article makes his skin crawl. He looks at Tai, who shrugs. The reporter might be right about sponsorship, but that doesn't mean Ollie needs to trot around revealing all of his secrets.

Ollie takes a breath. "No—"

"You're making a mistake," Alex says.

Tai speaks up. "Thanks Alex, Ollie appreciates it. But we might wait 'til he gets through Pipe Masters first and then have a chat with journalists."

"Your loss, kid." He moves away.

Ollie can't help but reply. "Not really." It's probably lucky that the party's loud and the guy's already out of earshot.

"You're going to have to talk to the media soon enough," says Tai. "But I reckon you can take a break tonight."

"Especially from him. Thanks, Tai."

"Not a problem."

Tai turns to talk with one of the older association guys about the boards Tai's grandfather shaped for him back when they still put balsa wood inside fiberglass. Ollie's heard this story a hundred times before—he could tell it himself—and he's hovering around Tai in a way that must be annoying. He didn't bring Tai because he needed someone to cling to in the sea of people. He steps away and surveys the room. There's a DJ and a little dance floor crammed with people. Ollie hesitates between the tables and the bar. It's stupid being on edge like this, alone in a room full of people he almost knows.

Ollie's relieved when a guy about his age steps over. It's less awkward when someone's talking to him.

"I wanted to meet you," the guy says. "I'm Ashton." He swoops his golden brown curls out of his face. They drop straight back into his eyes again. He tries again.

Ollie nods. "Nice to meet you," he says. "You one of the surfers?"

"Yes," Ashton says, a little stiffly. He pushes his hair out of his eyes.

"New haircut?"

"New hairdresser." Ashton shrugs. "I'm not used to it. She talked me into this, said it'd be cool. Mostly it's in my eyes. I hope it doesn't get in my way on the surf."

Ollie laughs. "I've got a pair of scissors if you need one. I'm Ollie Birkstrom. Though I guess you said you knew that."

Ashton holds out a hand. His handshake is firm enough that he might be trying to prove something, but that's okay; Ollie's glad not to stand out as the only loner in the room.

"Is this your first year on tour?" Ollie asks.

"No, no, it's my second. Scraped through in the top group last time around."

"Right. Nice."

The whole room has been on the circuit longer than Ollie has. He's way out of his depth. Worse, the way half the room watches him, he's pretty sure they know him or know of him. He wishes he had the benefit of either confidence or anonymity.

Ashton says, "Anyway, like I said, it's good to meet you. I've heard a lot of things." He blushes under his tan. "All good, of course."

"Thanks. I think."

"Just from magazines mostly," Ashton hurries to add. "There's been lots to read about you of course. There was that old profile piece in *Stab* mag. I have a copy. Everyone looked up to you back then."

Ollie doesn't answer. He's pretty sure the guy's not trying to be rude.

"And now the local paper's been raving about you getting through again."

"Not raving."

Ashton shrugs. "I've watched you surf. It'll be good to see you compete. It's pretty nice to see us Americans getting back up."

"And Hawaiians." Hawaii might not be its own country, but Hawaiians surf for themselves.

"So you brought Tai along?" Ashton asks.

Ollie nods. "Yeah." He's surprised by the question, but not surprised Ashton knows Tai. Tai knows everyone.

"He's your roommate, right?"

"Yeah." There's more here under the surface than Ollie knows. "That wasn't in the *Stab* profile," he says, trying to figure it out.

"You're probably right. I was just curious."

Ollie shrugs, but he's watching the guy. "Yeah, he's my roommate. Well, my housemate, along with a few others."

"Right. Yeah." Ashton blushes again. "The thing is, we got kinda close last year," he says, and everything becomes clear to Ollie. "You know?"

"Ah. Got it."

"Yeah. Tai hung with some of the surfers when we were in town for the comp. I guess you weren't around much."

"No." Ollie thinks about last year, when he didn't have many options, had been pushed out of some smaller comps, and hadn't qualified for anything. Nothing seemed possible for Ollie then, and all he wanted was distance from even the sound of the ocean. Instead he was stuck living with obsessed surfers two hundred feet from a famous break—which was probably what made it possible to drag himself back into the surf, but it still wasn't fun.

He avoided Pipe Masters that year. Tai hadn't, though. He'd kept quiet about it for Ollie's sake, but he'd watched the comp and then probably hooked up with a longish list of cute mainlander boys.

"He might have mentioned you," Ollie says carefully.

Ashton's eyes widen. "Really? He talked about you all the time."

Ollie senses a bit too much sharp eagerness and has no idea what to say. He's relieved when Tai approaches. Tai's timing has always been pretty much on point.

"Hi, Ash," Tai says.

"Tai Talagi, you look good. Really good." Ashton's gray eyes run up and down Tai. He takes a quick breath. "I was just—" His eyes have gone wider. "You know what? I was asking Ollie here if you two were here together."

"Together?" asks Tai quickly.

"Together together." Ashton is flushed.

Ollie blinks. That wasn't what Ashton had asked Ollie, but it was there underneath everything. Good for him for being direct.

Tai glances at Ollie, then back to Ashton. "No, dude. We're housemates. And I'm training him, when the fucker lets me. So he caved to pressure and brought me along to this."

Ashton's smile gets wider. "Oh well, good, that's great."

"Clearly I'm an excellent trainer." Tai grins at Ollie for a flash, and Ollie nods. "Plus, I heard there was an open bar."

Ashton laughs under his breath. "Which I figure you'll take advantage of." He glances across the room, then rests a hand on Tai's sleeve.

Ollie watches. He's never minded watching Tai flirt. Tai has a way about him that makes everyone want to be near him. It makes Ollie happy. It's not as if Ollie hasn't seen all of this before.

The only trouble is, usually when Tai starts flirting Ollie has people to talk to. But this is not a bunch of people he's known all his life, who know how to laugh and roll their eyes when he gets uncomfortable and silent. He's lonely here in the crowded room. There are still speeches to come, and a presentation. He can't take a walk down by the water and find some space. He takes a breath. "I'm going to get a drink."

He's not a big drinker, but with Juliana on, the bar is an easy place to be.

"Want another rum and coke?" she asks.

"Thanks, Ju."

By the third one, he's sitting on a bar stool, swinging his feet and watching everyone dance while exchanging comments with Juliana whenever she has a moment. The speeches are dull, but they're over quickly.

Ollie watches Tai talking with a bunch of the surfers. He's shaping a board in the air with his hands. Ashton's nearby, laughing with some of the other Americans. His eyes flick to Tai sometimes. Ollie's brain sticks on that. Ashton has something of Tai that Ollie doesn't have, and has never thought about having.

Ollie watches the other surfers too: famous faces and handshakes and sponsorship deals. In this room, everything seems far beyond his reach. He leans against the bar and tries to look confident and imposing to ease his melancholy.

"Ollie." Tai appears at Ollie's side.

Ollie didn't expect him, but he definitely doesn't mind. "Hey, Tai." Ollie's foggy with the alcohol and with the crowd, too. "Hi."

"You can't leave me alone in this crowd," Tai says.

He's laughing, but the thought that Tai would want Ollie around more than any other guy warms Ollie's insides. "I won't."

Tai eyes him. "Hey, you. You okay?"

Ollie needs Tai to understand. "Yeah, I'm not bad, only I'm not—" Tai is still, but the whole world is shifting. Ollie blinks, trying to keep everything steady. "I'm not as sober as I'd like to be. Not really."

"Okay. That's okay." Tai contemplates Ollie. "So, it's pretty late. I don't know, do you want to hang around here, or are you ready to check out our room, see how the other half lives? I've always wanted to find out if those rainstorm showerheads are as good as they sound."

Ollie smiles a real smile. "That sounds perfect."

CHAPTER
SIX

IN THE ELEVATOR, OLLIE LEANS on the wall with his back to the rail. The lights are bright, and the floor shifts uncomfortably, like the wrong kind of water. Tai leans forward to press the button for their floor. Ollie breathes slowly and watches, letting everything drift a bit. Tai's jaw is strong and shadowed. His eyelashes are long and dark as he blinks. It's strange to watch him this closely. Suddenly every detail seems important. Suddenly Ollie can sense the way Tai's whole body moves, even under his suit.

Ollie shakes his head. He's not sure how to get a hold on this. His tongue is thick and stupid in his mouth. "The thing is—" He lets the words come. "It's weird, but I guess I didn't see you before."

Tai laughs, "You've known me since you were thirteen, Ollie. I'm pretty sure you've seen enough."

"No, I mean, I didn't see, really see."

Tai looks carefully at Ollie, then away. His tongue flicks out to wet his lips. The elevator glides upward.

"Sorry," says Ollie into the space. "I just wanted to tell you. That. I don't know. That you're hot, and I guess that came as a surprise."

Tai keeps his eyes on the elevator numbers and huffs out an awkward laugh. "No problem, dude. And thanks. Um. You're surprisingly hot, too." His voice is mild, but hard to read, and Ollie is tipsy. He wants to giggle and cry and explain.

"No, but I mean it, Tai."

Tai looks at him then. "Okay." His eyes are wary. "Sure. Well, thanks." The elevator door slides open. Tai takes a quick breath and steps out onto the soft carpet of the corridor.

Ollie watches, then rushes to catch up. He's not accustomed to running after Tai. One of the Australian surfers, Brandon something, a tiny Asian guy, is leaning against the wall next to a giant decorative urn.

"Locked out?" Tai asks as they reach him.

"Oh." Brandon blinks at them blankly, then shakes his head to clear it. His eyes are tired. His hair is sticking up in a hipster ponytail of some kind. "Nah, mate. Hey, it's kinda possible this isn't my floor."

Tai smiles; Ollie tries not to laugh. "Do you need a hand getting to the right place?" Tai says. He rests a hand on the guy's arm.

The guy frowns. "I'm staying in the South Wing. Maybe I got in the wrong lift. Elevator."

Ollie nods and focuses. He works here; he can fix this. "You need to go back down to the first floor and then head across the bar past that fountain with the rainbow lights, you know? There's a set of elevators."

"Hope you make it." Tai's face is kind. Ollie's seen that look on Tai every day for years. And still its sweetness twists in Ollie's stomach. He blinks away the strangeness.

Tai stops at the door of their room and holds out his hand for the key card. Ollie fumbles in one jacket pocket, then the other, while Tai waits, eyes still. He takes the key card from Ollie and their fingers brush. They've touched a hundred times, shoved one another into the waves, shared drinks and squeezed into cars and surfed the same board. Ollie pulls his hand away. Tai doesn't look at him as he unlocks the door with a quiet snick. He pushes it open. The room is dark, the curtains are pushed back, and the wide window is open to the black and the rush of the ocean beyond.

They stand just inside. Tai reaches for the light switch beside the door.

"Leave the light out," says Ollie, on a breath.

Tai turns to him, then, in the dark, as the door closes heavily behind him. Ollie's buzzing and bright with rum. He's reckless. Tai is beautiful. He looks solid; his shoulders are wide in the suit. He's warm and certain. He's the most constant thing in a fuzzy, shifting world.

It's unworkable and idiotic, the idea of reaching out to touch Tai this way. It's beyond what Ollie has words for. But unexpectedly, here in this hotel room, alone with Tai and a little bit drunk, it all seems possible.

Tai's standing right in front of him. Ollie steps close to the boy he's known all his life.

"Oh no," says Tai shakily. He doesn't step back.

Ollie's eyes are heavy, fixed on Tai's lovely, familiar face. Tai's tongue flicks out to touch his bottom lip. "Don't say no," Ollie says. "Say yes." His voice shakes, but he acts more confident than he is, and moves in.

Tai closes his eyes. "God, Ollie."

There's almost no space between them. Just the dark room and the scent and sound of the ocean. Just the smallest breath. Ollie leans forward to close the too-small gap. He hesitates.

Then Tai's hand curls around Ollie's waist. As always, his palm is calming and anchoring thing on the small of Ollie's back. But this time it pulls Ollie closer, moves their bodies hard against one another. Ollie stumbles and shifts his feet. When he takes a breath, his lungs fill with Tai and nothing else.

Ollie's only kissed one person before. Still, even dizzy with alcohol, he knows how.

Their lips meet. Tai tips his head. His mouth is open, soft under Ollie's. Ollie runs one hand about Tai's neck. Tai's breath catches. All Ollie can think about is more and more and closer.

Tai's strong, Ollie knows, but he lets Ollie press him back, lets Ollie use his height and shift forward so Tai's shoulders and the back of his head hit the door with a dull thud. Ollie pushes into him, still kissing. He lifts one thigh and angles it between Tai's legs. Tai's whole body responds and Ollie welcomes his shuddering little intake of breath, the ripple of desire that pushes Tai's hips forward, right there, tight against

Ollie's. His mouth opens further to Tai's tongue. It's just a kiss; it's just Tai, who can never be a surprise, and still it overwhelms Ollie's thinking. Everything everywhere is rich and bright and strange and brand-new.

Tai takes hold of Ollie's shoulders and twists his body. All Ollie's breath escapes as he's pressed back against the wall beside the door. Tai's eyes are dark in the night and steady as he bends to kiss Ollie again. There's no air. There's nothing but Tai and the movement of their bodies together. Then, just as suddenly, Tai shifts away.

"Damn," he says in a low voice. He's still so close. He looks Ollie in the eye, and Ollie blinks and tries to focus. "Damn." Ollie stretches forward to try to kiss him again, but Tai steps back, leaving Ollie leaning boneless against the wall.

"I thought," says Ollie, "we could just—"

Tai groans and closes his eyes. "No. No way. We couldn't just anything."

"I thought—" Ollie stops and frowns.

"You're not thinking at all." Tai's voice is not unkind, but he steps back farther. He sounds resigned. "You're drunk, Ollie. You're not thinking, and I can't let this happen."

"I am thinking," says Ollie. He tries not to sound petulant, but sadness shakes his voice. He sighs, presses his lips together as Tai watches, still. They stand there, facing one another, for seconds that seem to go forever. Ollie tries for sensible. "I'm sorry, Tai."

Tai exhales. He looks exasperated and something else, something sweeter and wider and infinitely worse. "Go to bed, Ollie. Please. We need to go to bed."

Ollie stays still, then twists his mouth into the only smile he can manage. He stands upright. "Tai, I know you. You'd pick up any of those guys downstairs and fuck them. So why not me, then?"

"God damn," breathes Tai. "Ollie, *don't.*"

Ollie holds his nerve.

Tai sighs. "Because it's *you*, Ollie. And you're an idiot if you don't know that it's not the same." Tai's jaw is set, and his eyes are hot and black and sure.

Ollie closes his eyes and lets the room spin. Then he gives in. He moves to the bed and sits to take off his shoes. They've seen one another dress and undress a hundred times after a surf. But now Tai turns his back. Ollie wonders if everything has changed forever. He strips down to his boxers, walks across the room and into the bathroom to wash his face and brush his teeth. He half hopes Tai is watching. But when he comes out Tai is still staring out the window at the black ocean.

Ollie climbs into bed. The bed is soft, but perfectly sprung. It's far better than any of the beds at home.

He shouldn't say anything, but he does. "The bed's good. You could just join me." He's not making another play. They've never slept in a bed like this one, and this is Tai. Ollie will always want to share.

"I'll sleep on the couch," says Tai softly.

"Okay." Ollie lies still and watches the ceiling spin until he sleeps. He doesn't say *join me* again.

THE ROOM IS DARK. TAI hasn't had enough sleep. His eyes are sandy.

Before he lay down on the couch last night, he pulled the blackout curtains closed. Then he stared into the darkness for way too long. The sounds of the ocean were familiar but the room itself was not. And everything he was thinking was a mess.

He sighs. He should get up. The couch is comfortable, but he won't get back to sleep. Ollie breathes steadily across the room—close and so far away.

Tai rolls off the couch and pulls on a T-shirt as he crosses the room. He fills a glass of water from the bathroom tap and steps outside onto the balcony. The light is too bright and his sunglasses are back in the room, but he can't stand to close his eyes. When he does, all he can see against the back of his eyelids is Ollie and last night. Tai tries to block the memories. He watches as the ocean rolls over and over toward the shore, spread out before him. The sky is endless blue; the clouds are solid white. Tai breathes it all in.

Ollie shifts in the bed. Tai winces. There's no way this is going to turn out well.

Tai's spent years not looking at Ollie. Not in this way. He's spent years seeing him as a friend and a brother, sometimes as a competitor. He's made sure never to look and want more of him, never to touch him out of anything but that brotherhood. It's important. It's how they're keeping the Blue House together. So Tai's tamped down on even the thought of physical intimacy, afraid that it might wake something huge hidden inside.

He can't ignore those thoughts now. It's as though he's waking up, like pins and needles in a limb that was fast asleep. Tai groans with frustration. He thought he'd put all of this behind him.

But now he knows what, years ago, he was desperate to find out: what kissing Ollie is like. He knows the way Ollie pushes forward and opens his mouth and licks between Tai's lips. He knows the scent and sound and taste of him. Tai's fantasized before, when they were younger and he couldn't resist the thought. Now he has the reality imprinted on his mind. He wishes he didn't.

Tai's been out since he turned sixteen, about the same time he recognized he was at least half in love with his best friend.

His parents seemed untroubled by their youngest child's revelation. Their religion is important to them, but it's focused on love and singing their lungs out. Tai had all his sisters and his brother and cousins on his side—the whole Samoan community—which probably scared the surfing community into leaving him be. He was surrounded by friends, easily loved, safe in that, and most of the time nothing could touch him.

He hooked up with tourists, a couple of surfers from out of town. Never with the local boys. That was too close to home. He'd reveal his feelings to Ollie one day.

They were eighteen when Ollie's mom died.

It was a couple of weeks before Ollie was back at school, more before he came back to the beach. Tai left messages, sent texts, saved Ollie's homework. He turned up with food he and his momma cooked. He waited.

When Ollie called it was the middle of the night.

"It's not fair," he said.

Tai clung to the phone. He curled up under the sheets. "I know." He pressed the phone to his ear and listened to Ollie sob. "Do you want me to come over?" he asked.

"No. Not now."

When he returned to the beach Ollie looked thinner, longer-limbed. His eyes shifted between bright and dark like the ocean.

They surfed. They went back to normal—as normal as things could be when Ollie had lost his mom. Tai tamped down on the way he felt about Ollie. He'd spent way too much time half in love, anyway. He had to forget all of that and be there for Ollie.

One afternoon they were on the rocks at Sunset Beach. Ollie pulled his knees up and rested his chin on them. He didn't look at Tai. "There are all these things that I see, and for a second I want to tell her about them. Nothing special. Fucking stupid things, usually. Like the new dress shop at the resort. Or this one cat I saw with no ears. Nothing. To be honest, I'd probably have forgotten them all while I was out surfing. By the time I made it home I wouldn't have had much to say."

Tai held Ollie's hand. Ollie let him, tangling their fingers and resting their joined hands against the rocks between them.

For a while Ollie and Jaime lived with their cousin. She was kind enough but lived in a small apartment, far from the ocean. It didn't work out.

Living together was Tai's suggestion. "Momma and Pa are moving back to Samoa. I thought we could get a place. You, me. And Sunny needs a place where she can have her own room. We have jobs, I'm sure we can afford something. I can sort of cook. We'll take Jaime too. If they'll let us."

"They, you mean, like protective services? If they'll let us? We don't need to tell them," said Ollie, as though it had already been decided. "We're taking him."

The apartment they found on Lokoea Place was kind of a hole, but six months later this run-down blue bungalow on the beachfront came up and the four of them and Hannah walked over to see it.

"It's perfect," said Sunny, before they even went inside.

It was. The bedrooms were small and the shower walls were linoleum, the boards of the deck were rotting and the walls and windows didn't block the sounds of cars and people or the endless noise of the surf. But still. There was sun on the deck, there was space for everyone, and they could be in the water twenty seconds after opening the front door. Hannah and Jaime timed it on the day they moved in.

Tai learned to step back from any thought of Ollie beyond friendship. He learned to live with Ollie and not look at him. The Blue House was important. It is important. Tai wants to hold it together more than he's ever wanted anything in his life, even more than he wants Ollie.

CHAPTER SEVEN

OLLIE COMES OUT ONTO THE balcony. He's pulling on a T-shirt. He scrubs a hand through his hair, which is sticking out in every direction. It's unfair, more than unfair, how he can look gorgeous even when he's probably hungover and definitely only half awake, even when Tai is a strange combination of angry and confused and faintly, unexpectedly humiliated. Tai's kept some things secret for so long. He and Ollie kissed and now he's exposed.

Tai looks away, back out to the safety of the ocean.

"Hey." Ollie's voice is rough with sleep and the night before. It's infuriatingly sexy.

"Hey." Tai says toward the water, then sighs gustily. It's not as though they can avoid one another, and this isn't the kind of thing he can just let be. "Okay," he begins, turning to Ollie and leaning back against the rail. In the sunlight, Ollie's freckles stand out against his skin and his eyes are pale and blue and gray. "Okay, Ollie, I have to ask. What the fuck *was* that last night?"

It's Ollie's turn to look away. Tai watches his jawline shift as he thinks. He's known Ollie for a long time. He knows how much he can get tangled in his thoughts.

"It's okay," says Tai. He's giving Ollie an out. "You can tell me you were drunk. Just tell me that, Ollie."

"I wasn't that drunk."

Tai is both irritated and secretly, intensely glad that Ollie's willing to say it.

"It wasn't just— I guess I wanted to see what the fuss was. I wanted to know what it was like," Ollie continues.

"What? What it was like to kiss a boy?"

Ollie frowns. He speaks as if it's all so very obvious. "No. To kiss you, you fucker." He hesitates but then goes on. "I watched Ashton last night, the way he was with you. It hurt. It wasn't jealousy. It was—look, this guy I've never heard of knows parts of you that I don't know, and I wanted that too. To be important to you in a different way—to know that."

"Okay," says Tai. The thought of knowing Ollie that way is dangerously appealing. "I don't know what to do with that."

Ollie leans against the rail too, not close enough to touch. Not that Tai would reach out if he could. He's always careful about Ollie's edges.

The tide is coming in, and the noise of the surf is everywhere. Tai looks at Ollie: his familiar profile, his long arms folded across his body, his legs stretched out. Ollie lifts his face to the sky. Looking at the long arch of his throat, Tai can't swallow.

Tai says, "We have a whole life already, Ollie. Your career, the Blue House. There's a lot to lose. I'm not going to risk all that to be some kind of experiment for you."

"No, of course." Ollie turns back to him, struck. "I mean, that's not really—"

Tai wants to smooth Ollie's hair and trace his cheekbones. But more than that, he wants to redefine the space between them before everything explodes.

"Let's forget it. Please, Ollie?"

Ollie opens his mouth as if he's going to say something more. Then he shrugs. "Okay." There's nothing to say. At length, Ollie looks around. "So, we're here. The best resort on the North Shore. Want to head down and take a swim in one of the pools?"

It's a relief to say yes and finish this conversation.

The nearest pool has a palm-clad channel that runs by the force of underwater jets. There are a couple of fountains too. Ollie finds a deep point and dives in cleanly.

"Show-off," Tai mutters and cups his hands around one of the fountains to direct it to shoot Ollie in the face when he surfaces. Ollie splutters, then springs through the water to exact revenge. Soon they're both shaking water from their eyes and laughing. Ollie somersaults in beside Tai. Tai laughs. They can probably turn this around, turn everything back to the way it was.

Tai dives in and swims a lap underwater. Everything is quiet and aqua blue. Swimming is the best solution to confusion and emotion and last night's lack of sleep.

PIPE MASTERS STARTS FOR REAL on a cloudy Tuesday morning the next week. Ollie's nervous. It's a strong field, the top thirty-four surfers in the world. But somehow, from the start, Ollie's got this. It's as if he owns the ocean. All of his heats go smoothly. The waves are perfect tumbling barrels, typical for this break. They're everything he wished, and he knows them the way he knows himself.

On the afternoon of the fifth day, Ollie leaves Tai and the others up the beach and stands in the wet sand, facing the ocean.

This is it. The finals. His opponent is Marco Leederville, an American from the mainland. He's third in the world. He's both experienced and talented, and is one of Ollie's heroes.

"I'll go gentle on you, rookie," Marco drawls. Ollie looks into his quick, crinkled eyes and is certain he'll lose.

Early in the heat, Marco pretends he wants a wave while Ollie has position. Ollie's fooled. He takes the wave, which of course falls flat, as does Ollie's run on it. Marco laughs at him as Ollie paddles back out. Ollie's frustrated. He should've expected that. "Pick your own waves," he hears Tai say in his head. "Never watch what your opponent is doing."

Ollie takes a breath and refocuses. And then his board becomes an extension of himself, as if, through it, he knows how every wave will behave before it even lifts from the ocean. He takes two nice rides and then holds position carefully until he sees a perfect wave come in. He grins into the sun. That wave is his.

As he shoots through the blue, everything is loud and bright and exactly right. The world's just carrying him. He carves into the wave as it spirals over him in a tight tube. The wash chases after him, licks at the board, but he's going too fast for it, and his board is soft and mobile against his feet. He bends to fit in the space left by the water and turns to stay right in the pocket. The green room opens up. When he exits the tube, he skims across the surface and then turns up the slope again before letting the board escape the wave.

Ollie's paddled halfway out again before the horn sounds, signaling that the heat is over. The judges' score for Ollie's last wave is put up on the sign on shore. A wave rolls under his board. The last ride netted him a 9.4. Ollie adds up his scores. He adds them up again. It's more than enough to win him the final.

He stays out in the ocean, bobbing halfway between the waves and the wash. The cheers carry out from shore. He shakes himself and looks around. Marco's making his way in. He nods across the water. "Decent job, rookie. See you at the next stop."

And that's right. There's a next stop now. It's been a long time coming.

His body shaking, Ollie follows Marco in. He can see Jaime leaping around like a wild thing. Sunny and Hannah are hugging and dancing in circles. Tai is watching Ollie. His dark eyes are sweet even from this far away. They're still far apart, but they beam at one another across the sand as Ollie stands at the edge of the ocean.

He steps out of the water, hoisting his board under his shoulder. Right away he's crowded by photographers. "Top ride, Ollie," calls one. "Look over here and give us the hang loose, Ollie," says another. The camera shutters click and the flashes flash. Ollie tries to do as they ask.

"What are you riding, Ollie?" asks one guy.

Ollie grins at that. "My friend Tai made this board. Look out for him."

"We'd like to have a word," says a woman he doesn't recognize. "I'm with Hurley." Ollie glances at her, startled.

"Can you go up to the media tent first?" says a marshal of some kind. "You need to do some press."

"Billabong," says a tall guy. "Pretty sure you'll want to chat with us, Ollie."

From behind him, a voice says, "You want me to handle their questions?" When he turns Carise shrugs, but she seems a little nervous, as though she hadn't expected to be so bold. Ollie doesn't recall hiring her, but he probably will. He likes her. He needs someone to help with this stuff.

"Okay," he says.

She smooths her hair and turns to the corporates and reps, smiling professionally as they surround her and demand her attention.

"Okay, okay," she says. "I'll get to all of you."

"What do I do now?" Ollie asks her.

She grins. "We'll talk later. Go and find your friends and then get up to the podium to collect that massive trophy."

Ollie doesn't need to be told a second time. He's already looking through the crowd. He runs when he sees his family, gathers Tai and Jaime into his arms, and squeezes tightly until they're soaking wet too. The photographers snatch a photo. Hannah and Sunny pile in. Ollie can't stop smiling. He's won at Pipeline. The Pipe Masters. It's all of his dreams in one perfect, perfect day.

THE WIN ISN'T JUST A win. It's enough to get him a place on the World Championship Tour. Ollie's half shaken, half thrilled.

Ollie's renown as a junior surfer is helpful. Carise convinces *Rip* magazine to put up the airfare in return for a front cover article. Some of the prize money for winning the round will go for accommodations, but the rest of it's put straight into the household account. No one in the Blue House has seen that much money. Tai arranges for the car to be tuned. Hannah fills the kitchen with food and replaces the microwave. Sunny gets all the overdue bills paid.

"I can't believe it," she says, coming out to sit with them. She looks back at the Blue House with easy pride. "It's pretty nice to know they won't cut off our electricity for three whole months."

Even after that, there's still so much money it makes Ollie feel short of breath. He's finally doing something. He'll have to think hard about this sort of stuff; he needs to be responsible for everyone's sake. He's proof that, in surfing, you can be on top of the world and then slump and be no one. But now, for a short time, it all seems clear.

OLLIE'S NOT GOING TO GO off on the world tour blind. He's watched it for years, first on the television in his mom's apartment, sometimes in the middle of the night. It's different to watch now, though, knowing he's going to be part of it. He keeps pausing the DVD to work out who's who on shore. He sits close to the TV and watches the surfers, but he also watches the judges and the interviews. All the big guns thank a coach and a team. They seem to have people to carry the boards and the trophies and the surfers themselves, if they do well.

All the things he won't know how to do buzz in Ollie's head. He'll need to navigate events and attitudes and heat times alone.

"Hey, want a lift?" says Hannah from the doorway. Ollie lifts his head, startled. She smiles. "Hey. Tai sent me back from Nalu. He thought I'd need to tear you away from the TV. We're done with setup and people are arriving."

"Okay," says Ollie. He doesn't stand. He's still thinking.

Hannah says, gently, "It's your party, babe, you can't be late."

They're giving him a big send-off at Nalu Kua Loloa. Everyone comes along: the local surfers, Maile and Maribel, and some of the older crew.

Maile makes a speech. In the middle of talking about how long she's known Ollie, how hard he's been working, she tears up. "You can't blame me for crying. I'm proud," she says. "Ollie's like my little brother. I've watched these kids grow."

Sunny gives a speech too. "Here's to our North Shore boy set to take over the world!" she finishes. There's a cheer as everyone raises a glass.

Ollie smiles. It's encouraging; he wants to do them all proud, but his stomach is churning and his nerves are fluttering.

Halfway through the party he finds himself alone with Jaime.

"What's wrong with you?" Jaime asks, and though it's his little brother voice, it's still sweet that he noticed.

Ollie shakes his head. He doesn't have an answer.

"It's cool," says Jaime. "Everyone's scared about stuff like this. It's a big deal."

"Yeah." says Ollie. "Yeah. But I wasn't this worried until I started watching last year's tour on those DVDs Webby loaned me. It's all so professional."

"That's kind of the point of a pro tour?"

"But it's more than that. I mean, they've got their crew, they've got a coach, sometimes a caddy. Some of the big gun surfers travel with physios and board shapers, Jaime. And I'm going to be among them all. Me."

"You've done great without any of those things," Jaime says. "You'll be okay."

Ollie sighs. "Plus, I'm not great with crowds."

Jaime laughs. "I'd noticed, dude." He eyes Ollie. Ollie glares back. Jaime says, "Okay. How about this. Take Tai with you."

Ollie shakes his head. "Nah. Nope. Tai needs to stay here. I can't."

Sunny bounds over but slows down when she sees their serious faces. "What's up, buttercups?" she asks.

Jaime answers. "I'm telling Ollie that he should take Tai on tour with him. He's freaking out. Much to my shock."

"Be nice," says Sunny.

Ollie says, "And I'm telling Jaime that Tai needs to stay home." Ollie can't imagine going away and leaving Jaime alone. At least if Tai's here—

Sunny narrows her eyes. She says, "We can handle it without either of you, Ollie. You know that, right?" She grabs Jaime around the head. "Jaime would be fine without you or Tai. He's got Hannah and me."

"I can't just take Tai on tour," says Ollie. But the thought makes every breath come more easily. "Can I?"

"Well… we can pay the airfare out of that ridiculous sum of prize money," says Sunny. "Or maybe you can convince the magazine to pay for two coach fares. You'd never fit in with the business class people and all their fancy suits and laptops anyway."

Ollie stands still, staring at her, then at Jaime.

"Go find him," Sunny says.

Ollie goes. Jaime comes after him, saying, "Just a second, I'll come with you. You'll forget to tell him it was my genius idea."

It's not a huge café, but it is full. They find Tai behind the counter talking with some people Ollie barely knows. "Can I steal you for a second?" Ollie asks Tai.

"It's important," says Jaime. "Serious stuff."

"Sure. Sorry guys, the champion calls." The three of them head into the corner of the galley kitchen.

"So?" Tai prompts them.

"Ollie wants to ask you something," says Jaime. He bounces a little on his toes. It's endearing to see his excitement, though it might also be due to the thought of six weeks living alone with Sunny and Hannah, who have such an easy relationship with him. Even with Tai he'd have had an easy go of it. The worst thing is, Jaime might prefer life without Ollie in the house.

Ollie says to Tai, "Sunny and Jaime and I were talking and—we thought. Well, I was hoping you'd come on tour with me."

Tai's eyes widen. "What?"

"He wants you to go with him, Tai," says Jaime. "He needs a coach and someone to handle all the people and stuff."

"Oh…" There's a pause. Tai frowns. "You'll have Carise. And. I can't, Ollie. I can't just disappear . I've got stuff on and I can't leave Mai in the lurch at the café, and the flights would be so expensive."

Somehow it never occurred to Ollie that Tai might say no to him. "Oh," he says.

Jaime rolls his eyes at them. "Dude," he says to Tai. "We're talking about a world surfing tour here. You *need* to go. You'll get six weeks surfing on the other side of the Pacific. You'll be in places you've been annoying me by talking about my whole life—places right across Australia, and that fucking terrifying wave in Tahiti. Think about it. This is a once in a lifetime thing." He glances at Ollie. "Well, maybe not once in a lifetime, but you know what I mean."

Tai nods, weakly.

Jaime goes on. "Anyway, I can help at the café. I need some money. Fashion isn't free, you know,"

"But the flights. And—"

"Sunny has a plan, and you guys can share a room, easy," Jaime says.

Tai still hesitates. And however much he wants Tai there, Ollie's not about to push it. He says, "It's cool. It was just an idea."

"It's an awesome idea. Fuck it, Tai," Jaime says. "My brother needs you there. We all know he can barely cope as a human without you."

"I can cope fine," says Ollie. He presses his teeth into his lower lip. "Seriously, Tai. It's cool."

"And instead of being there, you'll be watching from home as he messes up. You'll feel like shit. You know it's true," Jaime persists.

Tai looks between them. He breaks into a smile. Ollie's chest eases. "You're right, Jaime. It's an awesome idea. Fuck it. Okay."

"I knew he'd see sense," Jaime says.

Ollie meets Tai's gaze as Jaime thumps both of their shoulders simultaneously.

"We're going on tour," says Tai. He grins, and things seem as if they could be okay. Better than okay. Ollie's going on tour. He's going on tour with Tai. This will be incredible.

CHAPTER EIGHT

TAI CRACKS HIS EYES OPEN to a bright, blank Australian hotel room ceiling. The other bed is empty, its sheets flung back. Sunlight streams in through the half-open curtains. One curtain's got itself caught in the wind and billows through the open balcony door.

Ollie's outside on the narrow balcony. He's slim, silhouetted against the bright sea and Southern Hemisphere sky. His hair is lit up so it looks like a scruffy, crooked halo around his head. He's chewing his nails.

It's their fifth day in Coolangatta, on the Gold Coast of Eastern Australia. They've spent their days trying to get in a free surf on the couple of gutless waves that have popped up around the rocks. Every day the water's flat, and the competition is on hold. It's frustrating. Ollie's watched the water obsessively. He's chewed his fingernails and has snapped at Tai a few times for no reason.

Their hotel room is on the north side of the hotel, facing up the coast over miles of beaches, with the city and green mountains behind them. From this high up, it looks a bit like home, but the coastline stretches too far to the north, and the air's different: cooler and lighter and less fragrant.

Ollie's leaning over the balcony railing to see more of the ocean. His body is stretched out, tapering from his shoulders to his narrow, muscled waist. He's lovely to look at. Tai sighs and shakes his head. It's been worse since Ollie kissed him, harder to be in the same space as Ollie without noticing his physicality.

"Morning," Tai calls out. He yawns and arches his back, lets his spine curve into place.

Ollie turns his head. "Morning. It's another flat one out there."

They're used to being in this space now. At first it was weird for the two of them to be together in a pristine room with wide white beds, amazing water pressure, and maid service. The only time they'd stayed in a hotel room like this before was the night they kissed. So the whole first day they got here, they scarcely looked at one another. Ollie skirted Tai in the room, keeping more space between them than he usually did.

Things have settled. They've lived in the same house for years; they've been inseparable since they first met. However much things change, time together at home is always going to end up domestic and ordinary. The only difference is now they're on the other side of the Pacific.

Ollie steps into the doorway. "You were out late last night." He leans against the doorframe and chews on his thumb; his body is at ease even when his mind is clearly distracted. Tai blinks at the familiar ache. "Was some sort of party happening downstairs?"

"Nah, not really, I just sat talking with the guys. Some of the veterans stayed up and a couple of guys who know this break. Ashton and that guy Brandon, too, remember from the hallway at the resort? The lost Australian? All of them reckon the comp's going to start today."

Ollie frowns, thinking, and looks out and down to the ocean again. "I don't know, Tai, it's still flat. At least from way up here. There's hardly any surf at all."

"Yeah, though we can't see what it's doing at Snapper Rocks. That's where the best of it will be. Apparently you can get a little bit of surf with the wind onshore like this."

"Okay," says Ollie dubiously.

Tai sits up on the edge of his bed. Because of the two-week competition window, the league needs to start the competition soon, otherwise there won't be enough time left to finish. "It's not like I know for sure," says Tai. "I'm letting you know what I heard."

Ollie nods. "And do your new friends have much to say about how to surf it when it's dead flat?"

"They're keeping that information close to their chests." Ollie sighs and walks to sit on his bed, facing Tai across the gap. Tai goes on. "I'm taking it as a compliment. To you. They know a real threat when they see one. Usually I'm more persuasive."

Ollie laughs a little. "Yeah, yeah, yeah. We've all heard those stories, Tai."

It's ordinary teasing, but it's become awkward in the last weeks. Tai blushes. He throws a pillow at Ollie's head. It glances off and bounces on the bed. Ollie grins and things are back to normal-ish.

When Tai finishes in the shower, he wraps a towel around his waist and uses a second one to towel his hair. He opens the door. Steam billows into the main room.

Ollie is on the edge of the bed, with one leg stuck out in front of him. He's got a bandage half wrapped around his ankle. It's hanging loosely around his foot.

"Shit." Ollie unwinds it and starts over.

Tai tucks the towel more tightly at his waist. "Let me do it. You're making a mess of it."

Ollie hesitates, and Tai wonders if he's going to reject the help. "Okay. Yeah, thanks."

Tai takes Ollie's foot in one hand. Ollie's breathing pauses.

"Giving you trouble?" Tai asks to ward off any awkwardness that comes with touching Ollie when they're alone. If they were on the beach, this would be easier.

"A twinge. Nothing to worry about. But better to be safe."

"Yeah, you don't want to favor the other one." Tai pulls the bandage tight. "This all right?"

"Good, thanks."

Under Tai's fingers, Ollie's ankle feels all too human – tendon and bone and skin. Tai doesn't linger, just wraps the bandage around the joint and up and down, maintaining the tension. Ollie studiously looks away from him.

"All done." Tai pats Ollie's foot and lets it drop to the bed.

"Thanks," says Ollie again. His phone buzzes and he glances at it. "You're right. It's like the guys said. We're on today."

Once Tai's dressed, they head to the dining room for breakfast. Their table overlooks the water. They sit opposite one another. Some others from the tour are eating, but everyone's got their game face on, so no one chats.

Toward the end of the meal, Brandon stops by the table and claps Tai on the shoulder. "Told you we'd be competing today, man," he says.

"Morning, Brandon," says Tai. Brandon's easy to like. Tai's happy to see him. "That you did."

Brandon has his longish black hair pulled into a topknot on the crown of his head. He stretches out a hand. "So you're Ollie, then."

Ollie nods and shakes his hand. "Nice to meet you."

"Brandon Hong. We met, but I honestly don't blame you if you don't remember. I was that dickhead who was lost in the hallway of the resort. You had other things on your mind."

"Oh," says Ollie. He glances at Tai. He's waiting for Tai to fill the gap in conversation, but Tai's tongue-tied. They *were* distracted, but Brandon seems to be making a huge assumption. Ollie says, "I'm surprised you remember much."

Brandon grins and taps his head. "It's one of my superpowers. Okay then. Well, I'll meet you in the third round if things go well for both of us."

"Sounds good," says Ollie

Once Brandon's gone, Tai downs his orange juice. It's time for business. "Let's go through this one more time." Ollie rolls his eyes. "Don't roll your eyes at me," Tai says. "What's the strategy?"

"Same as ever. I keep a lookout for the right wave and until then I wait it out."

Tai contemplates. "Don't wait too long, though, Ollie. There' aren't many good waves out there today."

They both watch for a while. The surf's uninspiring.

Ollie shrugs. "Okay, so I hold on for an okay wave, anything maybe waist height. I push on that." He takes a breath, and Tai watches it catch in his chest.

The silence between them is full of nervy energy. Tai shakes it off. They don't need to have this conversation. Ollie already knows everything Tai knows. "You'll be great, Ollie. Just pick your own wave. Don't let the others talk and put you off your game." Tai glances at his watch, knowing before he sees that it's time to go. "Are you done? We can grab your boards and get over there."

As he stands, Ollie is paler than ever; his freckles are stark against his skin. Tai hates to see him nervous. He's watched Ollie face monster waves on Pipeline and beat the best in the world in comp after junior comp in Hawaii, and one time in California. But this is the world circuit, they're far from home, and the waves are flat.

"It'll be okay," Tai says. He knows better than to touch Ollie when Ollie's like this. Ollie needs to be in control of his own skin. "You got yourself here because you're the best," Tai says. Ollie nods, but doesn't look at Tai. "You're gonna be amazing."

OUT ON THE OCEAN, OLLIE's tense. He lets the veteran get a couple of waves and hold position on him for ten minutes. The pressure builds and Ollie takes off on the wrong wave.

He paddles out again, but he's stuck waiting while the other two have position. They can choose their waves. For another five minutes there's nothing worth catching. Ollie does his best on a weak knee-high wave but there's not much he can do. The horn sounds to indicate the heat's over. Ollie comes in third, way out of the running.

He walks across the sand. His body is drained and his muscles tremble. The disappointment is heavy and huge in his chest. He can't even look at Tai. "I have to go," he says when Tai approaches.

Tai's grimace is apologetic. "Okay. But first you need to get to the press room."

"Fuck." Ollie's not good with the media at the best of times.

"I know." Tai's sympathy is clear. Ollie is half warmed by it and half irritated. He doesn't need sympathy. "It won't take long. Then you can get away from all of this." Tai's hands shift at his sides, but he doesn't reach out to touch Ollie. Ollie's grateful for that.

"Right," Ollie looks down at the sand.

In the press room, a guy in a polo shirt holds out a microphone.

"Ollie! Rough day."

"Can't win it all."

"Was it a fluke at Pipeline? A one-off thing?"

Ollie takes a big breath. Everyone around is competition. It's time to fake the confidence he doesn't feel. "Nope. Wait 'til you see me tomorrow."

The next day Ollie scrapes through heat two when his opponent fails to find a decent second wave. It's a win, but it's not encouraging.

For days after that, the ocean is flat. There's nothing worth catching. The league makes the call for a first lay day, then a second and a third. The scoreboard on the beach reads, "On hold."

Ollie and Tai spend the time training as close to the rocks as possible despite the crowds, trying to drag some energy or even a simple ride out of the lack of swell. It's frustrating and unrewarding.

"At least this few days' lay time means we're not jetlagged," says Tai.

Ollie glares at him and doesn't bother to reply. Tai's positivity could sometimes use a break.

The third night of the delay, they're in their beds early. Even with the balcony windows open to the regular pounding of the waves, Ollie can't sleep. He lies on his back, and then shifts unhappily to one side, then the other. He turns his pillow over and rests his cheek against the cool side, facing away from Tai's bed. He rolls back onto his back. There's nothing of interest to see on the ceiling.

"That's it," Tai's voice comes out of the dark. There's a shuffle as he sits up on his bed. "I'm calling the concierge. Tomorrow we're renting a car."

"Why?"

"We need to get the hell out of here. You've worked your ass off getting nothing out of the tiny waves. Let's take a breath and enjoy being here. It's Australia, Ollie. Our teenage selves would kick our asses for hanging around on flat surf when we're here."

"They would."

"Ashton says there's a better swell up at Noosa. Nothing huge, but at least we'll get a surf. You and me and our boards. No one will be watching, or no one who matters anyway. We can drive there first thing."

It sounds perfect, of course.

But Ollie says, "I can't, Tai, I need to practice here. Someday they'll get the comp started again and this is the surf I need to win on."

"Yeah. But." Tai switches on his bedside light. Ollie blinks against the glare and then leans on one arm and focuses. Tai sits cross-legged. He scrutinizes Ollie and chews on his lip. "You'll never win the heat if you don't get back some sort of joy in the water and your board. You're forcing it, Ollie. You need to forget the competition for a day, stop churning it over in your head, and just surf." He nods with all the earnestness Ollie's seen in him since he was thirteen. "Anyway, wherever we surf here, it's all the same ocean."

It's the same ocean at home too. And Ollie and Tai have been in it a thousand times. It stretches all the way north and east, endless miles of it, then wraps around Oahu and beats against the shore right near their house. Ollie settles into the thought. "You're probably right."

"Usually." Tai grins. "At least where you're concerned." He calls reception and speaks pleasantly to the concierge. Then he switches out the light and settles down in his bed. Ollie closes his eyes. The water moves its almighty weight all the way from here to their home. It's easier to sleep now.

THE NEXT MORNING, THEY STRAP their boards to the roof racks of a rental car and drive away from the hotel just as the sun touches the long horizon.

Tai masters driving on the left side of the road in an instant. They don't talk much as they drive. They keep the windows down and turn the radio up. Tai sings along, drumming his palms against the steering wheel. Ollie hums under his breath and sticks his bare feet up on the dashboard. The sun warms them through the windshield. He wriggles his toes.

It's late in the morning when they drive through the ocean-side bush and scrub of the national park near Noosa. Tai parks where a few cars are pulled off the road. They put on their flip-flops. Ollie unstraps the boards from the roof. It's a bit of a trek in, walking around the headland along a rough sandy track. They follow the track all the way to a granite-edged bay, then make their long way down until the tiny beach appears. The beach is edged by green-gray scrub and dark rocks that thrust their way out of the ocean and curve around the sand.

It's too late in the day for the water to be glassy smooth, but it's still clear. Better than that, the point's producing some nice mid-sized waves where a sandbar kicks out from the shore.

Ollie glances at Tai.

"Good, yeah?" Tai smiles broadly. He looks immensely proud of himself.

"Perfect," Ollie says, returning the smile.

Out in the deep, they sit upright on their boards and watch the waves. They let their legs dangle beneath them and get accustomed to the movement of the ocean. The swell isn't huge, but there's a long break and a nice sharp edge to play with as the water moves over the sandbar.

They don't work on anything at all. They just surf, and let the water take them where it takes them. On one wave, Ollie gets snapback after snapback, lifting his fins out at the peak and letting the spray surround him. As he paddles back out he watches Tai do a lovely aerial, flying over the top of the lip and letting his front foot bring the board back to the water. Ollie hollers encouragement.

Later, as Ollie takes a wave in, Tai shouts over the noise of the ocean, "I'm starving."

Ollie hasn't been very hungry on the tour, but right now he's ravenous. "Me too," he shouts, though Tai probably can't hear. Ollie lets the wave take him as far as it can, then grabs his board and heads up the beach. They've got lunch they bought in town at Surfer's Paradise and left knotted in its plastic bag and hanging from a tree at the top of the beach.

Ollie throws a towel down in the shade under a couple of trees, then sits cross-legged and unpacks the sandwiches. The drinks aren't sweating anymore, but they aren't warm. The sand's dry this high up the beach, so it might blow around and get into their food, but it's cooler here out of the sun.

Ollie watches Tai leap off his board in the wash and make his easy way up the beach. He's so sure of how his body moves. There's a brightness to the air around him. Ollie probably looks like an idiot, but he can't stop grinning as he watches. He hands over a can of soda. Tai flops down in the sand.

"Thanks." Tai throws back his head and swallows half of it.

"This was a good idea," says Ollie.

"Did you doubt it?" Tai takes a bite and chews. He swallows. "I saw you were getting some awesome snapbacks on the top of those last few. Your fins were way clear of the water."

Ollie nods. It feels good down to his bones to get it right in the water again.

They finish in silence, with just the ocean and air and squawking sea birds. "Shall we head back?" asks Tai a bit later. "Or have one more go at it?"

It'll be a long trip back to the hotel, first all the way up the walking track and then the drive. It's going to be dark before they get back. The competition could be back on tomorrow and Ollie needs to rest up for it, but he looks at the ocean with its line of waves and can't resist. "Let's go back out for a few."

Tai nods, unsurprised and smiling. The Australian sun is still hot and it beats down on them. Ollie pulls out the sunscreen. It's warm and liquid as they put it on. Tai leaves a streak down one side of his face and Ollie reaches to rub it in before he thinks. He blushes.

Tai shifts away. He stands. "I call dibs on the first good wave." He grabs his board and runs out.

"No chance." Ollie hoists his board and follows Tai over the sand and into the surf.

It gets dark on the drive home. The lights of Surfer's Paradise are a beacon, sky high and backed by the expanse of black ocean.

They leave the boards downstairs in the lockup.

"You shower first," says Tai once they're upstairs. "I'm going to sit out on the balcony."

Ollie groans with pleasure as the warm water batters his shoulders and arms and rushes over his aching body. The heat seeps into him. All the salt and sand pours down the drain. Every part of him feels good. At length he turns the water off and shakes his hair so it sprays the shower walls.

He steps out. The towel he grabs is huge and rough in exactly the right way. It's been a long day. His eyes are heavy and his muscles are weary.

"Your turn," he calls to Tai before collapsing onto the bed. He pushes back the covers without getting up, just shoves them down under his body with his hands and feet, then covers himself with the cool sheet.

Tai comes in as Ollie closes his eyes. His voice comes softly. "'Night, Ollie." Ollie settles in deeper. Between waking and sleep, he hears Tai's tread across the room. Everything is easier with Tai nearby. Ollie is warm and heavy, sweet and safe as he's dragged into sleep.

CHAPTER NINE

THE SURF'S LIFTED A LITTLE the next day, in time to start the third round. Ollie's in the last of the three-man heats.

Out on the ocean, there's not much worth catching. Even on Tai's board, Ollie is clunky. He's sluggish on the first wave he catches, too heavy on its face. The wave only gets him a 4.9, which will never compete. He steadies himself as he makes his way back to the zone, then finds the rhythm of each set's height and weight. He waits it out on his board, paddling steadily and ignoring the other guys' chat until he has priority. His next wave springs to life. The third is better again. He's putting together a decent combined score.

He paddles back out. The Pacific swells under him, moving as it does at home. Time ticks down. And suddenly he's on a fourth wave. This one is flawless: The board clings to his feet, the wave shifts perfectly, he carves through over and over. He even gets some real air on the top lip, letting his body fly while his feet control the board.

The horn ending the heat sounds as he slides off the front of the wave. It's over. There's nothing more anyone can do.

At the water's edge, Tai bumps his shoulder softly into Ollie's. Ollie takes a steady breath and stands still, leaning into Tai. It's a rare thing for Ollie, to want this kind of contact. He feels Tai's glance before Tai relaxes into it. They stand together to wait for the judges' final scores.

Ollie used to watch video of himself over and over, perfecting his moves, getting a sense of the way all his choices were working for people watching from the shore. It's important to know what the judges see and what they'll value. He hasn't done that in a long time, and he's not sure he can tell what worked out there anymore.

"That was good, right?" he asks.

"That was good," says Tai. "It was really good." The light in his eyes is at once so fond and so amused that Ollie has to turn away.

When the scores come through, Ollie's taken the lead. It means he'll skip the fourth round and go straight through to the quarterfinals. Ollie turns to Tai. He doesn't know how to move.

Tai laughs aloud and tugs him into a close hug. "Told you that you did good."

Ollie grins and shoves him. "Shut up." He pulls Tai back into a quick hug. He's into the quarterfinals of his first world championship event; he's made it to the top eight.

People watched from all over the world. Strangers. Tai's parents and sisters in Samoa. The kids back home. Before Ollie and Tai do anything else, they call the Blue House. It's afternoon there, but everyone managed to watch. Jaime and Sunny squeal with delight through Jaime's cell phone.

"I was just yelling at the TV while you did nothing," says Jaime. "There were some good waves, too. What the fuck were you waiting for? A tsunami?"

"I was keeping position," Ollie answers. "So I could pick the best one. It's strategy."

Jaime says, "Right, of course," as if he's always known that.

"Quarterfinals now," says Sunny. "You're the best surfer in the world."

"I'm not sure that's how it works," says Ollie, laughing. "So guys. What's going on at home?"

"Not much," says Sunny.

"I'm being an angel," says Jaime. "Obviously."

Tai asks, "Did you get our postcard?" They'd sent a picture of Snapper Rocks sticking out into the ocean.

"Yeah. It's up on the fridge," Jaime says.

Ollie's pleased they kept it. "How's school?" he asks.

"Good," says Jaime, and that's clearly all Ollie's going to get.

"Well, do your homework, okay? No parties. This is an important year." Tai eyes him and Ollie turns away.

"Yes, Mom," Jaime says. It stings. Not just the mom thing, but also the fact that Ollie is working so hard, has been working hard at everything for Jaime, and the kid will never appreciate it.

"I'm so sorry for *caring* about your education," Ollie snaps.

"Hold on there, Ollie," says Sunny quickly over the phone. "Jaime's all good."

They don't leave things there, but the conversation never quite comes around to the early enthusiastic ease. Ollie hangs up. He's dissatisfied and worried. But it's hard to stay down when he's through to the quarterfinals of his first world tour event.

They walk toward the media tents. Halfway there they run into a couple of other rookies.

"Great heat, Ollie," says a Brazilian rookie Ollie has seen around on tour. "Brandon and I were talking about your board. It's a good-looking ride."

Ollie beams and sticks out an elbow at Tai. "That's all this guy. Makes all my boards."

"Nice."

"We'll be at Burleigh Head tonight if you two want to come," Brandon says. "It's about twenty minutes south of here. We can get a fire going on the beach."

"Cool," says Tai. He glances at Ollie. "You wanna go?"

"Sure," Ollie says. It's a relief to be so at home among these people. He didn't expect that.

"You guys need a lift?" asks Brandon.

Tai shakes his head. "Nah, we've got the rental car from yesterday."

A bunch of people have gathered on the quiet beach when Ollie and Tai arrive. Most of them are the younger crew: Ashton and some of the Californians and some Aussies and Brazilians, including some of the women on tour. The temperature is cool, especially for the Hawaiians, but it's not cold. Still, the guys have already lit a decent fire in a pit in the sand, between the dunes and the surf.

Ollie sits beside Tai near the bonfire and wraps his arms around himself. They're perched on a single log, close together. It's not as if there's no room to spread out. There's a whole empty beach, with their one glowing campfire and the ten or so of them sitting around it. But Ollie feels a pull to be close to Tai, and it's heightened by Ollie's relief and happiness and by being so far from home, way out here on a whole new continent.

Ollie accepts a drink from the backpack they'd brought. He's relaxed, deeply relieved, with a good surf behind him. It gives him a break in the competition pressure.

Over the ocean, the stars are bright pinpricks. The horizon is one shade of darkness meeting another. If Ollie turns around, though, the sky is streaky over the mountains where the sun dipped moments ago. The fire flickers between them all; its glow ripples across everyone, lighting faces and making the whole world look pretty. Especially Tai.

Ollie doesn't dwell on that thought.

He turns to Beatriz, one of the women on tour. She has powerful, tanned shoulders. She could take anyone on.

"I saw you surfing today," Beatriz says. Ollie wishes he could say the same. He hasn't watched much of the women's comp. Sunny would yell at him for failing at feminism. "You were good," she says. "Very nice air."

"Thank you," says Ollie. "Uh, I've heard of you, of course. But I wish I'd seen you surf today. I didn't watch much that wasn't directly relevant to my heat. Pretty shortsighted, I know."

"Because of nerves?"

"Yeah, I guess. I felt like I had to stay focused. This is my first time on tour. I don't know what works yet." It's nice to talk to someone who won't gain a competitive advantage if he admits his fears.

"You'll work it out," she says. "You're quite the surfer."

On Ollie's other side, Brandon and Ashton and Tai are leaning into one another, talking. Ashton says something, and Tai throws his head back. His throat bobs as he laughs; his face is bright as he looks around at the group.

Across from them, one of the Brazilians plays guitar. Ollie doesn't recognize the song even when a couple of others sing along. The beach is wider and the sand finer than on the North Shore, but every beach is a little like home. Ollie misses the Blue House; he misses the surf and the palms and the shoreline he knows so well. He misses Jaime and Sunny and Hannah. Still, though he's as far from home as he's ever been, Ollie's comfortable. These are his people, too. He leans back on his arms and looks up into the dark.

He's watched the night sky since he was a little kid, but down here in the Southern Hemisphere he doesn't recognize the hundreds upon hundreds of stars. The Southern Cross is up there. Ollie tries to orient himself.

Tai shifts toward him, then looks up and follows Ollie's gaze. The warmth of Tai's body settles into Ollie's heart, grounds him. Ollie leans into him a little, and their arms brush to the elbow. The contact simmers in the air between them.

Unexpectedly, Ollie knows what he wants. "Come back to the hotel," he says quietly to Tai. He pitches his voice low. It hums across the tiny space between them. No one else can hear him over the pounding surf and the sound of the music. It's easy to be bold in the dark of a beach where Ollie's never been before. He's shocked by that same boldness.

Tai startles and his body shifts a little away from Ollie's. Without the contact, Ollie's skin cools. Tai frowns, puzzled. "Um. For sure. Of course. You need your sleep for tomorrow."

Ollie doesn't say anything for a stretched-out moment. Tai shifts his head. His eyes are almost black as they meet Ollie's gaze in the firelight. Each tiny detail aligns. "Oh," Tai says, low and surprised.

"Come back to the hotel," says Ollie again.

Tai sucks in a breath. It's clear that this time he knows what Ollie means. "Okay." Tai's voice is a raspy whisper. His fingers brush against Ollie's accidentally, but the touch is full of promise. It runs under Ollie's skin and up his spine.

They get up from the sand as one and stand slightly apart. No one's watching them. Tai speaks up. "Hey, guys. We're getting out of here. See you tomorrow." Ashton glances up at them, then away. Brandon smiles.

"Later," says Ollie to the group in general. He adds, "Do good in the morning. Let's get some rookies through to the next round."

Ollie and Tai walk across the sand toward the car, keeping not too close and not too far from one another. They can pretend that everything's normal. But Ollie can hardly feel his feet, and his heart beats hard and fast.

CHAPTER TEN

TAI STARTS THE CAR WITH fingers that only shake a little.

In the passenger seat, Ollie winds down the window to the night. His profile is pale; the streetlight outlines it in white. Tai makes a U-turn, then heads onto the road that leads back to the hotel.

They don't touch on the drive. It's easy not to. Tai's not reckless, not with Ollie. They've always kept space between them when they were alone, and for now Tai needs to be absolutely sure of every move he makes toward Ollie.

When Ollie scans his face, electricity fizzes in Tai's chest. He holds the steering wheel and keeps his focus on the road stretching out in front of them, lit by irregular streetlights and the car's headlights. The buildings of Coolangatta and Surfer's Paradise rise in front of them, lit with scattered lights all the way to the top. It takes far, far too long to get through the outskirts of town to their hotel, but part of Tai wishes it would take longer.

The hotel parking garage is underground, down a ramp. Tai parks. They're surrounded by gray concrete walls and fluorescent lighting.

Even in this light Ollie is fine-boned and lovely. Tai's whole body is alive with that ever-present tide, pulling and pulling when Ollie's around. Ollie draws him in.

Tai wants this. That means he needs to take care. "Ollie," he says into the silence. He'd thought he had a plan, but the words he expected to say are long gone. He sighs and just asks, "Are you sure?"

Ollie doesn't answer, but he unbuckles his seatbelt and lets it retract. Tai follows its path with his eyes. Then Ollie leans in slowly, slowly. He's within a breath of Tai but doesn't close the gap. "I've been thinking about this," he says. Tai resists moving closer. Ollie's breath is soft on his skin. Ollie half shrugs. "I don't seem to stop thinking about it. So, yes. I'm sure."

Tai closes his eyes. When they kiss it's slow; it's full and rough-lipped with sun and salt.

Tai's heart races. His skin is electric, his blood warm. He's spent years kissing strangers and convincing himself that a kiss would never be like this, as if everything that's always been caught inside him is bubbling over. As though all of it matters. He closes his eyes and lets himself taste Ollie's lips, while his brain says, over and over, "Ollie" and "Please" and also "Oh, shit."

His seat belt is tight across his lap. He moves back, leaving Ollie blinking at him, and undoes it with shaking, certain fingers. Then he releases a breath. "Let's go upstairs."

At the door of their hotel room, Ollie takes Tai's hand. Both their palms are sweaty. Tai unlocks the door with his other hand. Once they're inside, the door closes with a steadying thump behind them.

The curtains are open wide, and outside the vast span of the world is mostly black—black sky, black ocean and dark-shadowed mountains.

Tai turns his body to Ollie's and opens his mouth to speak, but says nothing. Anything that comes to mind seems silly and awkward. He's always been direct about sex with other boys. But this is Ollie, and he's forgotten how to be anything but ridiculous. It's difficult to think straight. He can't tell why Ollie wants this.

Ollie's hand is warm. Tai squeezes it, checking that it's real.

Ollie's face quirks into a half smile that's both amused and a little embarrassed. "Too weird?"

"I suppose. But that's not what I was going to say."

"Let me guess. You wanted to check if I was sure. Again." His voice is both exasperated and fond.

Of course, Ollie's pretty much right. Tai blushes. He doesn't resist smiling as he moves forward to kiss Ollie. He runs both his hands up Ollie's sides. Ollie's breath catches beautifully. Tai's never let himself daydream such things.

Under his T-shirt, Ollie's back is warm and faintly damp and smooth to touch. Ollie leans forward and opens up to the kiss.

Everything is hushed and brand new, but also strangely easy. They know one another's bodies with the intimacy of a thousand days of surfing and waxing boards and doing chores and staring helplessly under the hood of the car. They've spent years together.

Still, Tai could not have expected so much from this usually careful, edgy boy. He holds himself back, torn. He wants to take everything slowly. He longs to draw his fingers reverently over muscles he's never touched this way. He'd like to taste every inch of Ollie's skin. But if he takes his time, they'll both stop acting on instinct. Neither of them want that.

"Ollie," he says tentatively.

"I'm right here. Trust me." Ollie kisses Tai again, silencing him.

Tai walks Ollie backward, directing him toward Tai's bed. They're still kissing as the back of Ollie's knees bump against the mattress. Ollie sits as Tai watches. Then he lowers himself onto his back and scoots up the bed a bit. Looking up from the bed, his eyes are wide, steady, and blue.

They're both still fully clothed. Ollie's shirt hikes up, revealing an inch of pale skin that Tai's seen so many times before.

"Okay?" Tai asks as he puts a knee on the mattress beside Ollie's legs.

Ollie rolls his eyes impatiently. "Tai. You can seriously stop checking. Believe me."

Tai isn't exactly sure what to do with the combination of irritation and desire that flows through him. "Fuck off," he says. He drops his body over Ollie's to kiss him, hard. There's a stunned noise from Ollie's throat. It's sweet, like nothing Tai has ever heard. It makes him feel smug. And suddenly, hearing that helpless noise again is all that's on Tai's mind.

Tai has thought, theoretically, about Ollie's experience of sex. But he's never asked, and Ollie is always quiet about things that he considers private. Still, Tai knows Ollie and he's pretty sure Ollie hasn't done much with anyone; not that he can tell from the way Ollie's moving, his hips rotating, his mouth mobile. Tai doesn't resist the soft moan Ollie draws from him.

He focuses on reading Ollie's body. He watches the stretch and yield of Ollie's muscles, listens to the way his breath hitches when Tai's fingers trail across his mouth. He doesn't need to ask whether this is all okay when Ollie answers that question with every tiny noise. Tai slots his thigh high between Ollie's legs. Ollie's hips strain upward.

However much Ollie might be Ollie, and therefore different in Tai's head from anyone before, Tai's body has the same needs it's always had. He craves that involuntary rhythm and the inevitable, electric release. As Tai pushes forward over and over, Ollie responds. His whole body arches, his hips churn. Their bodies rock together.

Tai kisses under the angle of Ollie's jaw. Ollie huffs shakily, and his head rolls back, throat bared. Tai's amazed; Ollie's beauty makes his heart hurt.

Tai shifts his hips to align their cocks and rhythmically presses Ollie down against the bed. The sound of their breathing and fabric against fabric rubbing back and forth, back and forth is intimate and unmistakable. Tai lifts his head. He wants to watch, wants to stay here forever, wants to wrap himself up in Ollie's gaze. This is the only secret they haven't told one another.

Ollie's eyes, now gray and green and unfocused, are on Tai's. Then he seems to forget himself, and his eyes roll back in his head before he shuts them tightly. Tai understands. The encounter is intense, even for Tai. Ollie's protecting himself in a small way. But he's still here in the moment. His brow is furrowed with concentration; his mouth is twisted and frozen in pleasure and need. His breath escapes in tiny pants.

"God," breathes Tai.

Ollie breaks apart, loses control. And Tai is a part of it. The joy simmers brightly up and down Tai's spine. He wants to slow down. If he never has this again, he'll remember forever.

"Ollie. Hold on for a sec," Tai says. "Hold on with me."

Ollie keeps his eyes closed but nods and stills.

Tai shifts over, reaches between them, and slides his hand under the waistband of Ollie's board shorts. His fingers graze Ollie's belly. Ollie's eyes flick open to meet Tai's for a fearful, wanting moment.

"Tai." His voice cracks. "Please."

The angle is awkward and Tai's wrist is going to ache, but he skims his hand farther down, trailing past Ollie's rough curls. This pulls a low, achingly long groan from deep in Ollie's chest. The groan sinks into Tai's heavy balls and his cock shifts where it's pressed against Ollie's hipbone. Then Tai wraps his fist gently around Ollie's cock and runs it slowly back and forth. The soft skin moves over the shaft inside.

"Oh god," says Ollie brokenly. "This. You—" He thrusts into Tai's hand, out of any kind of rhythm. His hands flutter to his face, then back to Tai's shoulders. "God, Tai," he gasps again.

The words are nothing, just Tai's name on Ollie's lips, but they explode in Tai's heart. He kisses Ollie again and again with his fist wrapped around Ollie's cock. Every time Tai breaks away for a breath, Ollie's lips chase mindlessly after him.

Tai sweeps his thumb across the head of Ollie's cock. He spreads its moisture over his palm, holds tighter and starts pumping. Ollie's hips buck upward irresistibly, over and over again. His eyes are open but blind.

"Come for me," Tai says. Ollie is so beautiful. "Let go for me."

Ollie's lower back arches upward. His body spasms and shakes, and he comes, spilling in bursts over Tai's hand.

"Oh god." Ollie blinks sightlessly at Tai.

"Oh god," echoes Tai, amazed. He holds Ollie's cock for a cooling, comforting moment, lets it soften a little in his hand as Ollie's breathing eases. Then he gently draws his hand out of Ollie's shorts. His palm is wet with come, but he has no concern for that. His cock is swollen. He rocks against Ollie.

"Let me," says Ollie after a panting minute. He tries to reach his hand between them.

Tai shakes his head. "No. Please. Stay like that and—"

He's almost there, his breath rough in Ollie's ear, shamelessly rutting against him to get the friction he needs. But then Ollie rolls his hips up, shifting everything around just as Tai was about to come. Ollie's hipbone presses sharply against Tai's cock, and Tai groans with frustrated need. He considers wrapping his hand around his own cock and getting himself off, but Ollie strokes Tai's back, presses close, and keeps rolling his hips. That sends a ripple of pleasure through Tai. He focuses and thrusts harder into Ollie, rhythmically keeps time with Ollie's movement, and lets his body seek its end. Pleasure coils tightly. Trapped in his shorts, his cock strains between them. He's at the edge of control. He breathes Ollie in and finds the perfect angle as he thrusts and thrusts. Release is there, just out of reach, just in reach, so devastatingly close.

Then Ollie lifts his head to mouth at Tai's neck. His lips are hot, and his teeth press delicately into Tai's skin, in a tiny, breathy nip. Such a small thing, yet it sends shivers through Tai's nerves. Tai lets out a gasp and throws back his head. Tai's hips shudder forward and the orgasm blazes through him, running electric down his nerves and bones and leaving him slumped, vibrating, gasping against Ollie's hair.

They lie there, Tai heavy against Ollie's body, their chests pressed together and heaving. The air is humid where it's caught between them. It takes a minute for their heartbeats to slow and steady. Tai becomes aware of Ollie watching him. Ollie's hand is covering his mouth. His eyes are clear on Tai's face, clear and soft and watchful.

"Ollie," Tai says. He means so much more. They stay still, breathing in sync. Tai's eyes trace Ollie's familiar, elusive expression. He has never seen anything so beautiful. Under his gaze, Ollie blushes. There's everything to say, but the truth is, there's no way to say it. Time stretches out strangely.

"I'll get a cloth," Tai manages. "You must feel kind of messy. I know I do." It's not at all what he wants to say. He rolls off the bed and stands up.

When he returns from the bathroom, hopping a little so he can pull on clean boxers, Ollie's there, exactly where he was when Tai left. He lies quite still, uncovered, and stares at the ceiling with wide eyes.

"You okay?" Tai asks.

Ollie looks at him. "Yeah," he says. "Yeah."

Tai's heart settles. He reaches out carefully, but Ollie shakes his head and takes the cloth from him. "Thank you." He's shaky as he stands, but he visibly steadies himself and walks naked to the bathroom.

They were in Tai's bed, so Tai stays there. He sets the alarm clock. When Ollie returns he has his boxers on, too. He stops across the room. He looks uncertain.

Tai says, "I've set the alarm so we won't sleep through the early heats." It's hard to keep eye contact. "Come back to bed with me. If you want to."

Ollie's eyes widen. For a thudding moment, Tai's certain he'll refuse. Then Ollie presses his lips together and nods. In the ambient light, his skin is so pale it's ghostlike, and his eyes are bright and sweet. He climbs into bed. Tai's surprised when he doesn't leave space between them. Instead he shifts close, and stretches out his lovely body alongside Tai's. He presses his face into Tai's shoulder. His breath is warm and soft on Tai's skin.

They lie together, barely moving. Ollie's breathing slows and steadies. Tai stays still in the dark and lets sleep take him, too.

OLLIE WAKES BEFORE THE ALARM. Tai's behind him, pressing his breath and warmth and solid, sleeping life against Ollie's back. If Ollie rolls over it will all be real.

The curtains are wide open, and through the big windows the day is pale and gray above the steely stretch of the ocean.

Ollie holds himself motionless. He's not sure if he should feel anything.

He can't regret last night. It's hard to think beyond that, the forgetfulness of tumbling apart in someone else's safe hands, of falling into a place where he no longer needed to hold himself together. And Tai right there, knowing everything that Ollie's ever been. The thought of it sends shivers across his skin, even when he tries to tamp down on it. His body is unwound in a way he never expected.

Ollie breathes slowly. His world has shifted, and Tai's still in the center of everything. Ollie watches the horizon and doesn't let his hands follow the path across his body that Tai's hands took last night.

"Morning," says Tai out of the quiet. His voice is rough with sleep.

Ollie closes his eyes. He can't postpone this. "Morning," he says. He doesn't roll over, though, as he asks, "How could you tell I was awake?"

He can hear the shrug in Tai's reply. "Your shoulders. Your breathing." Ollie holds his breath, though Tai must understand why he's doing that, too. Tai almost always knows what Ollie's doing. In the past that's been reassuring, but right now it's terrifying.

Ollie hears Tai move behind him and imagines Tai's shoulders stretching out. He listens as Tai pushes back the sheets and stands to walk across the room. The bathroom door closes. Ollie rolls onto his back and doesn't listen further.

When Tai comes back, he says, "Hey. Do you want some time to yourself up here? I'll go down and watch the morning heats. You can have the room, get some space if you want it." His face is open but somehow unreadable.

Ollie should be relieved. Instead, he's unfairly frustrated. For once, it isn't time alone that Ollie needs. "I'll come with you," he says. "If that's okay?" He's not sure he's ever asked. They've always presumed on the welcome between them.

"Of course it's okay." Tai's smile is a little unsettled, but it's still Tai's smile.

In the elevator on the way down, Tai watches the floor numbers change. Ollie glances at Tai, then the floor.

They stand together for the first few round-three heats. The waves have picked up. It makes for more of a show, and means there are a bunch of locals around. Some of the guys are getting good air.

Ollie will face one of these surfers in the quarters. It's good to scope out how they surf. He tries to get a sense of their strengths and weaknesses, at least as much as he can tell from shore. Though he came to the beach with Tai, they don't talk much. After a while, Tai moves off to chat with the other surfers.

Ollie can't help but watch Tai through the crowds of people. Tai moves easily. There are new ways Ollie knows Tai, and he can't keep them out of his head. He feels stupid and obvious.

When it's Brandon's heat, Tai stands right out at the water's edge to cheer. Ollie stands farther back. He doesn't know Brandon well, but his disappointment is real when Brandon is knocked out by a fellow Australian.

As Brandon steps out of the water, his shoulders droop. His board looks heavy under his arm. Tai says a few words, meets Brandon's eyes. He squeezes Brandon's shoulder and takes the board to walk him back to the media tent.

However messy this whole thing might be right now, Ollie is proud to be around Tai.

When Tai returns, Ollie moves down to the water's edge beside him. They watch Ashton's heat together. It's close, but Ashton's two-wave total is strong enough that he makes it through to the quarterfinals.

Tai cheers as Ashton bounds from the waves and pumps a fist. Once Ashton's disappeared into the media tent, Tai turns to Ollie. "You'll be called up in half an hour or so," he says. "Are you ready?"

Ollie nods.

"You're going to kill it out there," Tai says. His gaze flickers to Ollie and away. It's something he's done a hundred times before, but this time the energy simmers in Tai's veins.

"Okay."

"D'you want me to grab your board?" Tai asks.

"Nah, I've got it."

However Ollie tries to put the night before out of his mind, it comes to him in blazing flashes every time he blinks. When his fingers brush his lips he imagines Tai's lips against them and shivers. He remembers Tai's tongue moving in his mouth, that foreign thrill. When he smooths his shirt, he remembers Tai's fingers running up his sides. Everything feels tender and thrown wide open.

Forcing himself to focus on the surf, he heads to the stands and grabs his board. The weight of the board steadies him.

"Whatever happens today," Tai says gently, once Ollie's back on the beach, "It's all good. You've gone from a win in the first event to the quarterfinals in the second. You're going to be way up in the rankings. Everyone's talking about you. You've been amazing. So go out and have fun."

Ollie's form is good. His board responds to him. But the other guy is good too. It comes down to the right wave at the right time, and in the end, Ollie loses. It means the end of this competition. You don't get second chances in the quarterfinals.

Ollie walks out of the surf and lets Carise direct him to the people he needs to talk to.

He faces the cameras. "JP was the better man today," he says. "I'm honestly happy I made it so far."

When he exits the media tent, Tai's waiting between the sand and the road.

"Hey," says Tai.

"Hey." They walk across the sand together, not close enough to touch. Ollie says, "I thought I'd got to a place where I'd be okay with this. With not winning."

"Yeah. I get that."

"I mean, it's the quarterfinals. That's pretty good."

"It's more than fucking good, Ollie. You did better in this comp than most of the seven billion people in the world."

Ollie glares at him, frustrated. "They weren't in the comp, Tai."

Tai shrugs. "See?"

"Some of them are babies, or ninety-year-olds, or live in the middle of Russia and it'd be too cold to surf even if they were near the ocean. And some of them prefer cycling or, I don't know, soccer."

"As hard as that is to believe." Tai picks up Ollie's board from the racks. "There's no shame in losing. Let's get out of here."

CHAPTER ELEVEN

THEY DROP THE BOARD AT the hotel and make their way to a bar a little way back from the beach. Ollie doesn't want to hang out where all the guys are, and this place is sufficiently uncool not to attract them. Music blares from a jukebox. People have lined up coins beside it, saving themselves a chance to choose songs. The pool tables are all in use. The floor is covered with giant carpet tiles in various awkwardly matched colors. Ollie orders two beers. Next to the bar, a stand of free postcards shows the bar's terracotta-wash exterior. Ollie grabs one. He borrows a pen from the bartender.

They sit out back on the tiled patio, next to giant pots filled with bamboo. Ollie writes on the back of the postcard. "Ugliest bar I've ever seen. Be glad you're underage."

"That for Jaime?" Tai asks.

Ollie nods. He signs, "Love, O." He'll get the hotel to mail it.

They sit in silence. Ollie fiddles with his coaster, folds it at the corners, then tears each corner off carefully. "It's like I need to prove I deserve to be here."

Tai scrunches up his face. "Ollie, you won at Pipe. You got into the quarters here. Honestly, you don't have to prove shit."

"I won on my home ground. I was lucky to get through the first round here."

"You know surfing's about the wave too, and luck. And persistence. You're twenty-two, you're the top ranking rookie on tour. You're fine."

Ollie takes a mouthful of beer. Tai's right. He still feels like shit. "You know, I was ready to throw this all in and get a certificate in hospitality. Back when we were home, before all this started."

Tai raises his eyebrows. "You were?"

"I told myself the wildcard comp was my last chance," Ollie says. "I talked with the resort about studying and working my way into management."

"And now?" Tai asks. Ollie hears tightness in his voice.

"Now I couldn't give it up. So I guess I'd better keep on winning."

"Seems like it," says Tai.

"D'you think it'd be easier if I'd thrown it all away?"

Tai shrugs. "Easier maybe. But it wouldn't be what you want."

"Yeah." They sit quietly. "So what do you reckon? We should be at Bells Beach in a week or so for the next round."

They plan their way down south: some time at the beaches nearby and then a flight to Melbourne and a drive around the coast to Bells.

The bar is filling up. It's safe here. They can be anonymous so far from home, among strangers who talk in Australian accents and hardly notice two Hawaiian boys sitting too close together. Tai's talking about boards. Ollie listens, but more than that he watches Tai speak, watches his hands trace pictures in the air.

Somehow they shift closer on their stools. Ollie is caught up in Tai's hands and face and shoulders. When their knees brush, the connection feels inevitable. It's frightening and irresistible. This is how Ollie imagines drowning feels at the end—not the thrashing and struggling part, the part where a person is pulled softly under the water, unable to breathe and not caring anymore. Ollie moves closer.

Tai looks at the place where their knees touch. His speech falters, then he goes on. He's talking about rear fins—freeing them up, snapping them out of the waves. He doesn't move away.

Tai's the best person in Ollie's world, and yet Ollie's always kept a distance between them. He's always made sure he stands by himself.

That is habit, ingrained in him. But there's more to it. Even before Tai came out to him, Ollie was pretty sure Tai was gay. But it seemed disrespectful, and plain weird, to assume that being attracted to boys meant Tai might have any interest in Ollie. Sure, now and then it was obvious that Tai wanted to touch him. But Tai is comfortable touching everyone, strangers and lovers and friends. It makes touch safe. So Ollie can lean into Tai and still keep up that tiny distance. Once Tai was cheerfully hooking up with guys, just random tourists and surfers, Ollie was surer than ever that Tai's sexuality had nothing to do with him. Tai was Tai, and Ollie wouldn't read anything into that momentary awkwardness when they were alone.

Right now, that awkwardness isn't a dangerous thing. Before Ollie can think himself out of it, he leans forward and places a careful hand on Tai's leg, right below the hem of Tai's shorts. He grazes his thumb carefully across Tai's knee, brushing over the hair and warm dark skin and the bone beneath.

Tai looks down at Ollie's hand. When he lifts his head to meet Ollie's gaze, there's a deep frown between his brows. "Ollie," he says. "Hey. If you want to try this out, stuff with guys, then that's cool. You know I'm never going to get in your way. But you should do that with someone else. Who's not me. Where there's less—you know. History and stuff. Less future too. And not so much family that we need to keep holding onto." He exhales shakily and keeps his eyes on Ollie's face.

Ollie's hand is still on Tai's leg. He doesn't move it. It's oddly easy to be brave. "Okay. If you don't want this, then that's fine. Of course. No question. Just say the word."

"It's not that I'm not—" Tai takes a little breath, "—interested. It's just that there's a lot more going on here. You've worked for this surf tour your whole life. The last thing I want is for you to be worrying about me while you're supposed to be winning a world title." He lifts Ollie's hand from his thigh but holds onto it longer than needed. "Not just that. We share a house and a life, and we have to put that first. I'm not about to let five years of work go, bring a whole lot of tension home, just because you're a good kisser."

Ollie nods. "Yeah. Okay." He feels a tiny thrill, knowing Tai enjoys kissing him. He has to be careful. "I understand, Tai. But maybe we could try something."

"Oh no, that's never good," says Tai under his breath. He bites his lip. Ollie lets his thumb move against Tai's wrist, catches it in the string of shells tied there. Tai looks at Ollie's hand and still doesn't move away from it.

Ollie's cheeks heat up as goes on. "Last night was—" He hesitates. Even with Tai, Ollie's always kept physical things very private. He lets go of Tai's wrist and worries at a thumbnail with his teeth. "God. This is stupid. Last night was new for me and it was good. It was really good. Maybe because it was you. And today." There are so many things he wants. He keeps going, though he might be rushing in a bid to get this all over with. "The thing is, I thought maybe we could keep doing this for a bit."

"Doing this," Tai says.

"Make it into a tour thing."

Tai rubs a hand across his face before echoing. "Make it into a tour thing."

"Are you being intentionally slow?"

"Are you being intentionally unclear?"

They're silent. Tai runs his hands down his thighs and leans into them, shifting his body toward Ollie.

He says, "So, let me see if I have this right. We hook up? We keep hooking up while we're away on tour."

"That's the idea. We do things."

"You mean things like sex?" Tai presses his lips together, amused. He's not really teasing, though, so Ollie can't mind.

Ollie nods. He feels stubborn in a good way. He liked his experience of sex. He wants that experience to continue. He keeps talking. "Yep.

That's what I mean. We do things like sex. We're sharing a room anyway, so it makes sense. And you can't really bring guys home, can you? I figure you must miss that. So you could explore this stuff. With me. If you want to. It won't do any damage to all the things we're trying to protect if we keep it a tour thing. Everything's different away from home. And last night was—" He swallows. He wants to say a million words. "It was good."

"Good." repeats Tai. "Yeah, you said." His expression is a little worried, a little amused, a little turned on. And underneath it is something dangerous and beautiful, huge like the Pacific. There's a long pause. Ollie doesn't fill it. "Okay," Tai says. "All the reasons this is going to be a fucking disaster seem to have got lost in my head somewhere."

There are certainly conversations they should have, about how they're going to work this out when it's all done and they're at home, when it's not just two of them in a place where no one knows them. But Tai looks down for an instant. His eyelashes are long and dark against his skin. His shoulders press against a T-shirt Ollie has seen a hundred times. There's already a catch in Tai's breath. Ollie aches with the simple sense of how much he wants to touch him.

They leave their empty beer glasses on the bar table and walk back to the hotel, both knowing what will happen once they're there. That knowledge adds a layer of mindfulness and self-consciousness along with a dizzying hum of anticipation. When Ollie's arm brushes against Tai's, Ollie moves away. He's not sure he knows how to touch, not out here in public, and anyway this intimacy isn't something that's ready to be shared with the world.

The evening is warm. Their route home is mostly flat, past high-rise apartments and shops. People are out on the street, shopping and walking about, spilling out of bars and laughing. One time, Tai steers Ollie past a group of smokers with a light touch at his elbow. But the buildings and crowds aren't what Ollie sees. He glances out at the ocean and lets its vast, layered beauty calm him, then he looks at the curve of Tai's steady profile. His heart stutters.

They cross the tiled floor of the lobby and step into the elevator without looking at one another. But as they pass the tenth floor, Tai's hand slips down between them and brushes intentionally against Ollie's. Ollie curls his fingers, wrapping them around Tai's. The contact ripples all the way through his body. One breath, two breaths, three. When the elevator doors open, they move apart quickly, as though they need to keep this hidden. Tai shakes his head and releases a little laugh at himself, and Ollie smiles at the floor, but neither of them says anything as they walk to their room.

When the room door closes behind them, Ollie looks directly at Tai. They stand still between the doorway and the bed. Then Tai smiles. "We should be getting used to this," he says.

Ollie lets his mouth twitch into a smile of its own. "What? Get used to standing around in dark rooms together?"

Tai lets out a breath. "Something like that."

He steps closer and runs two deliberate fingers up Ollie's arm. The feeling ripples right to Ollie's spine. He doesn't bother to try to breathe.

"Your skin's still sticky with salt from the comp," Tai says, as if he's trying to work out what happens next. "Do you want to take a shower before—?" He stops. "Do you want to take a shower?"

Ollie doesn't hesitate. "I'll shower if you come with me." He turns toward the bathroom. He knows Tai will follow.

FROM THE BATHROOM DOORWAY, TAI watches Ollie. The tiles are cream with accents of turquoise-blue and green. They're Ollie's colors, and next to them Ollie is as beautiful as ever.

The shower is easily big enough for two. Ollie reaches past the glass door and turns on the water. It pours through the huge central shower head and fills the shower like rain. Quickly, without looking back, Ollie pulls his shirt over his head. The muscles in his back ripple under the skin. Then Ollie drops his shorts to the floor. He steps into the shower, but then dances back out with a muffled exclamation. Water drips from his long torso and pools on the floor.

"Cold," he explains. He wraps his arms around himself, appearing ill at ease. He's blushing and pouting; his skin is blotchy red and his mouth is clamped in a frustrated line. Tai presses his lips closed over a smile. Ollie rolls his eyes at himself. "I'm not very good at this," he says.

"I'm gonna have to disagree with you there," says Tai. He adds, "But you know what? I probably need more evidence."

Ollie's smile is a tiny, amused thank you. "You reckon?"

"I reckon."

The shower's still running. The room slowly fills with steam. The glass fogs, and the tiles fade.

Ollie checks the temperature of the shower, then steps in and lets the water flow over him. He's facing away from Tai, and the water runs down his back and over his ass. Tai waits. He's spent enough time naked with other people to be sure of himself, but Ollie isn't like any other naked human.

The shower door is still open. Ollie looks over his shoulder in a clear-eyed invitation.

"Coming?" he says. And this face, this invitation—Tai couldn't have expected it and he's never seen anything he wanted more. He strips quickly, dropping his clothes into a neat pile, and steps in. He pulls the glass door closed behind him.

He blinks a spray of water from his eyes. Ollie is smooth and wet in front of him, still facing away from Tai.

A miniature bottle of body wash is on the shelf in the shower wall. Tai slicks his hands with it and reaches for Ollie carefully. The steam swirls around them, smelling of fancy hotel bath product: lemongrass and lime. Tai washes Ollie's salty skin, running his hands over his muscular shoulders, around his body, across his flat stomach. He wants everything. Ollie slowly relaxes until his body is loose and easy under Tai's mobile hands. Ollie sighs sweetly. Tai's chest echoes with the vulnerability of that sigh.

"This good?" Tai asks.

"So good," Ollie says to the wall.

"You're okay?"

Tai can almost see the eye roll. "Yep."

Ollie turns around so they're face to face. The shower is a tiny secret universe with only two of them in it. There's nothing awkward in keeping their gaze steady on one another. They breathe in sync. This boy who's opening up in front of Tai is his reserved, edgy Ollie.

Ollie reaches out to Tai. As they lean in to kiss, his hands run up Tai's sides, flutter over Tai's ribs, and touch Tai everywhere, too quick and not knowing where to land. He smooths them around to the small of Tai's back and then up over his shoulder blades. He pulls Tai closer and traces the sun, the ocean, the turtle on Tai's tattoo. When Ollie leans away again, his eyes are wide and dark, raking over Tai as if he's filling his mind with him.

Ollie's gaze and his restless touch make Tai greedy. He steps forward, crowding closer into Ollie's space, putting his hands on Ollie's soapy shoulders. Ollie falls back as Tai presses against him. He gasps as his back makes contact with the cold tiles. His gaze, irritated, fiercely blue and turned on, catches Tai's. Tai smothers a laugh. He kisses Ollie's lips again, and they open under him.

Tai could do this for a long time: kiss Ollie's lips, needy against his. He knows how to sense the pleasure under the surface. He could stop thinking about anything save this moment and their combined breaths, save Ollie's simple enjoyment and his own. But as their bodies press together, Ollie's cock is hard and slick against his hip. Tai doesn't resist rocking against it. There's need here too, beyond the pleasure, and that's not slow at all.

The trouble is, this tour hookup thing could end at any time. They're here in one another's space, and, even with the tour as a timeline, Tai can't trust it to last.

He kisses Ollie once more, briefly, then slides his hands downward to hold Ollie's wet hips as he lowers himself to his knees.

He sits back onto his heels and looks up. Ollie's slim cock juts out at eye level. The tiles are hard and cold. It doesn't matter, though. He's done this before, gone down on his knees for hot young surfers and wide-eyed tourists. He wants this so much more with Ollie. This is worth sore knees.

When Tai meets Ollie's gaze, Ollie looks both amazed and unsure. He bites his lip.

"Don't worry, I've got you," Tai says. Ollie nods silently.

The water tumbles from Ollie's body and rushes over Tai's face and lips. He breathes carefully through his nose as he leans to lick up Ollie's inner thigh and mouth over his balls. He flattens his tongue against Ollie's cock and runs it carefully around the head. Ollie whines. He rocks forward, almost butting Tai's face. Tai clasps his hips tightly, his arms bent and thumbs digging into the curve of Ollie's hipbone. Then he opens his mouth to take Ollie inside. The warm water forms pools between them, sitting where their bodies meet and flowing down Ollie and over Tai. Tai starts sucking Ollie, long and slow and smooth. There's a second when he has to remind himself to breathe around Ollie's cock and the water flow, then he drops his jaw farther and lets Ollie push deeper as he sucks.

Above him, Ollie's thigh muscles tremble. Tai looks up: Ollie's got his own hand pressed against his mouth. He's biting his knuckles. Tai smiles a little around Ollie's cock.

"You're gorgeous," he says. With Ollie filling his mouth, it's probably indecipherable. A tremor runs through Ollie. His knees begin to buckle, and Tai holds onto his hips firmly to prop him up.

"Oh god," Ollie says faintly.

Tai moves back a little, releasing Ollie's cock from his mouth, and Ollie's head drops against the tiles as he moans a protest. His chest rises and falls.

"Fuck," Tai says, before he bends back to his task. "Look at you. Come for me, Ollie. Please." Ollie's hips jerk forward into Tai's mouth. His whole body is rigid and shaking as he obeys. Tai closes his eyes to hold onto it all and swallows and swallows.

Ollie seems out of it as Tai stands, supporting Ollie between himself and the shower wall.

"Bed?" Tai asks.

Ollie nods.

They wash together. The water pressure beats against Tai's muscles. They dry off quickly as they leave the bathroom. Ollie's cheeks are pink and his eyes are clear, flicking to Tai and away again over and over. They drop both towels near Tai's bed. Their skin is damp as they lie down on their sides facing one another. Across Tai's belly and chest and back, the air is a startlingly cool contrast to the heat of his skin. He's smug and so brightly turned on. But he lies still, letting the distance sit between them until Ollie reaches out, strokes Tai's shoulder with a shaky hand, and then pushes Tai onto his back. Tai shivers appreciatively under Ollie's gaze.

Ollie pauses there. "I haven't done this before," he says. He looks adorably serious, as if he's working things out, or studying for some test. "I want to, though." He lowers his eyes as though he can't quite bear to meet Tai's eyes, then slides down Tai's body, kissing his chest and belly, his face frowning and intent.

"Wait," Tai says suddenly. "Wait. Stop." This is awkward and stupid. "Sorry." He should have thought about this before now. Ollie sits back quickly as if struck, as if he did something wrong. Tai hurries to explain: "I'm sorry, but I have done this before. So I think—" He sighs and his skin heats. "I'm just saying that I haven't been tested in a bit and I need—to get a condom—" He stumbles over the words. This is not getting better.

"Oh." Ollie's face is frozen. "Yeah." He sits back on his feet; his eyes are wide as Tai gets up to rummage in his bag. Once he's found the condom, he glances at Ollie.

"Right," says Ollie. "Okay. There are condoms in your bag."

"Yeah." Tai opens the packet with quick fingers and rolls the condom efficiently over himself.

Ollie bites his lip. He swallows noticeably. Tai can't tell what he's thinking.

"Sorry," Tai says. "Sorry, it's just… I want to be careful. I'm careful about this stuff. I know it's boring."

"No," Ollie says. "It's not boring." He adds, "I kind of think it's hot."

He moves slowly, staying on his knees but curling his body over as he lowers his head and takes Tai's cock between his lips. At first, Ollie's mouth is warm and soft and gently sweet. Tai resists pushing forward into him. Ollie has no experience of this. But then his quick tongue curls in and traces the vein that runs along the bottom of Tai's cock. It's unexpected and Tai bucks helplessly into Ollie's mouth.

"Sorry," he mutters, but Ollie takes it as encouragement. He sucks harder, hollowing his cheeks. Tai's ready for him now, and holds himself still on the bed. He moans before he can think. Ollie's mouth tightens around his cock.

Tai lifts his head off the bed to watch. The sight of Ollie bent over him, putting all that extraordinary, lovely focus into his pleasure, makes him moan again. He drops his head back onto the bed and grips the covers with his fists. Ollie's warm breath huffs through his nose as he swirls his tongue, then bobs his head down to take Tai deep inside. It's imperfect and inexpert and beyond incredible.

"God, Ollie," Tai says. He wraps his hand around the base of his cock to help out, but Ollie pushes it away roughly and replaces it with his own.

Tai arches, lifted irresistibly off the bed. Ollie glances up, his eyes blue across the expanse of their bodies. Tai doesn't let himself close his eyes. He's not going to miss a second. The orgasm runs through him, sending tendrils of pleasure down his arms and up his spine. His mind is full of Ollie, Ollie's eyes and tongue and breath. He's shaking. He's amazed.

Ollie wipes his mouth with the back of his hand. It's so ordinary, and still the sexiest thing Tai has ever seen. Tai pants as he peels the condom off and wraps it in a tissue, then drops back onto the bed.

"Fuck," is all he manages to say, and as he turns his head to Ollie lying beside him, Ollie's answering smile is both blushing and pleased with himself.

CHAPTER TWELVE

TAI WAKES EARLY THE NEXT day, to sunlight filtered around the curtains and to Ollie warm with sleep beside him. The sight and the recollections that come with it are almost unbearably lovely—they swell in Tai's chest. He can taste Ollie on his lips.

He can't afford to get used to this. They agreed. *Just while we're on tour.* Tai hasn't spent five years building a family only to ruin it because his irresistibly attractive best friend is exploring his sexuality. Doing this only makes sense if they can get back to the life they've spent so long creating. That life matters. It matters more than sex.

Tai refuses to fool himself. Letting go of this thing between them will be at least as terrible as he imagines. But when he looks at Ollie curled softly in his bed, he knows he's already all in. However much this will ache in the future, he's not about to give up the five and a half weeks stretching ahead of them. They get to enjoy this. It could be incredible. Tai can handle everything else later.

Under the sheets, he rubs his feet together, an old comfort. His feet are smooth but not soft, tough after hours spent walking up and down rough sand and clambering across rocks. He moves his toes to tuck them beneath Ollie's ankle and drops back into sleep.

When he wakes a second time, Ollie's eyes are open. They're warm as they rest on Tai, gray-blue like the sky outside.

"You know what I was just thinking?" Ollie says. His voice sounds loud, breaking into the silence of the morning.

"Do I need to worry?" Tai says, though he could never really worry when Ollie's gaze is so sweet on him.

Ollie shakes his head. His lips are pressed together as though he's holding onto a smile. "I was thinking that they do room service here. There's absolutely nothing we need to do all day. We could get breakfast in bed and stay here. Forget about everything else for a while." Ollie's bites his lip but his eyes are wide, hopeful and teasing. It's enough to make Tai kiss him and press him into the mattress greedily.

THE POSTCARD ON THE BED is a picture of Bells Beach at sunrise. Tai saw Ollie grab it in one of the convenience stores in town while they were buying other essentials. It shows a little crescent of golden cliff curved around the big, barreling southern ocean surf.

Ollie writes in his neat script. Tai rolls over and hooks his chin over Ollie's shoulder to read. He breathes Ollie in.

There's no point in flying home between tour stops when the surf league has the competitions bunched together in Australia like this. Instead, they've been waiting for the next round of the competition, surfing a lot and not sightseeing even a little, exploring one another's bodies for almost two weeks. Two weeks of Ollie inviting him to their room after dinner with a quick-eyed smirk only Tai can translate, two weeks of kissing Ollie on the privacy of their balcony until Ollie's soft and needy and ready to push Tai toward the bed.

Ollie's skin is beginning to be as familiar as Tai's own. Tai had seen Ollie's body before, of course, but now he knows the particular curve of Ollie's back under his palm, the way Ollie gasps as Tai nips his collarbone. Now Tai's traced the freckles across Ollie's shoulders. There's so much new intimacy in the knowledge.

There's ease, too, in drawing pleasure out of someone else, in knowing, without words, what will happen next. Out on the ocean they rarely need words to communicate. That ease is reflected when they touch.

Tai reads the postcard as Ollie writes tidily.

Hey Jaime—There's not much of a town, not much to do here except surf. Works out okay for us, but you might get bored. You'd love the drive in from Melbourne though and the cliff face is gorgeous, all orange and gray and it falls straight into the ocean. It'd be worth painting. Hi to S and H for us, love, O

"You do know that your brother has an email account," Tai says. He's had plenty of emails from all of them, just about everyday shit. He kisses Ollie behind the ear and then stretches out on his side with his head on his hand to look across at Ollie. "I mean, the kid's sixteen. He's on it all the time. Even my mom has email, though to be fair she only talks in capital letters."

Ollie huffs and whacks Tai over the head with the postcard. "I know Jaime has email." He rolls onto his back and into Tai's space. The side of his torso lines up against Tai's chest and belly. He stretches his legs across the bed, the muscles in his thighs flex, and Tai doesn't resist touching. He runs his palm up over soft leg hair and lightly freckled skin. Ollie takes a shaky breath but goes on, speaking to the ceiling. "I guess… we can't argue in a postcard. It's simple. It's me writing to him, sending him something. Nothing about what either one of us should or shouldn't be doing. It seemed like a good idea. Plus I know he liked the first one we sent."

"Because he stuck it to the fridge at home."

Ollie nods and blinks. "Yeah." Tai runs his hand upward and strokes Ollie's chest. Ollie shifts comfortably. He says, "I miss him. I miss all of them."

"I know. Me too. We'll call them today."

Tai misses home often. He misses the Blue House kids. He misses Maile. But when he's honest with himself, it's more than that. He misses having something to do.

Here there are no boards to shape or people to feed. Here he's just part of Ollie's crew—not that he'd give this up, not for anything.

Ollie wraps his hand around Tai's upper arm and turns his head to press a kiss there. Tai's heart stutters and settles. He has to pause before he can speak. "You didn't mention how you're doing in the comp," he says. "On the postcard."

Ollie's managed to make it through to the quarterfinals here, too. He's thrilled about it. Tai's beyond proud. It's a great result, for the third time in as many events. Ollie's been getting noticed for the risks he takes, for being willing to get big air and do moves on sections where others might play it safe.

"They'll have watched it on TV," Ollie says. It's true. Tai imagines the three of them sitting on the floor cheering. Other people will have watched too: his mum in Samoa, who yells at the television as though she can change things with a combination of will and sheer volume; his dad and sisters, though more quietly; Maile and the other surf kids back home in Hawaii.

Tai says, "I was glad to see you made it through this time." He lets his thumb brush over Ollie's far hip. "Into the quarters."

Ollie frowns at him, puzzled, which makes sense. "What?"

"Obviously I'm happy you're winning. But I mean, you know, we started doing this thing we're doing. I'd have hated for that to have been caught up with any kind of losing streak. I didn't want you to worry that we'd need to stop doing this so you could win." He rubs his thumb over Ollie's hipbone again.

"Oh," says Ollie, as though the thought had never occurred to him. "You were worried about that?"

Tai shrugs. "Of course I was. It's your first ever tour. You're here after a couple of years down time. It's not exactly the best time to start having sex with one another."

Ollie watches Tai for a long moment then rolls into him. "Lucky it's all working out," he says with a grin.

Tai kisses him, tracing from his lips to his jawline.

Ollie goes on. "I don't know. It's possible that I'd be a total mess if I was only thinking about was the waves and the comp all the time." Tai breathes against Ollie's neck. He hadn't thought of that. "These things fit pretty well. Getting a sense of different breaks across the planet, learning how to navigate that in a competition. And learning the stuff here," Ollie's blushing a little, "in bed with you."

Tai traces the waistband of Ollie's boxers, but Ollie shakes his head and rolls away.

"I have a meeting with Carise," he says. "We're talking the serious stuff. Do you want to come up the road to the café with me?"

Tai considers. "Okay. Sure."

Carise is seated and frowning over a folder of papers. She has her hair in multiple braids with flowers clipped on either side of her head. Two coffees sit in front of her, one for Ollie and one for her. Carise half stands as they approach the little café table.

"I'll get you something, Tai," she says. "Sorry, I didn't know you'd be here."

"Not a problem. I'll get it." Tai walks over to the counter.

When he returns to the table with a chai, Carise is saying, "Their offer will be significant, Ollie."

Ollie looks stubborn. "It's not negotiable," he says. Tai wants to whack him over the head. He doesn't know what's going on, but he worries when Ollie's so quick to shut things down.

"Okay. Okay, your call." Carise takes a breath and moves on. "Everyone's impressed with your form, Ollie. Including me. I loved watching you in the third heat. You completely ripped it."

After breakfast is over, Ollie and Tai walk back to the hotel along the shore road.

"What were you talking about, when I came back with my tea?" Tai asks.

Ollie glances at him quickly and shrugs. "Not much. Billabong's been in touch with Carise about sponsorship."

"But. What? That's amazing, Ollie." It's the way forward, sponsorship. The comps pay, but even in the best of times Ollie can't win everything. Sponsorship is money you can count on. And Billabong is one of the big guns.

"It's not an option. I'd need to ride their boards. Exclusively." Ollie doesn't look at Tai.

"Oh." Tai thinks of the board he's currently imagining for Ollie. He's always shaping a board for Ollie in his head.

Ollie says, "I couldn't do that. I ride your boards."

Tai's touched, but he doesn't want to get in the way. He's not supposed to be the thing holding Ollie back. "You know—you don't need to," he says. "Billabong's got Butter Boards now. They make a sweet six-footer that might really work for you." Ollie grunts. Tai says, "I don't want you to miss out on sponsorship because of some loyalty to me."

Ollie grins at him. "Don't be an idiot. Listen, you know I'd do anything for you. But this isn't for you; it's for me. Your boards are the best. I'm the best I can be on them. I know them like I know myself. I don't want Billabong sponsorship. But even if I did, it's about the surfing first. There's no point in competing if I'm not riding the best."

"I don't know that they're not better than mine. You haven't tried the others."

"I've tried enough. Your boards work for me. And they're Hawaiian, too. That's important." There's no room for argument in Ollie's voice. "I told her it wasn't negotiable."

Tai doesn't say anything. He understands and he appreciates the confidence. Shaping is the thing he brings to this world, the thing that's just his. But sponsorship would bring a lot of money, and they could use it. They could save it for when Jaime goes to college. Or keep it for the day things go downhill and they can't afford to pay the electricity. It's been surreal to live these weeks without any thought of whether they can afford dinner out, or room service, or those replacement sunglasses that made Ollie look at Tai with quick intent. But the money won't last forever.

Still, there's no arguing with Ollie. And when he's insisting on riding Tai's boards while taking on the world's best, Tai doesn't want to argue.

"Okay," says Tai when they're back at the hotel. "I want to get some new wax on a couple of the shortboards. Help out?"

"Sure."

They take the boards down and set up shop near one of the faucets at the beach. There's a basketball court nearby. Some of the surfers are playing ball. Tai lifts a hand in greeting, then strips off his shirt to start clearing the old wax. The sun is warm on his back as he works. He runs his hands over the board to check the smoothness.

"You got some basecoat?" Ollie asks after a bit. He's rubbing the last of the old wax off the rail.

"Yeah, sure." Tai grabs some from his kit and hands it over. Ollie reaches out. His fingers brush Tai's and hold there a bit longer than is needed. Tai shivers.

"Chilly?" asks Ollie, teasing. His eyes reflect the bright sky.

"I'm good." Tai grabs another stick of basecoat from the bag. Before he gets back to work, he lets his eyes rest on Ollie, whose body is bent over a board. His shoulder blades shift under his shirt. It's not as if Tai can touch him right now. A bunch of surfers are on the basketball court, strangers and friends and rivals in all directions. But he longs to run his hands up under Ollie's shirt and feel the ripple of Ollie's muscles under his skin.

"I heard from Maile," Tai says to break his train of thought. "Jaime's doing well at the café. If he keeps it up she might fire me."

"Unlikely. Maile's like your third big sister." Ollie runs his fingers carefully over the surface of his board. "Hey, you got any topcoat?"

Tai reaches into his kit. "Yep." As he hands it over he says, "Where've your waxes got to?"

Ollie grins. "I have plenty. I just thought it'd be fun to make you share." He lets their fingers brush, then runs the pad of his thumb deliberately over Tai's knuckles. Tai pauses, suddenly breathless. Ollie grins at him and goes back to his board, applying the topcoat in long diagonal strokes.

As they finish the boards, a basketball bounces by. Brandon runs to grab it, and then throws it at Tai's head. "Come play, guys," he says.

"Basketball?" Ollie says. "Have you seen Tai, Brandon? Basketball is not his game."

It's a challenge and it's ridiculous. Tai shakes his head. "You got something to say about my height, Birkstrom?" Ollie's eyes sparkle back at him. "We're in," Tai says to Brandon.

Brandon high-fives them both. Tai follows the others to the court, shaking his head.

In the morning they go out to Bells for a quick pre-dawn surf. The sun is breaking over the horizon. It turns everything gold: water, sand, cliffs. The waves are tipped with light and twisting into powerful barrels with huge slopes. Tai watches Ollie ride one smoothly, his body crouched and ready, his moves fluid and graceful. His heart aches: Ollie's a joy to watch. Now that Tai knows his body intimately, watching him surf is even more of a privilege.

When Ollie paddles back out, he meets Tai's eyes. "Did you enjoy that?" he asks with a quirk of his lips. His look is knowing. Tai's diaphragm tightens in response. They've always had an immediate understanding, a way of knowing what the other is thinking, especially on the ocean. But now each look is colored in a new way.

Ashton and Brandon are on the surf, too. Brandon surfs well; he's compact and focused as he curves down the long slope. Ashton's surfing is flashier, full of quick turns and snapbacks with all the fins showing. But the truth is, nobody notices anyone else when Ollie takes another ride, fluid and bold at once, getting air as he turns a 360 and catches the wave neatly under his board. Tai glows with pride.

OLLIE'S UP AGAINST ASHTON FOR a quarterfinals spot. The wind's swung around to the west and there's an underlying groundswell, so the waves come in nice five-foot sets. Ashton has seniority, but Ollie's form is good. He has a handle on the waves from the start. He wins the heat easily.

Ashton doesn't glance at Tai or Ollie as he heads out of the water. Tai hugs Ollie. Ollie grins against Tai's hairline.

Afterward, in the rec room, Tai stands in the doorway talking with one of the veterans about shaping. Ollie's eyes follow him as he speaks. As they finish, Ollie says, "Hey, can I steal you for a moment, Tai?"

His voice has a contained energy, a simmering intensity. Tai follows Ollie to one side of the room.

They're surrounded by people, but there's some privacy in standing close to one another. Tai can't think about who might be watching as Ollie says, quietly, "You were over there shaping a board, with your hands waving in the air. And I couldn't stop thinking about how those hands feel. On me."

Tai raises an eyebrow. "Oh yeah?"

Ollie's confidence is alluring. "Oh, yeah." He grins, sharp and fierce. "So come upstairs."

"Okay. Absolutely."

CHAPTER
THIRTEEN

IN THEIR ROOM, OLLIE REACHES for Tai immediately. He doesn't stop smiling as they kiss. Tai's lips move in an answering smile.

Ollie's sure of himself in ways that surprise him. It turns out he's pretty good at sex. He gets it. He's spent so much time reading the ocean, taking note of tiny shifts in the wind and the swell, so of course he knows how to read the ripples in someone's body as it moves beside or above or beneath his own. Ollie's proud of that focus, his sense of detail; he knows it lifts his surfing game. In sex, the details matter in a different way: the private hitch of Tai's breath, the way his eyes dilate, the scrape of his fingernails across Ollie's back. It's beautiful. He doesn't want to miss any tiny thing.

They kiss between the door and the bed. Ollie's unwilling to break away. It's a relief to be near Tai, as close as they can be, with bodies and tongues and hands all moving thoughtlessly together. Ollie is clumsy with emotion, and desperate for more contact.

As they reach the bed, Tai stays standing. "What do you want?" he asks, hushed.

"I want—" Ollie pauses. It seems both simple and vast. They've spent time exploring one another's bodies and pleasure with hands and mouths. He wants to know all the ways Tai can touch him. He wants all of Tai's self-assurance and physicality.

He's blushing as he speaks. "I want to know what you feel like inside me," he says quickly. He speaks too quietly, and as Tai glances at him, Ollie thinks he's going to have to repeat himself. He blushes more deeply. "No, not—don't worry about it," he says, taking a step away.

Tai exhales. His eyes are steady on Ollie. "So wait, you don't want that?"

"No. Yeah." Ollie huffs out a sigh. He's exasperated with himself. "I—fuck, Tai. Are you going to make me say it again?"

When he looks, Tai's eyes are deep and warm, his pupils huge. Tai takes Ollie's hand in his. His voice is rough. "I want to hear everything you want. Say it again. Please, Ollie."

Going into this, Ollie was aware that Tai knew what he was doing. He knew Tai, and he knew that Tai would be both skilled and generous as he touched Ollie. But he hadn't known the flip side of that. How huge it would be to give someone else pleasure. He hadn't known there'd be this dizzying joy in watching Tai ask for something, and in knowing he could give it. Ollie's not sure he's ever wanted anything as much as Tai's voice breaking over him as he says, "Please."

Ollie takes a breath, bolstering himself. "I'd like you to fuck me," he says, with his eyes on Tai's.

"Okay."

They've had nights of fumbling with clothes, of half-dressed rutting. They've had afternoons with one of them swiftly removing the other's shorts as though the whole thing might be over far too soon. This is different. Ollie is fully clothed as he sits to carefully untie his shoes. He's self-conscious. He looks up as he slides his shoes off and watches Tai. It's not a huge room, but there's plenty of space to stand apart from one another, not touching as they undress. Ollie tries not to count his buttons, his breaths.

Then they kiss, all that warm naked skin pressed close, and Ollie couldn't count buttons if he wanted to.

Ollie steps away from Tai to lie down on the bed. He tries not to hold his breath. This is Tai; they've fallen asleep on the couch together, covered one another with sunscreen, wrapped one another's injuries. Now Ollie's laying himself out naked on a bed. But he lets his eyes run over Tai's compact, muscular form, his wide shoulders and the tattoo, ocean and turtle and sun, and everything is way less weird.

The practicality of sex confronts him now, though. Ollie can't avoid imagining all that Tai can see as he slips a pillow under Ollie's hips. However much Ollie wants this, the action is deeply and intrusively personal. Ollie lifts his head to try and gain a degree of control. He watches Tai uncap the lube. Ollie's breath puffs shallow in his chest.

Tai kneels on the bed beside Ollie's legs, closer but still so far away. He runs one warm dry palm from Ollie's knee up over his thigh.

All the air goes out of Ollie. "Tai," he says, half entreating.

Tai bends forward and kisses Ollie's chest briefly, then sits back on his heels again. "Take a breath for me. Then let it out and relax your body."

Ollie does, and while he breathes out Tai presses a single cool finger against his hole, pushing a little so it moves up into him. Ollie gasps and clenches around it. They've had a lot of sex in the past weeks. Tai's not tentative with Ollie's body anymore. But he's being careful now.

"Don't fight this," says Tai, meeting Ollie's eyes. He rotates his finger a little; it's probably not far in, but to Ollie it feels huge. He lets himself sit with it, closes his eyes.

"Ready?" says Tai. Ollie takes another breath and nods. As he exhales this time, Tai's finger slides deeper inside. Tai lets out a breath that sounds like a groan.

Ollie's hips roll against Tai's hand, taking Tai's finger farther inside. The world is focused on one tiny part of his body. It's splitting his whole self in pieces. "More," he says.

Tai's huffs out a kind laugh, and presses a second finger against Ollie's hole, then a third. Ollie's body stretches around them. He switches between feeling awkward and overwhelmed. He wants everything he can have right now.

"You want more?" asks Tai.

Ollie opens his eyes to answer. "Of course I want more," he says, trying not to sound impatient.

"Okay then. Hold on there." Tai's amused but his voice holds softness and deeper emotions too.

Tai sits back. He pulls a condom on with the efficiency of someone who's done this many times before. Ollie closes his eyes and breathes. Then Tai's body shadows Ollie's on the bed. He settles his weight between Ollie's legs and kisses Ollie's lips. Ollie's too on edge to open up to it fully, but the kiss is safe, like home.

"I've got you," says Tai, against his lips. Ollie can't quite smile, but he kisses Tai and lets his thighs drop open around Tai's hips.

When Tai pushes inside, achingly slow, Ollie turns his face into the bed. He knows he's moaning at the fullness and the relief; his voice vibrates long and softly in his chest, but he feels far away from it. He's amazed and overwhelmed, taken apart by Tai filling him, by the intensity of Tai's body as part of his own, by his own openness.

Ollie's cock is bobbing up between them, sometimes brushing against skin. He's mostly hard but he's pretty sure he can't come this way.

"It's okay," says Tai above him. Tai puts all his weight on one arm and lifts a hand. He runs his thumb over Ollie's lips. Ollie presses his teeth into Tai's thumb thankfully, letting it ground him, then grabs Tai's wrist and pulls it against his mouth. He mouths Tai's shell string and pulls it between his teeth. He bites down. The string is delicate, just a single fine line across his mouth, and somehow that steadies him. All the details are stark and clear: Tai's breath on his neck; Tai's hips thrusting and stuttering forward; the stretch as Tai grinds deep inside him.

Ollie arches his back, trying to get pressure on his cock. Then he reaches between them and wraps his hand around himself. His hips thrust up over and over. A bright, spilling warmth runs up Ollie's spine and down his limbs. When Ollie comes, Tai does too. Their bodies shudder together.

"Thank you," says Ollie, overwhelmed. "Thank you."

Tai exhales on a fond laugh that holds as much gratitude as humor. He slumps forward, worn out and heavy on Ollie's chest. He lifts his weight to roll away.

"Don't go," says Ollie. He keeps his eyes closed and runs his hand down Tai's back to cup his ass. "Stay here for a bit." He doesn't want to be clingy, but he's warm and vulnerable and unbearably close and he can't imagine wanting Tai to give him space.

Tai shifts closer. Ollie curls into him happily. He opens his eyes. There's a deep mark on Tai's wrist where the string bracelet dug into his skin. Ollie turns his head to kiss the spot, over and over. They settle into one another and into sleep.

In the morning, Tai looks muscular and gorgeous across the bed in the sunlight. He lies on his side with his head propped up and runs one hand down Ollie's body. Leaving bed, leaving Tai at all is the last thing Ollie wants. But Carise wants a breakfast meeting. He looks at the clock and groans.

"Don't you want to come along?" he asks as he rolls away from Tai and sits up.

Tai lies back with his hands behind his head. He drawls, "Nah, man. This one is all you. I'm just gonna lie here and think of you."

Ollie dresses reluctantly.

"Bring me back a pastry," says Tai as Ollie leaves. "I'll need to get my energy up." He's lying back on the bed with the covers pulled to his waist. He tucks one arm behind his head and slides the other suggestively under the sheets.

"You're an asshole," says Ollie. He closes the door behind him with a bang, mostly to stop himself from turning around, going back in there, and plastering himself to Tai for all time.

The breakfast bar is in a room that looks out past the street to the water. Ollie's starving. He fills a bowl and a plate and sits opposite Carise. He stretches his back. His body feels good.

"I've got a plan," Carise says without preamble. "For you."

Ollie nods around a mouthful of granola. He swallows. "Hit me."

"Okay. I've been talking to a couple of people. You love Hawaii and you're pretty stubborn about your boards." She pauses for his acknowledgment.

"Yeah," he says. It still makes sense to him. If he's going for a world title, why would he let someone else choose his board?

"I'm going to use it to position you."

Ollie raises his eyebrows.

"Here's how it sits. You're a Hawaiian kid with a heart for your home and you believe that Hawaiian boards are the best in the world. You want to be the top of your game. So, you won't negotiate with the bigger board companies, you want the autonomy to choose your own."

"Okay. That's true." He leans forward, interested.

"I can use that as a selling point with other sponsors. Vans is interested. I'm talking with them to get the best deal, but, see, you can get sponsorship without giving up your choice of boards. For Vans you'd need to do some photo shoots with their gear. Maybe wear the shoes when you're around." Ollie shrugs. He owns some Vans anyway. "You're someone people recognize; a few more wins and all the surfer kids will want to be you.

"And Paradise Beverages in Honolulu have this coconut water. I talked with their people. Plus there's a granola bar company and—basically I'm going to find a way for you to have sponsorship without giving up your boards or your state."

It's a great plan. "I knew I liked you," he says happily.

THEY'RE USED TO COMPETITION DAYS now. Tai enjoys them. He and Ollie head to the beach together but they don't talk much. Ollie watches the sets, working out which ones to push on, which ones to avoid. He's got a board they borrowed from another Hawaiian surfer. The big swell that was forecast has come, so the ones they'd brought were no good.

Tai watches from shore as Ollie surfs on the unfamiliar board. He sits a bit heavy on the wave, his turns slower than usual, but he's competent. It's a surprise when Ollie misses out on the top spot in the first round. It's not alarming, though. The winner goes straight through to round three, but Ollie has another chance to make it through at round two.

"It's just one more round," Tai says to Ollie. "Don't get worried." They've been through this before.

But there's nothing Tai can do as Ollie's knocked out in the second round, hanging back on the good waves and not scoring above 6.5 on any of them.

He waits for Ollie on shore as usual. "Nothing quite came together," says Tai as Ollie walks across the sand. Ollie scowls at him. "Dude. It's one stop in the competition," adds Tai. "There are plenty more to come." Ollie walks away. Tai rolls his eyes at his back and follows.

He stands back as Ollie is interviewed in the media room. He can't help but hear, though, when a reporter starts with, "So, Ollie, your dream run has ended." The reporter's smiling. Ollie isn't.

When Tai finds Ollie again, out on the surfers' deck where the media can't get to him, his face is stony, his jaw set in cool anger. Tai never wants to see that again. He doesn't think as he pulls Ollie into a hug. His hands slide up and down to rub over Ollie's back. Ollie stands stock-still, muscles tense, and then almost shoves Tai away.

"Not here," he says. His voice is low and hard.

Tai blinks. "Sorry." He's grown accustomed to being allowed to touch Ollie. He'd always been careful, before. Embarrassment sits hard on his chest. "It was only a hug," he adds, trying not to sound like a child. It wasn't about sex. It was about sympathy.

Ollie freezes. Their eyes fix on one another; Ollie's are bright with frustration. Then Ollie turns away from Tai and walks through the crowd of people and the big light-up signs advertising surf brands and out of the room.

"Shit," Tai says. He stands where he is as the room moves around him.

Someone steps up beside him. "Sorry to see that." It's Ashton. "Is Ollie okay?"

Tai's face is frozen. "He'll be fine. I'll just give him some time. How did you go today, Ash?" He sees Ashton wince and doesn't need an answer. "I'm sorry," he says. If Ollie weren't here, Tai would have watched Ashton surf and known not to ask. Of course, if Ollie weren't here, Tai wouldn't be either.

Ashton takes a big mouthful of his drink, polishing it off. "What can you do?" he says. "You can't always win. Have to be able to handle that in this game. Want a drink?"

Tai shrugs. "Sure." It's not as if he wants to go back to the hotel room, whether Ollie's there or not.

"Ollie's been riding a sweet board," says Ashton after they get their drinks. "Rumor has it you made it."

"Yeah." Tai doesn't want to talk about Ollie right now, but talking about boards is different. "I've got this shed at the back of my place. It's all set up. I've been doing it for a while now."

"You've got good hands," says Ashton. If there's suggestiveness in his tone he's hiding it well. "That's awesome. You should talk to me about setting up a business, you know. My mum runs this surf place, started up in Portland but it's huge now. We're weighing viable options, you know, exclusive boards and stuff. You could maybe talk to her about it."

"Thanks." Tai takes a drink. "That sounds useful."

"I'd buy your boards either way, Tai. You're a born shaper. So. Tell me about you and Ollie." He flicks his hair out of his eyes. It's a nervous gesture despite his confident smile.

"What do you mean?" Tai asks guardedly.

"You guys are... well, it appears to me that you're together. Right? Or something? Fucking? I guess it's all a secret." When Tai doesn't answer he goes on. "Tai, I know you, I like to think I do. You're an up-front kind of guy. Even within the surfing community you've never hidden anything like this. So what's happening?"

"It's not like that," says Tai shortly. "We're not—we're not together. It's a short-term thing."

Under his curls, Ashton seems nothing so much as sweetly concerned. "I just want you to be happy," he says. It's nice to hear, even if Ashton has it all wrong.

Tai smiles weakly. "I know, Ash. Thank you. But honestly, it's not what you think with Ollie. Things are a bit complicated, because we've been friends forever."

Ashton's eyes are firm on Tai. "Also, because you're in love with him. You always have been."

Tai's throat is tight. He looks away. However he feels about Ollie, he's not about to share it at a party. And not with Ashton. He hesitates, then says, "I'm not, Ash. At least, not in any way that will make a difference." He exhales. He can't think about Ollie right now. "Leave it alone, would you? Please." He turns back to Ashton as he says it.

"That's not an answer, Tai." Ashton's silver-gray eyes flash quickly, a brief moment of temper, in the crowded room. "You know, I could tell, even when he wasn't surfing, you've always been dazzled by that boy."

"It wasn't ever really your business, though." Tai's not trying to be cruel. Ashton lost today too. He's got to be hurting. It makes sense: hurting and looking for reassurance in his own way. He's just not looking for it in the right direction.

Ashton glares at him. Then he gives him a sudden, unhappy smile. "Yeah, okay. I had reason to think it was gonna be, though." He's sweet, and lovely to look at; it's not as if Tai didn't notice all of that last year. He just didn't have space to think about it. He never really has, not with Ollie in his orbit. "It's a shame," says Ashton.

"I'm sorry, Ash—" Tai says.

Ashton shakes his head roughly. "I'll talk to you later, Tai."

He walks away. Tai watches him go, then glances around the room. Ollie's still not there. Tai sighs. He's not going to chase after Ollie, not if he's not wanted. He heads over to the bar and orders a beer. Brandon and some of the rookies are at one of the tables near the window. Tai gets talking to them. When Brandon goes back to the bar, Tai orders another.

A couple of hours and several drinks later he makes his way up to the room. It's dark. Ollie's not there. Tai flicks the lights on and sits heavily in the armchair. He thinks about going back downstairs, but he figures the only people who'll still be up and drinking are those guys who were knocked out of this round of the competition. Tai's disappointed enough about Ollie's loss. He doesn't need to take on everyone else's feelings.

He watches the clock between the beds and tries not to worry.

It's almost an hour before the door opens. Ollie steps in.

"It was a bad day," Ollie says before Tai can speak. It sounds as though it's going to be an apology.

"I know," says Tai.

"I figured of all people, you'd know I sometimes need space."

"Yeah."

"Then what happened?" asks Ollie sharply. His tone sends needles along Tai's spine.

"I made a mistake about what you needed. A simple mistake. You didn't need to act like you did."

"I was on edge, Tai. I'd just lost and you were right there, like you always are." Ollie's voice rises.

Tai's briefly furious. "I've given you space, Ollie. Your whole life I've given you fucking space. But this past couple of weeks you've wanted to be with me as much as I've wanted to be with you. Don't tell me you haven't. I know you."

Ollie says nothing, and Tai can't read him. Resentment swells in his throat.

"I came along on tour because you asked, Ollie. But I'm not just gonna spend my time following you around. I'm your friend, or whatever we are, not your caddy."

"That's not fair," says Ollie shortly. He looks ashamed, though. "I don't think of you that way at all."

"Tell me, then," says Tai, though right now he's not sure he wants to know what Ollie thinks of him.

Ollie deflates. "Tai, I'm miserable and you've been drinking. Can we leave this be tonight?" He meets Tai's gaze directly. Tai shakes his head and lets his shoulders slump. Ollie's right. Now is not the time.

"Fine," Tai says. "Fine."

It's the first night they've slept in separate beds since they started this thing. Tai stares into the dark and listens to Ollie breathe. Though he's more experienced than Ollie in some ways, he's never done this before, never wanted something he couldn't have, never come back for more. It's a terrible, terrible thing. He misses Ollie's touch in his bones.

CHAPTER FOURTEEN

OLLIE DOESN'T SLEEP WELL. HIS bed is lumpy and awkward. The waves sound different from those at home. Each time he wakes in the night, he reaches for Tai with his eyes closed before he thinks. But when he opens his eyes, he can make out Tai across the room, asleep. He's lying on his back. His face is traced by silver blue moonlight. It looks smooth and untroubled, at ease. Ollie has no idea what he's dreaming about.

He watches as Tai sighs and rolls so he's facing Ollie. Tai's asleep and too far away in the other bed, so there's no bright gaze or quick understanding, no earnest reassuring words either. But there's a vulnerability to him that touches Ollie. He stares across the space between the beds and watches Tai's soft, young face, his long lashes, the way the pale light catches his dark cheekbones and parted lips. Tai's beautiful, of course; everyone knows that. But Ollie's only recently started noticing.

They're flying out today.

Once the sky starts to lighten, Ollie gives up on more sleep. He climbs out of bed and pees in the little bathroom. Then he reaches around the curtains to slide the glass door open and step out onto the deck. The dazzling gold of sunrise is touching the far-off horizon. The ever-present Australian parrots are waking up and starting their noisy pterodactyl screeching.

Ollie watches the Indian Ocean stretching east of them. It's not his ocean. And there's no point in counting the waves here, not anymore. But he can't help himself as he stands there. The rhythm settles his heart and lets him think.

He knows he's not like everyone else. He's always had to keep a bit of distance. It's not coldness, not really. It's experience. Touch is a prickling distraction at best and raw pain at worst.

Yet it was Ollie who reached for Tai that first time, and he's reached for him over and over since. Every time it's been dazzling, but also effortless. Ollie trusts Tai, and that's part of it. But it's not just that. When he's with Tai that way, Ollie doesn't need to think. Everything stops. Tai's careful touch is welcome, even though it's overwhelmingly intimate.

But last night Tai reached out to hold him in front of everyone. Ollie was full to the brim with disappointment and frustration, and Tai touched him in front of all the competition. Ollie was exposed. He's always trusted Tai not to do that.

The sun's still low in the sky, the scattering clouds yellow and pink, when Tai appears in the doorway. He rubs a hand across his face before he looks at Ollie. His eyes are dark and concerned, but he moves across the deck and leans against the railing before he speaks. Even just awake and clearly worried, he's comfortable in his skin, sure of himself and the way his body moves. He looks like something Ollie needs.

"Morning," Tai says. The birds are keeping up their raucous song, and Ollie can only just hear him.

"Hi." Ollie tries to smile at him, but he's sure it looks like a grimace. He wraps his arms around his body. One night without Tai in his bed and his whole body longs for something he can't have. Not forever. Ollie's way more caught up in this thing than he needs to be.

The way Ollie sees it, Tai knows all about sex. He's known for years what it's like to share breath and sweat and desire. It's never seemed to touch Tai, not deeply. For Ollie, sex is different. As soon as Ollie fell into bed with Tai, Ollie's whole self, his skin and his heart, were invested in something way bigger than anything Tai's ever wanted.

Ollie doesn't want to lose Tai. But he doesn't know what to do about it. He pushes the pad of his thumb against his teeth.

"How did you sleep?" he asks Tai.

"Terribly." It seems so simple when Tai says it.

Ollie can't help the spurt of happiness, however unfair. "Me too." After a pause he says, "Fuck, Tai, I don't like it when we fight." It's the smallest part of what he's feeling, but at least it's true.

Tai smiles and Ollie sees gratitude in his tired eyes.

"We need to pack," says Tai after a while. "The car's leaving in an hour."

Ollie nods agreement. Still, they stand there for a long time, watching the water, close to one another but not quite in contact.

It's a surprisingly long way from Australia to Tahiti. Tai's eyes are dry and sandy in the recycled air of the plane. He squeezes them tightly shut.

Ollie's beside him, his shoulder pressed close to Tai in the narrow seats. Tai's trying not to think about the cooling space between them last night or the not-quite truce this morning. He opens his tablet to run through all the stuff he's downloaded on the wave at Teahupo'o. It takes his breath and makes him nervous. Thick-lipped and relentless, it's not the height of the wave that's impressive, but the weight. Heaviest wave in the world, they say. Sometimes it looks as if the entire ocean is hanging over the lip, ready to pound surfers into the reef below. The thought of Ollie on that wave—

He turns the picture in Ollie's direction. "Take a look at this, a real look. We've got some time before the contest, but we'd better get you out near it as soon as we can."

"Okay," says Ollie.

"Not to surf, just to get a feel for it."

"I'm pretty sure I'm supposed to surf it."

Tai can't tell if he's being willfully obtuse. He lets his fear turn into frustration. "Don't be stupid. It's, like, the most dangerous wave on the planet, Ollie. No one surfed it until fifteen years ago."

"Bro, I know." He doesn't quite roll his eyes as he turns back to the tiny screen embedded in the seat in front of him. He has the flight path up there, an image of a giant plane making its slow way across a blue and green map of the Pacific.

Tai lets out a breath. He knows Ollie is on edge. Tai gets it, of course, but he doesn't know how to fix it. He hates not knowing what to do. This is their last tour stop before heading home. Everything's ending.

Tai pitches his voice reasonably as he says, "If you want to come through this stop with a good ranking, you need to think about this shit before you get on the wave. It's a fucking monster."

Ollie looks back at him irritably. His lips are pressed together.

Tai can't help but go on. "Ollie. You won't get through this round just on talent. You need to think."

Ollie's eyes spark brightly in the dim airplane. "I know that. Fuck it, Tai, stop treating me like I've never surfed a big wave before."

It stings, partly because it's true. Pipeline's a dangerous wave, and Ollie's been surfing it since he was a grommet. Tai's more worried than he should be. "I'm trying to help," Tai protests.

"Well, you can stop. I'm not some project for you to look after. I'm not a kid."

Tai leans away from him. "I know, Ollie. God," he says hotly and mostly to himself. But he's uncomfortably aware that he treats Ollie like that, some days. The difficulty is, he's not always sure what he's good for if he's not looking after Ollie.

When he turns back, Ollie has turned away again. Anger bubbles in Tai's blood. He leans closer and hisses, "Ollie." He puts his hand on Ollie's arm to get his attention.

Ollie jerks his arm away and turns quickly, his voice rushed and low. "Stop it, Tai." He puffs out a frustrated grunt. "Don't touch me."

Tai freezes. It's only with Ollie that Tai feels as though he's too much. "You're an asshole."

There's nowhere to go in a tiny plane. The seats keep them pressed together. Tai tries to lean farther away. Ollie sits rigid and cool beside him. When Tai glances across, tears edge Ollie's eyes.

Tai softens. He sounds rough to his own ears as he says, "Hey. You brought me here, Ollie. What's my job if it's not getting you all the information I can?" He pauses. "I'm not helping you because I think you're a kid, I'm helping you because that's what I'm here for." He pauses, catches his breath. "Trying to help, anyway. But hey, this is our last stop before we head home. I'm not going to let another fight ruin what's pretty much been the most awesome time of my life."

He turns back to his tablet. Next to him, Ollie puts on his headphones to flick through music channels. After a moment, Ollie reaches out to Tai without looking and loops his pinkie finger under the shell string tied to Tai's wrist.

IT'S LATE WHEN THEY REACH the little Tahitian resort. The air's heavier than Tai's used to at home. But after the cool dry of the airplane, its mugginess is a welcome comfort. The ocean's dark and close, lapping up against the black sand beach that stretches out past the lights in front of the cabin. Of course, it's almost dead flat at the shoreline. If they want to see the wave, he and Ollie will paddle out about ten minutes or take a boat past the reef.

There's not much around. Just the cluster of wooden cabins and a big central restaurant that's mostly open to the water. The mountains jut straight up behind the buildings to knife-edge peaks. They're rough and black under the night sky, covered with palms and tropical scrub. It's nowhere he's ever been, but the whole thing reminds Tai of home.

In their room, Ollie writes a postcard to Jaime. He pushes it across the tiny table for Tai to read.

I know, J, I sucked at the fourth stop. Hope you haven't disowned me. But now we're in Tahiti getting ready to surf Chopes, so at least we have that. Haven't seen the wave yet but we've all seen the pictures. Tai goes whiter than me at the thought of me riding it. But I'll be fine. Love, O

"I'll be fine," Ollie says to Tai, repeating himself.

"Yeah, I know." Tai wishes he could slow the whole world down.

There's no way they'll surf in the morning. Tai can't tell by the sound of the wind or the waves, but all the reports say that the swell out past the reef is huge and will stay huge, too huge for competition. They're the kind of waves that even experienced big wave surfers take their lives into their hands to ride at all.

They share a bed without discussing it, not looking at one another as they slip in on either side. Tai goes to sleep with one hand on Ollie's hip. Ollie twines his fingers in Tai's.

Tai wakes too early. The light in the cabin is exquisitely pale. The sun isn't up. Ollie's lying on his side across the expanse of sheets. His eyes are open, gray-blue and slightly guarded as he blinks sleepily at Tai. The wind shifts in the trees. There's no rush to do anything. Tai meets Ollie's gaze for a long uncertain moment. It hurts to want to touch and not really know how.

Ollie stretches out a long arm and cups Tai's cheek. He moves closer, shifting his body across the bed.

They lie still. It's warm, even this early. "I don't want to think, Tai," Ollie murmurs into the quiet. "Or talk. Not right now."

"Okay."

Tai moves his hand to weave his fingers with Ollie's where they lie flat on the sheets. It's hours before they need to be at breakfast; so much time stretches out before them. However much they've been prickling and cutting at one another the past couple of days, this is still Ollie and, for this last week, they still have this.

Ollie lifts their joined hands and kisses Tai's fingers. His eyes are heavy with sleep. Tai shifts closer and closes his eyes. Then he stretches out along the length of Ollie's body and nuzzles Ollie's shoulder, kissing up to his collarbone. He lingers, tasting salt, flattening his tongue over the bone beneath Ollie's skin. Ollie sighs sweetly.

They kiss.

"Good morning," Ollie says as Tai's cock presses against his hip. "Can I?" He reaches for Tai, and Tai almost laughs aloud despite his worries, the weight of silence, the closeness of the other cabins.

"Of course," he says. *Of course.*

Ollie's eyes are compellingly lovely as he slides down Tai's body. He keeps them open as he works a condom over Tai's cock, then closes his eyes. He exhales as though in relief as he opens his mouth then swirls his tongue low around Tai's balls. He takes Tai's cock into his mouth. Tai lies back with a pleasured sigh.

Tai's body is heavy and dreamy, but as Ollie drops his mouth all the way to Tai's crotch and draws him deep inside, desire coils tightly in Tai's belly. Ollie pulls off and sucks Tai down again, in long steady tugs. Tai gasps. He lets the pleasure build in his spine, moves his hips mindlessly. He comes before he expects it. The pleasure explodes low in his cock, skimming across all his nerves and bringing him alive, making him hazy and grateful.

Ollie rolls him over onto his front. "Okay?" Ollie asks.

"Yeah," Tai breathes, settling into the new position and turning his head so his cheek presses against the mattress. Ollie lowers himself against Tai's back. Tai closes his eyes, stretches out long and pliant under Ollie's body as Ollie grinds against his ass. His cock slots between Tai's cheeks and slides back and forth, deeply intimate and suggestive. Tai groans. Ollie thrusts forward, his breath coming in rough muted pants. He presses his mouth against Tai, muffling his pleasure in Tai's skin. His hips stutter. He grunts softly over and over, then comes across Tai's lower back with his teeth pushing focused points of pain into Tai's shoulder. Tai lets him catch his breath, settle the shaking. Then Tai rolls over, sticky and gratified, to hold Ollie close. He's half-hard again but drowsy with it. He longs to say something that matters, but he doesn't know how. He moves back into sleep with Ollie warm and sated against his side.

It's an extraordinary thing, the space not to think. Ollie finds it every time they have sex. He listens to Tai breathe beside him. Tai shifts and wraps an arm around Ollie's waist; his knees butt against Ollie's thighs.

When Tai makes a move to get up, Ollie pulls him back to the bed. "Stay a little longer," he says.

"Breakfast will be over in twenty minutes," says Tai, though he comes back willingly.

"Give me ten of them." Ollie knows Tai won't resist.

Half an hour later, they're sitting on the cabin stairs munching pastries they'd grabbed at the last minute from the closing buffet.

"I know I'm not the expert," Ollie says. "But I think we're kind of good at—you know—the sex thing."

"I know." Tai pauses long enough that Ollie turns his head. He watches Tai's lips then meets his eyes. Tai says, "What if we didn't stop?"

"What?" Ollie manages. The world around is a blur.

Tai rushes the words. "What if we kept going when we got home? It's not an accident that we're good at this. We're comfortable with one another. We've known each other for such a long time. We enjoy it. It doesn't need to be a big deal, you know."

Ollie freezes. This *is* a big deal. He can't help how huge it is in his heart.

Ollie's well aware of how differently they think and feel about sex, how easy it is for Tai and how complicated for Ollie, which is part of why this has to stop when they go home.

Tai watches with a worried frown. He says, "It'd be okay. I mean, we could keep it to ourselves."

Ollie says the first thing that comes to mind. "First, have you met Sunny? And Jaime? The house isn't that big. There's no way we could keep this to ourselves." He goes on. "But even if we could—no. No way, Tai."

Tai's face drops. "Okay, okay," he says, raising his hands. He sounds defensive and hurt. But it's easier to deal with that now rather than later, when the emotions become even huger and Tai moves onto some cute mainlander and Ollie's a mess.

Ollie continues, "We can't. We really can't. Making it just while we are on tour made sense. Have you forgotten about our house? *That's* our family. It's everything we have. We can't risk it. Jaime'll have nowhere to live. And the girls. We all need that home." He takes a breath. "No. We talked about this. We agreed this would end with the tour."

"I'm not talking about risking anything, Ollie," says Tai with heat. "I'm talking about something simple." He turns his head away. "Fuck it, I wasn't about to turn up at your bedroom door reciting poetry and giving you flowers and shit. I thought it'd be fun." And that is precisely the problem. Tai thinks it would be fun.

"I know, but it's a bad idea." Ollie wants to cry, but it's a gorgeous Tahiti day, he's on his first world surf tour with his best friend, and he's getting what he's asking for. Crying wouldn't make sense.

THEY TAKE A BOAT OUT to the wave the next morning. There are five days until the contest, and Ollie plans to use every one of them to get his nerve up for this monster.

The weight of the wave makes him breathless. All the things Tai told him are true, but in real life it looks about a million times more hazardous than Ollie anticipated. He meets Tai's eyes as they follow the others out of the boat and into the lineup.

"If you're not scared, you're stupid," Tai says. He's planning to sit on his board on the inside, though Ollie imagines part of him is itching to have a ride too. He has a waterproof camera to film Ollie. Ollie wants to hold his hand, just for a second, but they're in public. He gives Tai a thumbs-up instead.

They've reached an unspoken truce. These are the last few days they'll have. Ollie can't resist reaching for Tai. So they touch in the dark of their room. They don't talk about it. They talk about surf and boards and injuries coming off the reef. They talk about the wave Ollie has to master. They don't talk about home, not as much. They don't talk about leaving the tour behind.

BY THE TIME THE CONTEST begins, Ollie's ready. Teahupo'o isn't like most of the waves. The whole point here is to stay in the tube. It's huge and dangerous, but Ollie's been dealing with that since his first day on the North Shore. He holds his nerve. He makes it all the way to the finals and comes in runner-up to one of the Australians.

Part of him is euphoric with the success. The first stage of the world tour is over and Ollie's done better than even Sunny and Jaime could have dreamed. He's excited to go home to a place he knows deep inside. Home is safe.

But another part of him is terrified. Home might be safe, but there he and Tai have to go back to being friends. And he's not sure he remembers how.

For the whole of the next day they're surrounded by people. Tai shakes hands, or slaps shoulders, or yells goodbye to someone who was a stranger five weeks ago. Ollie watches from the outside. Maybe both of them are intentionally avoiding time alone.

That night, as they close the door to their room, Ollie says, tentatively, "I know we're not on the same page."

"But this is our last night," says Tai. The full force of his dark gaze brings tears to Ollie's eyes. "Come here," Tai says. "Please. Come here, Ollie."

He pulls Ollie to him for a kiss. Ollie goes easily into his arms; his body melts into Tai's. Later, they move against one another in the dark, seeking the rhythm of that ancient and unthinking pleasure. There's not much left to say.

They wake with Tai's alarm at six and head across the island to get a plane home. On the bus, Ollie keeps his eyes resolutely away from Tai's lips. They've already had their last kiss.

CHAPTER FIFTEEN

FROM THE PLANE, THE HAWAIIAN Islands are small and green in the vast crinkled stretch of the Pacific. Ollie doesn't look at Tai as the plane descends. It's easier to keep his eyes fixed on home as it comes closer through the tiny window. Honolulu grows bigger and bigger. Toy cars and buildings, beaches and streets come into view. The clouds rest heavily on the mountains above the city. This is what Ollie's world looks like from above.

Landing in Honolulu is rough. The plane sways as it lines up with the runway. It tips left then right. Ollie's heart stutters fast and loud in his chest. For just a second, Tai digs his fingers into Ollie's forearm on the armrest between them, and Ollie places a grateful hand over Tai's.

When they land with a thud, some of the passengers clap. Ollie blushes as he pulls his hand back and places it in his lap. He's home now. It's time to go back to real life.

"Aloha and welcome to windy Honolulu," says the flight attendant over the intercom. "It's 6:45 in the evening and the temperature is a balmy 85 degrees."

As the plane is pulled up to the gate Tai says, "We're home."

"Yeah. Look at that."

There's a pause, then, "It was an incredible trip, Ollie. Thanks." Tai looks down to undo his seatbelt.

"I'm glad you could come," says Ollie. "It was—yeah." He half laughs at himself uncomfortably.

Tai looks at him at last. He exhales as he stands. Then he squeezes Ollie's shoulder. He grabs his bag from the overhead locker as people start to file out. Ollie follows him down the aisle.

Windy or not, strange and awkward or not, it's immeasurably comforting to be home. The air feels right.

Jaime and Sunny and Hannah are waiting for them in the terminal. All three bound over as soon as Ollie and Tai come through the glass doors with their luggage and boards. It's as if everything's back to normal, though Jaime looks blonder and taller than he did when they left. Sunny's hair is growing out; it's somewhere between green and her natural dark brown, and her face is bright. Hannah's unchanged, broad shouldered and serene; her smile is wide as ever.

"I can't believe you're home," Sunny says. "We've missed you. We've got so much to tell you."

"We've missed you too," says Tai.

The five of them hug tightly. Ollie is surrounded in a way that's both simple and safe. When Ollie's hand brushes against Tai's bare arm, though, he flushes and steps back again. Tai flashes him a quick glance, but no one says anything. They're used to hugs being weird when it comes to Ollie.

Ollie looks them all over with tired eyes. Jaime's wearing ridiculous tiger-patterned three-quarter pants, and his hair is swooped above his head.

"You look great," Tai says to him. He sounds genuine.

Jaime grins. "Unlike you two. You both look like you haven't slept in days."

"Thanks for that, bro," says Ollie.

"It was kind of a rough flight," says Tai. "That's all." He is unusually self-conscious. Tai's always been open about everything with the rest of the Blue House.

Hannah takes one of the boards under her arm. Jaime grabs another.

"When did you get big enough to carry that?" Ollie asks.

Jaime rolls his eyes. "Like, two years ago," he says. "But I can't be bothered usually." He sounds annoyed, but he stays by Ollie's side as they walk out of the terminal and across the lot to the car. There's comfort in Jaime's presence. It reminds Ollie that it's not just Tai who cares about him. It reminds him, too, that this whole family is relying on them for stability.

Even strapping the boards to the roof of the station wagon has the warmth and ache of familiarity. They toss the two suitcases in the trunk. Hannah sits in front with Sunny. Jaime slides into the middle next to Ollie, with Tai on his other side. The car seat creaks and sinks under their combined weight.

"So, what's been going on?" Ollie asks Jaime as they head through the pineapple plantations.

Jaime shrugs. "Not much."

"Come on, man, we've missed you guys," says Tai. "Tell us everything. Did you go to any good parties? Are things still on with you and Phoebe? I don't know—did you take up any new hobbies?"

Jaime tips his head and answers each question in turn. "Yeah, some. No, she's on with Dan. There was this art comp at school. Um. I did pretty well in that."

"Yeah?" asks Ollie.

"He means he fucking won," says Sunny from the front seat. She flicks the indicator and changes lanes. The steep green mountains loom over them as they head through the Tetsuo Harano tunnel. "The teachers were all shitting themselves. I don't think they expected it. We have got serious talent in our midst."

Ollie's impressed. He thumps Jaime's head with one hand. "You couldn't have told me sooner?"

"Ouch, I just— I didn't think you'd want—you were touring. You were surfing and competing on TV. I don't know, you're ranked third in the whole world. This was a high school art thing."

"Whatever, Jaime," says Ollie. "That's fucking awesome. We all have our own things, right? I can't even imagine being any good at that stuff."

"It's only a painting," mutters Jaime, but he's blushing and proud.

"So do we get to see it?" Tai asks.

"Yeah. I've got a photo here."

Jaime pulls out his phone, swipes it open and hands it to Tai. Tai gives a low whistle and hands it over Jaime to Ollie. The photo is tiny on the screen, but the painting is huge. It stretches across one wall of the café. Ollie enlarges it on the little screen. It's a series of postcard sized paintings, one next to the other, oceans and cliffs and lighthouses and waves.

"It's all these different views of the ocean from all over the world. Maile let me paint a whole wall in Nalu," Jaime says. "And it's got such a gorgeous view, so I wanted to add to that, you know, not do some impressionist desert scene or weird indoor portraits. But I also wanted to paint something that you couldn't see by looking out the window."

"That's—man, Jaime. Can we go and see it?" Ollie asks.

Jaime tosses his hair back in a practiced flick, but he's blushing again. "Sure. That'll work. I have the key here, in case you wanted to."

In person, the painting is even better than it is on the phone. Jaime's obviously chosen the different scenes carefully. He's put them together so they balance. Each tiny painting is intricate and independent but somehow fits into a beautiful whole.

"I recognize this one," says Ollie, not quite touching the wall. It's a painted version of the postcard they'd sent from Bells Beach: the gray and orange cliffs, the glowing ocean. The light looks amazing.

"I needed to get the idea from somewhere," says Jaime. He shrugs as though it's not a big deal. Ollie moves closer to him. His eyes prick with tears.

From the other side, Tai wraps an arm around Jaime's shoulders and squeezes tight. "It's amazing. You're amazing." He's so comfortable with his arm tight around Jaime.

Jaime ducks his head and presses his cheek against Tai's shoulder. "Thanks," he says. But he's looking at Ollie too, and Ollie's so proud he could burst. He turns from the painting to Jaime and back again. He wants to remember.

"So," says Sunny as they all climb back into the car. "Um. Yeah." She hesitates and that's a warning. Sunny rarely hesitates. "Guys, there are a few people coming over tonight."

Ollie can't help but wince. He steadies his expression as Tai looks at him quickly over Jaime.

Sunny catches his eye in the rearview mirror and says, "I'm sorry, babe, we couldn't keep them away. You know how they are. Everyone wants to celebrate your success with you."

"It's okay," says Ollie, pressing his lips closed. He stares out the window as they head around the water. This is not at all what he wants. He's only just finished the first leg of his world tour. They've been travelling for nine hours. He wants to sit in the quiet. He wants time with his family. He wants some space and his bedroom. He wants to think. "It's okay," he says again.

Tai narrows his eyes. "So what do you mean by 'a few people,' Sun?" he asks.

"You know, just the kids who know you guys. People who were supporting Ollie, watching on TV with us. Stuff like that."

"Sunny!" Tai protests. He adds, "Couldn't you stop her, Han?"

"Don't blame me, babe," says Hannah, turning from the front seat. "I just bought the beer."

"Hannah," Tai reproves her.

"It could be fun," says Jaime.

"It won't be too big. I'm sure." Sunny might be trying to convince herself.

Ollie knows they're being kind—not just his family, all of the people who want to support him. He resigns himself to the night.

A loud cheer goes up when the car pulls up in front of the house. Ollie's eyes widen. People are everywhere—up on the deck, spilling out onto the grass in front. Some are holding plastic cups of beer.

Sunny winds down the window to stick her head out and holler. "Shut up, guys! Come on. You'll scare the wildlife. I won't be able to get Ollie out of the car."

Tai meets Ollie's eyes. "You'll be okay," he says faintly.

Ollie shakes his head and plasters on a smile as he opens the car door.

FOR TAI, IT'S REASSURING TO see so many people piled into the Blue House: Maile and her husband Isaiah, the local surf kids, Sunny's family, the older crew, friends from school, people from both boys' work. Tai's been gone for a while, not long enough for the gathering to surprise him, but long enough that gratitude for everyone here spikes inside him, sweet and sharp.

Music pours from the open windows. People sit on the deck and on the stairs. The whole house spills out into the world. However exhausted Tai may be, this kind of energy will always buoy him.

He grabs a plastic cup of soda and heads out onto the deck. Maile's supporting herself on the railing, talking with some of the café folk.

"I can't believe you came," says Tai, giving her a hug. "You're due in, what, a week? I'll get you a chair."

"Dude, I've offered a chair. Or the swing. Or my knee," says Isaiah.

Maile glares between them. "Of course I came," she says. "And I can still stand up, boys. I'm fine." She bats Isaiah away. "We're psyched for Ollie. And for you, too. I know how much you put into this."

"Nah, this stuff is all him," says Tai.

"I'm happy for both of you," she insists. "And I'm happy you're back." Tai's stomach drops. He'd hoped Jaime had worked out.

Maile goes on. "Don't look at me like that. Jaime's been great at the café, but..." She eyes him hopefully. "Well, he doesn't have those magic fingers."

Tai laughs. "If you move down a step, I can give you a massage, Mai." He steps behind her. "I can't believe there'll be a little version of you two in a week."

While Tai works on her back and neck, Tex wanders past looking drunk or high. He grabs Tai's arm. "Your boy's doing good, yeah?" he asks. His grin is wide and relaxed.

Tai doesn't stop massaging Maile's shoulders. He wants to say, "He's not my boy." But he knows what Tex means. He grins instead. "He sure is."

Maile and Isaiah head for home and bed early. "I'll see you Tuesday," Maile says. "If I'm not in the middle of giving birth."

Tai talks with some of the guys they've surfed with since they were kids. Even while he chats, he has an eye on Ollie. He keeps his distance, though, and tries to avoid being obvious about it. It's their first night back. He'd hate for Ollie to spend the night crowded by Tai's concern.

It's almost eleven when he sees Ollie in the yard by himself. It's dark outside, but someone has strung strands of lights across the back wall and up one of the trees so the yard sparkles. The windows are open. Inside, the music is suddenly turned down. Someone picks up a guitar and starts tuning it.

Tai walks down the stairs and stops on the grass. He stays a few feet away from Ollie. Tai's working at it, but he's not sure he knows how to be near Ollie without wanting him.

Ollie lifts his head with a pretense of a smile. As soon as he sees it's Tai, he drops the act. His shoulders slump in a way that is a little dramatic, but also twines itself around Tai's heart.

"This isn't what you'd have chosen on your first night back," Tai says.

"You think?" says Ollie.

As hard as it is not to touch him, it's harder not to want to make everything easier. "I know, but it's kind of nice that these guys want to support you."

Ollie frowns. "I'm not ungrateful, Tai. It's just a lot." He looks up at the sky. "Don't you feel the same?"

"No, not exactly the same."

Ollie shrugs. "Well, I hate it."

The silence isn't comfortable. Tai's tired of the awkwardness already. "You don't need to stay."

"I can't *leave*. It's *my* party," says Ollie. There are dark marks under his eyes.

"I know who the party's for, dude. But these guys all know you. And you just got in from your first world tour like two hours ago. They're not gonna be mad if you crash in your room."

Ollie looks up. "Yeah?"

Tai resists moving closer. It's always been important to maintain Ollie's personal space, but it's never felt so unnatural before. "Yeah," Tai says. Ollie looks so hopeful, which is an improvement. "And fuck 'em if they mind, anyway. You're exhausted."

"Okay." Ollie stops still. His tone is conciliatory. "Thanks, Tai. Can you say goodbye for me? You know the people who matter."

"Sure. Of course."

"Thanks," Ollie says again. A car drives past and turns into a driveway farther up the beach. The moment stretches out. The wind shifts the strand of lights in the tree. Someone shouts with laughter inside. Ollie moves toward the back door. "See you tomorrow," he says. With a last look he goes inside, leaving Tai alone.

Tai exhales into the dark. Whoever has the guitar is playing a Drake song. He takes a steady breath and heads back in.

Eventually everyone leaves. Even Tai is glad to see the backs of them. It's been a long day. He helps the other three clear away the food and some of the cups and makes his way to bed. But once there, he stares at the ceiling. He rolls over, shifts uncomfortably. Ollie's down the hall, sleeping. Tai knows exactly what he looks like—his freckled skin washed out in the moonlight, his eyelashes soft on his cheekbones. Tai sighs. He rolls over again and buries his face in his familiar pillow. He misses Ollie, all the way to his core. He never thought this part would be easy, but he didn't know how lonely he'd be, even here at home, where he was never lonely before.

CHAPTER SIXTEEN

ORDINARILY AFTERNOONS AT NALU ARE quiet. But today Tai's got his hands full with sandwich orders, home-fried potatoes and greens, and an order of pancakes, all to go.

"Good afternoon."

He lifts his head. "Tadashi. What can I get you?"

"An herbal tea, please." As Tai turns to get it, Tadashi says, "You're busy here today. Do you finish soon? I'd like to talk with you about something."

"Sure. I might be forty-five minutes though."

"I can wait." Tadashi pays for the tea and reads something on his tablet, then leafs through a local paper while Tai finishes up.

Once he's done, Tai sits at his table. "More tea?" he offers.

Tadashi shakes his head. "Thank you, no." He takes a breath. "Tai, I considered what you said."

Tai tries to remember. "Oh?"

"About my being just another old surfer on the North Shore."

"That's not—" starts Tai, but Tadashi holds up a hand to make him stop.

"I considered and I believe you are right, Tai. So I've spent some time viewing shopfront spaces. I would like to open a local surf shop."

Tai says, "Okay." He's not sure he can help with this. It's the North Shore of Oahu. There are a lot of surf shops.

"I am aware there are other surf shops. But I think there's a space in the market. I want my focus to be gear, rather than clothes or accessories. This is why I came to speak with you. I'd like to involve you in my decisions about board selection, if you are interested."

"Right. Okay." Tai thinks about the boards he'd want to buy. He considers Tadashi carefully. An idea builds. "Have you thought about shaping your own?"

Tadashi says, slowly, "My own boards? Unfortunately I don't know how, Tai."

"No. I know you don't. But I do." Tai says. He spreads his hands out on the table in front of him.

Tadashi tilts his head slowly. "The board you made for me. She's the sweetest board I've ridden, Tai. And she listens to me."

"Yeah. I—I know what I'm doing." Talking himself up is uncomfortable, but the idea's caught hold. "I know I'm young, of course, but I've been shaping since I was fifteen, Tadashi. I've kept things small. I've had to; I work and surf, and with the house and everything. But while we were on tour everyone got to see Ollie's boards. And some of the guys were interested."

Tadashi's eyes are black and difficult to read, but Tai thinks that behind his calm is a developing glow of excitement. "I see. We could carve out a market among locals and surfers. Your Ollie's still using boards you shaped for him, yes?"

Tai nods.

"That's good name recognition you're building. This is interesting." He nods as he speaks. "I wonder if we'd need to start with a shopfront or whether the boards would sell better on alternative lines, directly or through the Internet."

Tai feels bowled over, but this is something he's had in the back of his head. He hasn't said it aloud, but this is his very own dream.

Tadashi says, "We'd need to put some thought into the raw materials, costing those out. And of course I'm not sure where you get your glassing done."

"Up at Rey's. These days I do a lot of it myself," says Tai. He's proud of his developing skill with the resins and tints and proud, too, of the eco-friendly resins they're using.

"Good." Tadashi nods. Despite his excitement, he seems more serious than usual. He inhales steadily. "I don't know what it is that you want in your life, Tai."

"Yeah. I don't—I guess I'm starting to know."

"I believe we could do this." Tadashi's tone is measured. "We'd be partners. You'd bring the boards and your skill. People everywhere will want to ride them. And I would bring the business experience." He frowns at Tai. "I've done things like this before. Well, on a larger scale. But I have the experience that you need for this. If you're genuinely interested."

"Right." Tai stammers, now that there's a decision to be made. "Yeah. I mean, it's definitely something I've thought about." He rubs at his face.

"We don't need to decide right now," says Tadashi with a little smile. "This is new. I only just came to you. I'll let you think and I'll take some time to get a business plan to you. You might want to consider what you want to be doing."

"I'm happy with this."

Tadashi bows his head. "Not now, Tai. I want you to think about what you want to be doing in five years."

Tai blinks. "Sure." Five years sounds forever away. A lifetime. Five years ago Ollie's mom died, and Tai's parents and sisters returned to Samoa. It's only been four years since the Blue House became theirs. Whole worlds can be built in five years.

Tadashi nods. "I believe we can make a go of this thing," he says.

Tai doesn't doubt that. He nods. "I think so too."

"WHERE'S OLLIE?" TAI ASKS AS he sits on the couch for dinner. Sunny perches beside him, sitting forward so she doesn't sink into the soft cushions. Tai rests his plate on his knees.

"He's gonna be out late," says Jaime. "Something about the waves at Waimea. He'll eat when he gets in."

"Right," says Tai.

He's not sure if it actually is weird that he doesn't know where Ollie is, or if it just feels weird in light of the last six weeks of constant, close contact. He's accustomed to knowing what Ollie's up to. But he'll get used to this too.

"Dinner's good," he says. Jaime's made a not-bad attempt at spaghetti Bolognese.

As he eats, he tries not to worry. It's hard to avoid seeing someone when you're living in the same house, but Ollie might be doing just that. The last couple of days, Tai seems to keep missing him. He'll come in through the door as Ollie's going out. Ollie will arrive home at the same time Tai needs to leave for work. But then, Tai's taken on more and more hours at the café now that Maile's due to give birth any minute. Tai needs the money and, more than that, he owes her for the weeks away she gave him with barely any notice.

Hannah plants herself on a beanbag, carefully balancing her plate. "Nice work, James," she says, waving a fork at the food.

"It's your recipe," says Jaime. "You can take all the credit."

"No way, kid—"

"I'm starting a business," blurts Tai, interrupting. It's not as if everything is in place, but he's positive about it and bubbling at the possibilities opening up in his mind.

Jaime looks at him quickly. "A business?"

"Nice. Of course you are," says Sunny. "You gonna be making boards?"

Tai's surprised. "How did you know?"

"You're predictable," she says with a shrug. "Not much else makes you this excited. Shaping, and surfing, and Ollie."

Tai can't think of a response. "Yeah," he says vaguely. He takes a breath and goes on. "So right, I'd be shaping boards. You know Tadashi Mako? He came to me with this plan to start up a business together. I need to find a lawyer or someone to review the paperwork, but I trust the guy."

"That's great, Tai," Hannah says. "Oh. Hey. Linda's a lawyer. My cousin. Probably yours too. You know, the one with the cats."

Jaime doesn't say anything.

Later, Tai's in his bedroom. He resolutely reads up on high performance eco-resins and doesn't wait up and worry about where Ollie is even a tiny bit. It's late when he hears the front door swing open. He rolls over to finish the article facing the window. Ollie stops in the kitchen, opens a cupboard, runs the tap for a glass of water, and walks quietly up the hallway. There's a knock. As Tai turns to face the door, Ollie swings it open softly.

"You awake?" he asks from the doorway. His voice is clipped.

"Yeah."

"I got a text from Jaime," says Ollie. He steps into the room. "He said you've started a business with that Tadashi dude."

It's not a big room. It's crowded with the two of them in it. Tai swings his legs around and sits up. There's something too intense about lying in bed with someone else standing in that small space, particularly when that someone else is Ollie.

"What's that about?" Ollie sounds tense and almost angry.

Tai tries to work out what's wrong. "Are you okay, Ollie? Where've you been?"

Ollie shakes his head. "I had to hitch a ride back from Waimea. But that's—Tai. What are you doing with this guy?" His voice shakes.

"With Tadashi? We're talking about a business, selling boards. I'd do the shaping," says Tai. "I thought you'd be—"

"Why didn't you tell me?"

"You weren't here, Ollie. Tadashi stopped by the café this afternoon. It was the first time I'd thought about it beyond vague pipe dreams. I'd have told you at dinner, only you weren't around." Tai's chest is tight.

Ollie frowns. "But how's it going to work? I mean, really, what do you know about this guy? And you're willing to trust him with your whole life. Just like that."

"Hey. I wanted to tell you first, Ollie," Tai says, frowning. He tries to think. "And it's not my whole life. It's an opportunity to start a business. It's making money doing something I enjoy. I can't keep making omelets at Nalu forever."

"It's your *future*, Tai." Ollie seems genuinely worried. "I don't want you to make mistakes."

Maybe there's truth in his concern. But mostly Ollie's taking the shine off this, diminishing what Tai is excited about.

"Yeah, it's my future. I've been shaping boards for years, Ollie," Tai manages. "Of course I want to take this chance. I figured after the past few months you'd understand that for sure. I need you to let it go and let me do this."

"But this should be something we do together. Why do you want this guy involved?"

Tai's so tired. "Because Tadashi's good at the stuff we'll never be good at. All that business stuff. We know nothing about it."

"We could've worked it out."

Tai looks at him, hard. "I don't get why you're being like this. Do you want me to succeed?"

"What the fuck, Tai? What are you talking about? I fought with my agent to get to keep your boards rather than use some huge conglomerate's collection. We all could have had thousands of dollars in sponsorship money, as many boards as I needed."

Tai tries not to yell. "I know. Of course, I know." He quiets. When he looks at Ollie, Ollie's face is closed off. "I've been following you around for months, Ollie, and everything—you've been amazing. I don't regret a second of it. But you need to let me do this one thing that's not part of you and me or your success. I can't just wait on the sidelines for you." He takes a breath.

"I never thought you should. I *never* thought that," says Ollie. There are tears of frustration in his voice. They stand still, facing one another. In the half darkness, Ollie's chest rises and falls. His eyes are clear and hard. The air is hot between them.

Even in this moment Tai wants to reach out to touch. Tai turns his head away as Ollie leaves. The door slams.

Tai closes his eyes on tears. He does understand. They've always shared their ambitions. It's strange to be starting a business without Ollie right in the middle of it.

A minute later Ollie knocks again. He steps in and stands still. Tai holds his breath.

"I'm being weird," Ollie says. "I—didn't expect you'd be making this kind of decision without me. I thought we were doing this stuff together. You've been part of everything I've done for so long."

"I know." Tai sighs. He's frustrated, still. "I know it's not your fault. You didn't plan it this way. But somehow it turned out that it was always *your* stuff that we've done. This shaping thing is something I'm excited about. There's something wrong if you can't be excited for me too."

"I'm sorry," Ollie says. "Truly, Tai."

There's a spurt of resentment, though he knows Ollie means the apology. "We've always supported one another. You've been great, talking to people about the boards. But it's not the same as supporting me in doing my own thing."

"Tai—" Ollie's voice cracks between them. "I want to be." There's silence, less electric than it has been. "I will be excited," says Ollie. "I was surprised, that's all. You've never—I never thought you needed anything like this."

"My own dreams?"

Ollie half laughs, but his eyes are red. "I'm sorry." He glances around the room as though he's just noticed how close the space is. "I guess I got used to having you all to myself. Things are changing. I don't think I like it." He smiles crookedly, and Tai can't stay mad. He never could.

He wants to push close to Ollie, eliminate the walls they've built between them, and explore that bright joy they discovered in one another. He wants to remind Ollie what they have when they touch. He doesn't.

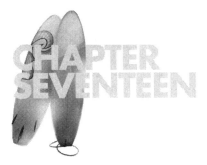

CHAPTER SEVENTEEN

IT'S EARLY, BUT TAI'S GOT the back door wide open so the breeze from the ocean can curl inside. He loves mornings like this in the Blue House. He pours cereal into a bowl and finds one for Jaime, who's taken to heading into school early and studying or painting or, Tai suspects, chatting with a girl in his art class.

Ollie pads into the room. He's bleary-eyed. His boxers hang low on his hips. His hair is sticking up in all directions. He blinks at Tai and Jaime.

"Morning," says Tai. Ollie always looks like this when he wakes up. It's both irritating and adorable.

Ollie nods an acknowledgment and gives them both a tiny smile. He leans against the kitchen counter to eat granola.

"The wind's from the north," he says as he finished chewing. "Kaisers is going off."

"But you hate Kaisers," says Jaime. Tai thinks the same thing.

Ollie shrugs. "I'm off to South Africa soon. The swell at Kaisers is enough like J Bay that it's worth going there for some practice."

It's hard not to be a little bitter, but it's not Ollie's fault that Tai has to work while Ollie gets to train for the next leg of the tour. That Tai's not going on.

"Drop Jaime at school first if you want to take the car." Tai says.

"Nah, don't worry about it. I'll take the bus. I only need one board today. Sunny can drop Jaime at school."

Tai suppresses a spurt of frustration. He's pretty sure he's being unreasonable.

He finishes his breakfast and heads to his room. Maile won't be in at Nalu 'til later. He needs to get going if he has to be there to open up. Nalu's always busy these days.

A FEW DAYS LATER, TAI is in the shed. It's a relief to be here, among his stuff, bringing all the things he's learned back home to his shaping. He examines his latest board critically then takes a planer to it. He used a template when he cut the blank, but now he sees something with a narrower nose. There's a knock on the wood to the side of the open door.

"Tadashi," Tai says with pleasure. He rests the planer on the benchtop and pushes his face mask to the top of his head.

"Will this one be our company's first magic board?" Tadashi asks after they shake hands.

Tai runs a hand around the board's edges. Ollie rides his first magic one. This one's not there yet. It's smooth, but it doesn't have the balance he wants. He'll fix it. "Could be," he says. He's getting a feel for how this one'll go in the water.

"Of course. Please, Tai. Don't stop what you're doing on my account," says Tadashi. Tai considers him, then picks up the measuring tape. He won't do the planing work while Tadashi's here distracting him—it needs to be perfect—but he can check some of these dimensions.

"How are you?" Tai asks. He notes the tail measurement in pencil on the board's surface.

"Good. Good. I've brought some documents for you to take to your lawyer."

"Okay." Tai hesitates. He's trying to pretend this is not all brand-new.

Tadashi considers him. "Has she done this kind of work before?"

"I don't know," Tai admits. "I'll check." He's embarrassed.

"The good news is I already have two investors interested. We can talk about what their involvement could be, whether we want them at all. What percentages they'll have. That kind of thing. But I'd like you to meet them with me first."

"Okay. Sure. I can do that."

Tadashi leaves a stack of papers when he goes. Tai flicks through them. He places them on the bench and looks through the door up to the house.

Jaime's doing well at school. Someday he'll head off to college, maybe an art school. Sunny's convinced the owner of the shop at the resort where she works to put her shell jewelry on display. They're selling well. Hannah's talked to the resort about a hospitality course that could change things for her. And Ollie's off to South Africa. Then in about a month he'll be leaving for the French Pro and the European leg of the world circuit. Tai tries not to feel that he's going to be the only one left.

He inhales steadily, then gets back to work on the board.

Late in the day, Tai visits Linda, Hannah's lawyer cousin. Before he leaves her office, Tai signs an agreement to start a surfboard business.

❧

TADASHI'S BUSY. IT'S JUST A couple of weeks before the money comes in. Tai buys a set of foam board blanks, gets a new electric planer, makes some choices about resins. Then he gets down to the business of shaping boards.

He's pulled the stands outside so he can shape in the bright afternoon sun. He's got the planer running. He's focused. When he looks up, Hannah's standing nearby. It startles him a little and she grins, amused.

"Hi," she says.

"Hi." There's no specific rush on this board, though everything is more urgent now that there's a business involved. Still, he hasn't talked with Hannah properly for a while. He rests the planer on the board and leans a hip on the stands. "So you did it, babe. You've got that course approved. You're moving up."

"It seemed like a plan." She sounds a little tentative. It's not as if her momma had time to give her a lot of support for her decisions. The Blue House might be chaotic, the five of them are still kids really, but at least they always back her. "It's either do the course or I could start my own tour bus company," she says.

"Tour buses?"

"Not just any old tour bus. I could take people to all the best shrimp trucks and cheap bars on the North Shore." There's a question behind her calm.

"You'd be amazing." He loves the idea. He can imagine her driving an open-air bus, charming the tourists with her mellow voice and all the stories of local life she's taken in.

She draws a slow breath. "I guess one day we might all be living our dreams."

"Terrifying, isn't it?"

"Yeah. I didn't really know I had any dreams until Ollie got the tour. And then you're out here running your own business shaping boards. I don't want to get left behind."

"Whatever you do, Han, you never will be. I'm happy things are happening for you, though."

She scrutinizes him. Then she pushes her hands down into the pockets of her shorts and steps closer. "Hey, tell me," she says. "What happened, babe? With you and Ollie. It's—" She scrunches her face. "Did you guys fight while you were on tour or something?"

"No. God no, nothing like that." Tai says. "We're fine, Han." He turns back to the board. He runs a hand along its smooth sides. In order to shape well he needs to think ahead. The fewer tools he uses, the less foam he'll take off and the less chance for error. He reaches for the planer.

"Put that down, Tai Talagi," Hannah says. "This is important."

Tai's surprised. Hannah's not much for pushing conversation. She usually lets the whole world flow by at whatever pace it wishes.

She folds her arms. "It's way past time to talk about this, Tai. If you two didn't fight, then what the fuck is going on? Because nothing's been right since you got back."

Tai tries to keep his face impassive, but he sees sympathy in Hannah's gaze and tears spring to his eyes. He blinks, hard. "Things got complicated for a bit. That's all." He turns his head away from her, out to the palms moving in the sky, but he doesn't go back to the board.

"Ah," she says. "Well. I know a little something about complicated relationships." She looks as though she's far away.

"You and Sunny." Hannah's pretty low key, but she's never hidden how she feels about her best friend. Not from Tai anyway.

"Me and Sunny. We're fine." She shrugs.

"Us too. At least, we'll sort it out." Tai takes a breath. "Really. It's gonna be okay." Maybe if he says it enough, it will be.

He looks at her again. "Talk to me," she says.

They use cut logs as stools in the backyard. She sits down on one. He sits on another nearby. "I don't know what to do, Han. It's not just about Ollie." It's painful to say Ollie's name. But that's ridiculous. "Everything's changing. All of us are doing new stuff. And that's okay. I want you guys to do the things you do best. And me too. And Ollie. It's all good. It's just—everything's different." She'll understand the fear in that.

"Yeah. We need to get used to it." She doesn't say anything for a while. "But about Ollie. You're telling me it'll be okay between you two?"

Tai can't really work out how to tamp down his own longing and the anger that keeps boiling up between him and Ollie. But he's optimistic. "It will be. Sometime." He tries to sound certain. "We'll get back to the way things used to be."

Her eyes are steady. "Is that what you want, though?" she asks. "To go back?" Tai's heart thumps fast. They sit in silence till she says, "Tai, are you sure Ollie knows how you feel?"

"How I feel?" Tai echoes. He's out of breath and sort of sick to the stomach.

"Yeah." She stretches her legs out in front of her, pressing her bare heels into the sandy ground.

"Of course he knows." He tries to smile at her but it feels all wrong on his face. "I'm starting to think everyone knows how I feel."

Hannah tilts her head. "Probably just me and Sunny. I don't know if Ollie knows anything much. He's Ollie. He's incredible, but there are some pretty huge things he misses. I reckon this is one of them. So have you told him? In actual words?"

"No." The thought is horrifying. "Fuck, no."

She narrows her eyes. "I don't know, Tai. Do you think maybe you should?"

"What, you want me to tell him that he's an asshole and I'm probably sort of in love with him." The words rush out, then drop heavily into Tai's abdomen. They'll never be unsaid.

But Hannah looks entirely unsurprised. "There's no 'probably' or 'sort of' about it," she says gently, as though it's the easiest thing in the world. "And he's only sometimes an asshole."

"Han. You have to know that I can't talk to him about this. This is Ollie we're talking about. I can't throw all of that at him. It's too much."

"Too much for him or too much for you?"

Tai shrugs. "Either. Both?" He's not sure if it matters. "Anyway I have told him. When we were in Tahiti I asked if he wanted—you know."

"You know?"

"I asked if he wanted to keep having sex." It sounds stark when he says it here. "With me," he adds.

She frowns, considering. "I'm pretty sure that's not what I meant when I asked if you'd told him how you feel. I mean, you know him better than I do. But think about it, Tai. Sure, you can say nothing, and things will go back to normal maybe. We'll get lucky and work hard so in another couple of years, five years, whatever, we're still all living here together."

She pauses. He looks back at the house, imagines Jaime home from college and Sunny's jewelry stuff spread across the living room. Imagines Hannah's tour bus parked out front and Ollie's boards lined up at the side of the house.

She says, "I can see it. You're there safely in your room with some guy's number, and Ollie's up the hall gazing out at the ocean; the rest of us are hanging around somewhere in between. And nothing's ever been said."

Tai stops thinking about it. She's right, but the idea of telling Ollie is insurmountable. "No, Hannah. Nope. I can't do it." It's supposed to be healthy to have put words to this whole mess, but part of him wishes he hadn't said anything. Maybe he's given too much of himself away. "It'd all go bad."

"Okay," she says mildly. "I'm not about to argue with you. It's your heart." She nods to his board. "I'll leave you to it." Before she goes she hugs him tightly.

CHAPTER EIGHTEEN

OLLIE HATES SURFING AT KAISERS. Jaime's right. Everyone knows that.

The surf's been good here this week, though. Day after day he's getting some long consistent waves, similar enough to the ones he'll face in South Africa. But unless it's raining, the ocean is crowded with tourists, and it's weird to surf and watch the skyscrapers of Waikiki. It's weird, too, to surf here without Tai. Ollie's so accustomed to him being nearby.

Not that Ollie has time to miss him, exactly. Tai's always there in Ollie's head. While Ollie trains, he hears, "Catch your own wave, don't wait around for the other guy" and "Remember, the board's another part of you." When he gets a good run he imagines Tai's loud "whoo" carrying across the water, and that bright, easy smile that's always focused on Ollie. Ollie shakes his head clear and paddles back out to catch one more before he needs to track down a bus on the main drag to take him home.

When he gets to his gear, piled up and sandy, there are a few missed calls—some from Sunny, one from Tai. Ollie dials Sunny's number while he pulls his rash vest over his head.

"Oh, you are alive," Sunny says brightly. "Well, good news. While you were out drowning or whatever, Maile had a baby."

"Nice."

"Yeah. A little girl. We're all going to visit tonight. You're coming. Get yourself home by six, Oliver."

Ollie looks at the time. There's a bus in ten minutes. He can make it. "I'll be there."

The second he arrives home, they all pile into the car. Tai takes the wheel to drive them to the hospital. Ollie sits in the back with Sunny and Jaime.

The nurse points them down the hall. The tiny hospital room isn't bad, but it's overcrowded with all five of them standing awkwardly around Maile and Isaiah and the tiny baby resting on Maile's chest.

Gazing down at the baby, Maile's face is soft with pride and love. Despite himself, Ollie is touched. He doesn't look at Tai.

"We've called her Cerulean," Maile says. "Like the color." This time Ollie can't help it. His eyes flick to Tai's and then away before either of them laughs.

"That's gorgeous," says Sunny. She's sincere.

"You want to hold her?" Maile asks.

Sunny coos over the bundle, then passes her over to Hannah, who studies the little hands and face with bright, wet eyes. Hannah offers her to Ollie, who shakes his head, blushing and embarrassed, so she hands Cerulean to Tai. However silly the name, Tai's face is sweet as he looks down at the little creature. When he lifts his head and finds Ollie's gaze on him, he smiles a tiny, awkward flash of a smile.

Ollie's only ever thought about babies as worth vaguely avoiding. They're pretty frightening for something so helpless. Ollie doesn't have much in the way of family, not like Tai and his scores of aunts and uncles and second cousins once removed, all of whom seem to have at least a couple of children.

During the ride home, Ollie stares out the window at the rough houses sitting on the land between the hospital and the beach. He thinks about the future.

Tai'll be shaping and surfing, successful. Maybe he'll have a family of his own. Ollie imagines him bundling a truckload of kids off to school and then heading out to Pipe to test his latest round-nosed shortboard. Everyone on the North Shore will want his time and his expertise and his boards.

When Ollie thinks of his own future it's less clear.

At least he can be sure of what he's doing for the next two months, though. He'll be at J Bay in South Africa soon, then in France. That's as far as he can stand to think for now.

⊕

OLLIE'S SALTY FROM THE SEA after an early surf. He peers into the pantry for something that'll work for breakfast. Tai walks into the room with a letter. He's wearing boxer shorts. His presence stops Ollie's breath. Maybe it always will.

"D'you know where the others are?" Tai asks.

"Jaime's just finished in the shower; I think the girls are around. What do you need?"

"I need to talk to everyone." Tai heads down the hall to gather them.

"What's up?" asks Hannah once they're all together around the kitchen bench.

Tai holds out a letter to the others. "It's from Jenny and Karen."

"Who?" Ollie asks, reaching for the letter.

"Our landlords," says Tai a little shortly. "Same ones we've had for the past five years."

Ollie refuses to feel bad. He's only met the women a few times. He scans the letter. "This is—" He lets Sunny and Jaime read over his shoulder.

"They're giving us notice," Tai says.

Ollie's shocked. "They can't do that."

Tai narrows his eyes. "Well, technically they're the landlords, so they can." Ollie turns back to the letter as Tai keeps talking. "They want to fix it up and rent it out to tourists. They'll make more money that way, I guess."

"But we've been asking them to fix it up for years," says Sunny. Her voice rises swiftly. "And now they're gonna kick us out and make it all pretty for fucking tourists?"

Ollie whips his head up and glares at Tai. "When did you get this?" he asks, waving the piece of paper.

"Today, dude. It was slipped under the front door when I got up just now." Tai holds his hands up peaceably. "We're on the same side, remember."

"Okay. So what do we do?" Hannah asks. She doesn't bother to read the letter herself.

"Can we fight it?" asks Sunny.

Worry is a storm, swelling inside Ollie. He looks at Jaime. The Blue House is their place. More home than anywhere has ever been. Ollie doesn't know what they'll be without it.

"I don't know. But we have some time," says Tai. "They gave us two months. We'll work something out."

They all stare at one another. It's not as if any of them have experience in fighting real life stuff like this.

"Mom and Jaime and I got evicted from our place in Honolulu," says Ollie. That's how they ended up here. It wasn't a good time.

"This'll be different," says Tai. "We get to decide our own stuff now. All of us together."

Jaime has school. Sunny and Hannah have to work. They'll take him on the way. They'll all talk about it tonight.

Ollie manages to swallow some breakfast at the kitchen table before he goes up the hall to shower. The bathroom door swings open as he reaches it. A cloud of fog escapes. Tai steps out. They stare at one another stupidly. Tai has a towel around his waist and drops of water on his chest. He smells clean and good. Ollie bites his lip and fixes his eyes on the intricate detail of the tattoo around Tai's upper arm. He tries to remember to take a breath.

"Sorry," says Tai. "I'm done in here. It's all yours."

When he meets Tai's gaze again, Ollie blushes to his hair. They move around one another awkwardly. Every careful, uncomfortable movement needles Ollie's heart. The air between them is electric.

"Fuck this," he says suddenly. He meets Tai's gaze and reaches out a hand to touch Tai's bare skin.

Tai steps back as though he's about to be struck. "Ollie," he says, low in the quiet. "Oh fuck. No, you don't." His eyes are black in the dark hallway.

Ollie blinks. He looks at Tai, then at his feet. "I want things to be back to normal," he says quietly. "I want things back."

Tai sounds exhausted when he says, "I know, and I get it. But we can't fix it this way. Nothing's changed. Right? And doing this won't make everything okay." He meets Ollie's eyes. Ollie can't quite get a hold of his expression: pleading and frustrated at once.

But what Tai says is true. Nothing's changed, and Ollie knows it.

In the shower, Ollie washes away the sand and rinses his salt-crusted hair. He can't resist taking his cock in hand. He tries not to think of Tai as he jerks himself off; he closes his eyes, but it's Tai's face and body that are burned on his brain. It's Tai's touch he imagines as he comes.

Ollie has no excuse to miss dinner that night. Sunny's made chicken and rice. Ollie sits next to Hannah on the deck with his meal. Tai sits cross-legged on the ground, a little apart from the others. He's quiet and frowning into his bowl. It's one of those rare nights when everything's hushed, save for the clink of silverware against their bowls and the relentless throb of the ocean on the shore.

"Maile could use some help with the baby," says Tai out of the blue. "Isaiah has to go back to work this week, so—" His voice catches. He has everybody's attention. Tai's watching Ollie when he says, "I think I'm going to go and stay there for a bit."

Ollie's breath is tight. "What? You're—what? Are you moving out?"

"Temporarily," says Tai. "Temporarily. Just for a couple of weeks. I'm coming back."

Hannah's voice is low. "Dude," she says. She glances quickly at Sunny.

"This is what you want?" Sunny asks.

"Maile needs some help," Tai says again. "She's family. It'll be good for her and for the baby."

Ollie can't speak. This isn't anything he thought would happen. He glances at Jaime, sitting in one of the plastic chairs and looking as horrified as Ollie feels.

"But—what about your stuff in the shed?" Jaime asks. "The boards and everything. You need to work on that here."

Tai turns to him. "I've got some of my stuff set up at Rey's factory," he says gently. "And Tadashi is finding a space of our own. So I'll work there sometimes. But Jaime, I'll stop in here too."

"But—" says Jaime again. His voice is small as he asks, "When will you be back?"

Tai finds Ollie's gaze, then turns back to Jaime's. "I honestly don't know, J. I'll stay with them while it's necessary. I don't want to make a big deal of it. This is temporary," he says. "I'm not leaving. Nothing's changed. The Blue House is my home."

"When are you leaving?" Hannah asks.

Tai lifts his shoulders. "There's not much point in waiting. It'd just—" He doesn't finish his sentence.

The next day Tai packs up the car. He straps his boards on top. Sunny will drive Tai over the headland to Maile and Isaiah's apartment, then bring the car home. Ollie doesn't offer to go with them. It's not as though Tai'll be that far away, just a five-minute drive. He tries to tell himself that this is good. Ollie's been thinking about the two of them taking some space. It might be easier not to bump into one another coming out of a steamy shower, for one thing.

This is short-term. Tai loves caring for people, and Maile needs his help. So maybe this isn't about Ollie at all, not really.

But in his heart, Ollie knows it is and is furious—with himself, with the whole mess they created but most of all with Tai, who should be here. He watches through his bedroom window as Tai and Sunny drive away. He wants to kick something.

OLLIE PULLS UP IN THE station wagon to collect Jaime from school. Predictably, Jaime's not outside. Ollie peers through the school gates, then sends a text message. Two minutes later he dials Jaime's number.

"Coming, coming," says Jaime as he answers. "Just packing up my shit."

A couple of minutes later he clambers into the car with a shoulder bag and a portfolio.

"You were in the art rooms?" asks Ollie.

"Yep." Jaime tosses his bags in the back seat. "Thanks for the ride."

"Not a problem. But I was thinking. You want me to start teaching you to drive, J?" Ollie turns onto the road home. Jaime hesitates and Ollie backpedals. "It's okay if you already have something worked out with one of the others."

"No. It's not that. I don't have something else worked out. Not at all. I was just surprised."

"Surprised that I thought I could teach you to drive?" Ollie asks. He turns onto Halaiweiale Highway.

"That you'd want to spend that much time with me." The answer stings.

"Hey," Ollie protests.

Jaime goes on. "I mean it might not be that easy, Ollie. I don't know much about driving. I might be shit. I don't want to fight with you."

"You don't need to be perfect on my account. You're learning." Ollie tries not to sound hurt. "It's cool, no big deal. But I'd like to help out. If you want. Anyway, you can have more than one instructor. Hannah's got a lot of patience. I can be the bad cop to her good cop."

"And Tai too," says Jaime.

Ollie nods. "Yeah, of course. Tai too."

Jaime glances at him. "You reckon Tai's moving back soon, Ollie?"

"I'm sure he tells you as much as he tells me." Ollie keeps his voice even, but anger bubbles beneath the surface. "It's only been a day since he went to stay at Maile's. You'll cope. We were gone for six weeks when I was on tour."

"You know this is different." Jaime huffs, dissatisfied. "What's gone wrong, Ollie? What did you do?"

Ollie is struck by the unfairness of it all. "Fuck, Jaime. This isn't my fault. I didn't do anything." He's angry, but he wants to be honest, too. "At least, it wasn't just me."

Jaime turns to gaze out the window in silence. As they reach the house he says, "But you can fix it, right?"

Ollie sighs. "I don't know. Honestly, Jaime. I'd do it if I could."

Jaime looks at him again. "Okay."

THE FOURTH DAY TAI'S GONE is a Saturday. Hannah and Sunny are both working at the resort. Jaime's ostensibly studying in his room.

Ollie sticks his head in. "Hey, J. I'm on my way out," he says. "I'll get in a surf at Waimea. You okay by yourself?"

"I'm not a kid," Jaime says without heat. It's a reflex.

"I know, I know." Ollie looks at Jaime's little frown and doesn't have to force a smile. "I didn't mean it like that. I wanted to let you know I was going is all."

"I'm good," says Jaime. As Ollie turns to go he says, "Hey, I was thinking, though. If you ever wanted someone to get some videos of you surfing, you know, so you can review them for any problems or post them to YouTube or whatever." He looks at Ollie hopefully. "I have this awesome camera on my phone. It's not waterproof but it has a great zoom. And one time you said how it was useful to see what things looked like from shore, 'cause that's where people sit to do the judging and stuff."

"For sure. That would be amazing, J."

Jaime beams. "Yeah?"

"Absolutely." Ollie woke up looking forward to a solo surf and some alone time when he didn't need to think, but Jaime's face is eager. It's like when he was eight and constantly trailing around the beach after Ollie and Tai. "What are you doing now?" Ollie asks.

"Nothing."

Ollie keeps his voice light. "You wanna come with me? There's some decent action pretty close to shore today."

Jaime nods immediately. "The light's perfect too. Give me a minute to get some shorts on, bro."

It takes Jaime more like fifteen minutes to get ready. Maybe twenty. Ollie mostly doesn't mind.

"You wanna drive?" he asks.

"Um. Okay."

It's a road they've driven over and over. Jaime signals and turns carefully. Ollie tries not to act worried.

"So what are you thinking for school? You applying to Hawaii Pacific?" Ollie asks as they park.

"Yeah probably, but—it hasn't got the best visual arts program."

Jaime sounds nervous. Ollie tenses his shoulders. He tries to think where else Jaime might want to go.

"I'm thinking I'll go to Carnegie Mellon," Jaime says. "They have the School of Design and Fine Arts and… "

"Carnegie Mellon in Pennsylvania?" There's no ocean there.

"That's the one." Jaime sounds closed off.

Ollie can imagine nothing worse. He thinks. "Okay… hey, this isn't some kind of weird attempt to find Dad, is it? 'Cause I can tell you from experience, Jaime. He's not worth it."

"No." Jaime's voice is clipped and pleading at once. "I don't even think about him. Honestly, Ollie. You're my family. You and Tai and the girls." He lifts his chin as he goes on, and Ollie sees himself in his brother's face. "I'll do fine arts or design combined with business administration or something. I want to work out how to make money doing the things I'm good at. Carnegie Mellon has all of that."

Ollie stays quiet and tries to channel Tai, who understands everybody, or Sunny, who considers every far-flung option, or Hannah, who never judges. Just because Ollie would hate being that far from the ocean doesn't mean Jaime's making a bad decision. "That makes sense, Jaime."

Jaime lifts his gaze. "It's a long way and, man, I'd miss home, but I'd visit. They have a scholarship program, or else maybe I can manage a loan."

Ollie studies him. "You know what, bro, you're the smartest one of all of us. Watch out or you'll end up supporting everyone."

"That's the plan," Jaime says and grins fiercely.

Ollie loves him so much. "It's not your job, though. We've got this, all of us, together."

They stay out for a few hours. Every time Ollie surfs right into shore, Jaime shows him a new clip of him out on the waves. Ollie should have known the kid could do this.

On the way back Jaime says, tentatively, "I like getting some time together, just the two of us."

"Yeah. Me too." Ollie thinks about it. Usually someone else would be along with them. Mostly that'd be Tai.

"I miss him, too," Jaime says as though he knows what Ollie's thinking. "But this is good. For us. For a change," He hesitates. "You want to talk about Tai?" He sounds like the kid he is, but smarter than Ollie knew.

"Nope, it's cool, Jaime. Right now I'd rather talk about you." They make it home, talking about Jaime's art and his plans.

OLLIE'S HEADING FOR HIS ROOM when Sunny sticks her head out of her bedroom door.

"Hey, Oliver, come in here," she says. "I want to talk to you."

He narrows his eyes but follows her into her room, where she flops on the bed. The windows are wide open, and the air is full of salt.

"Sit down," she tells him.

He scans the room and then sits at the end of the bed.

"Here's what we're gonna do," she says. "You're going to talk to me about stuff."

"God, what is it with you guys today?" Ollie asks the ceiling. "Okay," he says, after a pause. "What stuff?"

"You know what stuff. You and Tai stuff. Because here's how it is. I love you both, and he's moved out, and it is a fucking pain in the ass to live with you right now."

Ollie's quiet for a long time. Sunny doesn't press, she just lies back on her bed and contemplates him, almost kindly.

"Okay," says Ollie at length. "Okay. Okay. Fuck. So." He takes a breath. He should start at the beginning. "Okay. While we were away, Tai and I had sex."

"No shit."

Ollie starts again. "We had sex, Sunny, and it completely fucked everything up."

Sunny laughs, just a puff of breath.

"Don't be like that. I'm serious, Sunny."

Sunny sits up suddenly. "Right," she says. She means business. "Well, for starters it's not the sex that did that, you doof. Not all by itself." She leans toward him and sighs gustily. "Tell me what happened."

Well, we—it happened out of the blue one night while we were in Australia. There was a bonfire at the beach, and I'd just won the round, and Tai was there beside me looking so beautiful and safe and new. It was... kind of amazing."

Sunny laughs. "Go on then. I don't need a play-by-play."

"So after that first time, we talked. I had this thought that we could give it a go, having sex, just while we were on tour."

"Right. Sounds like fun."

He lifts his gaze. "Yeah, but it hasn't been. Or I guess it was fun at first, when we weren't thinking about it. But it got harder."

She laughs again, and he glares at her. "Yeah, yeah. This is not the time for dick jokes."

"Sorry. Go on."

"There's not much more to it. We came back; it's a mess. I wish we'd never done it." He's not sure that's true, but for now it feels about right.

"And now Tai's gone. We shouldn't have messed with things." He gets to the truth of it. "I'm just so angry with him, Sunny. And I'm angry with myself, too."

Sunny leans back on her arms and says slowly, "I know you two pretty well. Want to hear my guess? I reckon you messed it up because you weren't bothering to communicate. Also 'cause you're idiots."

"What? We communicate. We communicated fine before we had sex."

"Sometimes, maybe. On the water, sure. But I'm still right," she says. She lies back and props her bare feet up on the windowsill. She regards him upside-down. "Did I ever tell you that Hannah and I hooked up one time?"

"No." He's fascinated.

"Yeah. I propositioned her at one of the parties. It just, you know. She's so good and strong, those excellent shoulders—it seemed like something we could do. We both agreed it'd be fun. So we did it."

"You hooked up," says Ollie. He looks around the room. "Where?"

She frowns at him. "That is so not the point of this story. The point is, we talked about it. Afterward. Even though it was awkward and felt really hard."

"What happened?" The girls are comfortable together, the same as they've always been.

Her smile goes a little secret. "The sex was pretty nice, but it wasn't a moment or anything. I knew it wouldn't be almost right away. It was good, interesting, to connect with her that way and see what we could do. When we talked afterward, I couldn't tell what she was thinking. But I told her everything, said that I loved her but I wasn't going to have sex with her again. It was the best sex I've had. She's so—she's Hannah, you know. But I guess I'm not that into sex. And I don't think I want that kind of relationship. It was pretty awful, because she was hurt at first. But she's cool. We decided we had to be really clear, cut the ties quickly and not get tangled up making out or whatever, everytime we felt lonely or got a bit drunk."

"You didn't miss it afterward?" asks Ollie, remembering how hard it was to stay away from Tai after finally knowing what it was like to touch him. "You didn't want to have sex again?"

"I didn't. I think she did a little. But it's all good now. She's got that thing on with Ben, from the school. He's sweet. I was jealous about it for a little bit there. But we talked about that too. We're best friends. That's just as good."

"Yeah," says Ollie. He's seen the way Sunny and Hannah are together, tumbled all over one another half the time, Hannah rubbing Sunny's shoulders, Sunny flinging herself bodily at Hannah in greeting as if there's never been an awkward second between them.

Sunny says, "We'll be platonic life partners." She pauses. "I thought you might be asexual there too, Oliver, for a while. But I haven't missed the way you watch Tai. Hot," she says. "You guys are crazy hot for one another."

Ollie rolls his eyes, though not really at her. "That's not important, though, is it? If we can't get it together. I mean. Anyway, he's the one who moved out. He didn't need to do that." He's quiet for a time. "And now I don't know how to fix anything. I can't just call him up and say—what would I say?"

She frowns in thought. "What do you want out of this whole thing? How do you want this chapter to end?"

He gazes through the window above her bed. "I want things back the way they were before."

"Oh." Sunny wrinkles her nose at him. "Which before?"

"I want the Blue House back," he says.

"I don't think you've lost that, babe."

MAILE AND ISAIAH'S APARTMENT HAS white walls and huge open windows and ceiling fans and, currently, about eighteen aunties and uncles crowded together and sweating in the living room. Tai's known most of these people his whole life. He pours iced teas and coffees, passes around some food, then grabs a coconut bun and a beer and settles in next to Aunty Girlie. She's proud of her eighty-eight years. She knew everyone in the room as a baby.

Girlie hums with pleasure as she takes a bite of her bun. "How're your parents liking it back in Samoa, Tai?" she asks. "And your sisters?"

"They love it. I couldn't drag them back if I wanted to."

"You miss them?"

"Yeah," he says. "I talk to them a lot but, you know. It's not the same." He would love to have them here right now.

"You don't think of moving back there yourself?" Girlie asks.

He doesn't hesitate. "Nah. It's cool. My home's here." He's pretty sure of that. He's just not quite sure what home feels like anymore. He shakes his head to clear that thought.

"It's home for me too." Girlie tips her head like a bird. "Still, I sometimes think about getting out there and searching for more. Maybe heading over to the mainland to live close to my great-grandkids. There're three of them now. The twins and little Princess Tania. I'll show you a picture." She pulls out a phone and deftly skims through. "See there. Handsome things. All of them are the image of my Joseph."

Tai admires the children obediently. "They're beautiful kids. I didn't know your Joseph."

"No? How old are you?"

"Twenty-three."

"Well, you wouldn't then. He died a year before you were born. He was a good man. Beautiful and very kind. Big fellow. Huge feet, huge smile. I loved him." She appraises Tai. Her eyes are deep brown. "You been in love, Tai?"

Tai's cheeks flush. "I'm only twenty-three, Aunty Girlie. What would I know about love?"

"Hmmph," she huffs, dissatisfied. "I met Joseph when I was twenty." The room is full of noise, chatter and family around them. "It's not complicated. It's love. When you know, you know."

Tai nods silently. He's not sure she's got that right. Love is complicated. But that doesn't matter, really. Because, complicated or not, Tai does know. He knows that wherever he is—when he looks around this room full of family, or sits on the deck, or shapes a new board at the factory, when's he's out alone on the waves—half of his heart is wherever Ollie is. He knows that he's in love.

Girlie might find it sweet, if he told her. Girlie loves Tai and she's adored Ollie for years. But being in love isn't enough. This is not what they wanted at all.

Maile paces past their chairs, her pace and expression harried. The baby in her arms has set up a steady wail.

"Can I do something, Mai?" Tai asks.

"Teach me how to speak crying infant?" She glares down at Cerulean. "Use your words," she says to her intently, spreading the sentence out. "Use your words."

"Let me take her, Maile," Girlie says, standing up.

Maile hands Cerulean over. No one refuses Aunty Girlie, especially not when she's asking to hold a baby. With Cerulean firmly in her arms, Girlie starts up a surprisingly vigorous rocking. "There we are, little thundercloud," she says. "There we are."

Cerulean quiets. Maile shakes her head in amazement and sinks down in the chair next to Tai. "Thank you," she says to Girlie, who is muttering affectionately. "I knew she needed rest, but I think she was starting to sense the tension in my arms." She takes a steadying breath. "Communication is hard when you don't have a common language."

"Tell me about it." Tai sighs. "Sometimes even sharing a language doesn't help." He doesn't mean for Maile to hear, but she squeezes his knee sympathetically.

"I know." She leans her shoulder against his. Her undemanding weight is reassuring. "You'll get there."

Later, after everyone's gone and the dishes are washed, Tai flops down on his bed in Maile's spare room. He stays on his back and loops his fingers around the shell string on his wrist, enjoying its delicacy and strength. He squeezes his eyes shut tight trying to block out any thought of Ollie. Tomorrow he'll get out on the water with the boards he's been shaping. He has other loves and a whole life to get on with.

CHAPTER NINETEEN

Tai pulls Maile's pickup into the Sunset Beach lot. It's before dawn and the sky's still dark. The ocean is loud through the open window.

In another half an hour the lot will be packed with cars and vans. It's strange, almost awful to step out of the car here, to crunch loudly over the gravel in his flip-flops, to feel like a visitor. This place is home. For years Tai's simply walked across to the beach from the house, usually with Ollie, a surfboard, and no shoes. He wants to hide.

It's raining—one of those soaking, tropical rains. It doesn't put the surfers off when the waves are up, as they are today. But it does mean the chickens that usually roam the parking lot and grass by the toilet block are all in hiding. Tai can't help but look over at the Blue House. All of its lights are out. The palms above the house are silhouetted in black against the dark sky, whipping back and forth in the rain and wind. Tai squeezes his eyes tightly shut and lets the rain fall on his face.

He carries the boards to the beach one by one and lines them up on the sand. He's got four for trial, each of them slightly different. He's been shifting their fins and wants to know what that will mean in heavy conditions.

He grabs the first board. The fin cluster's spread out but farther forward than usual, so the ride will be smooth, but he should get some pivotal movement when he wants it. He dives out over the wash and paddles the long way around the break. The take-off zone is pretty clear for now, but the winds are offshore, and the waves are coming in long tidy tubes. When it gets crowded he'll have to battle for every wave. It's going to be a long day.

The first wave is sweet, even in the almost-dark. Tai paddles back out and stops, just resting on the inside shoulder. He's loved this break since he first saw it. Right now the sun is rising over the mountains behind him, turning the ocean silver and gray through the rain. He's not going to have his choice of wave for long. Already there are a few more paddlers in the channel. Tai watches as they come.

He recognizes Ollie's strokes almost before he sees the dark-covered body and white hair. It's less than a week since Tai left the Blue House for Maile's place. Seeing Ollie again shouldn't stop his breath. He tries to shake it off.

"Hey," says Tai as Ollie reaches the lineup. After all, they're friends. Friends talk when they meet like this, out on the waves.

Ollie lifts his chin in acknowledgment. The coolness of it stings.

It's a relief that Tai needs to keep his eyes on the surf. When he's catching a wave he doesn't need to think about much beyond the water, what it's doing, where it's breaking, and keeping the board beneath his feet. He looks out to where a wave is building, then checks for the other surfers. He's sitting pretty deep already.

He hesitates.

"That one's yours, bro," Ollie says beside him. It's the way they reassured one another when they first started surfing together, when they were some of the youngest kids on these waves.

Tai doesn't need to thank him. He's already paddling hard away from the peak until the wave picks up his board and propels him forward. There's no need to add any energy in this surf; he keeps himself positioned right and lets the water take him where it goes. He shifts his feet forward and turns to stay on the face. The board's pretty good. Not magic, maybe, but responsive. It'll be worth spending some time with this shape and placement.

A bit later, he's on the beach, switching over to his second board, when Ollie walks across the sand. Tai watches him and his stomach twists.

"Hey," says Ollie. His eyes flick away from Tai, and he tips his head to consider the board. He runs one hand over the nose. Tai resists stepping away. He resists reaching out and grabbing Ollie too.

"Hey," Tai says. "Howzit going?"

Ollie's eyes shift to him. His jaw is set. Tai's heart thuds. Once, twice.

"Mostly I'm angry, Tai. I'm so fucking angry that you moved out on us."

"I didn't—" Tai starts. This is not how things are supposed to go.

Ollie goes on, his voice low and focused. "Have you forgotten everything? It's supposed to be you and me, our family, in our house. The Blue House. Always. That's our deal. We're supposed to have one another forever."

It sounds perfect, of course. It sounds exactly like everything Tai has ever hoped for in his whole life. But it hasn't felt possible since they got home, and he doesn't know how to say that, yet. "Maile needed my help," he says.

"Don't lie to me," says Ollie quietly. "She doesn't need your help, Tai. She loves you like a sister and she's letting you stay because she's nice and because you freaked out."

"That's not—"

"It's not like I don't know you, Tai. But you moved out, and I don't get it. You've had sex with loads of other guys; it's never even made you blink to see them again. So it can't just be that. This is the one time you can't afford to freak out on me. And it's the first time you do." He draws a quick breath. "It's not okay. We promised that we'd stay friends for the sake of the house and for our family and—you promised me, Tai. And now you're letting it all go because—I don't know why. We were stupid."

There's nothing Tai wants to say to that. He tries, "I'm sorry."

"What?" Ollie breathes. He looks heartbroken, and that's unbearable.

"I'm sorry I couldn't stay. I'm sorry, Ollie." The tears have been sitting in the back of Tai's throat for days. The rain has started up again so everything is wet anyway.

Ollie exhales heavily. When he goes on, his voice is softer but his eyes glint. "You can't tear everything we've worked for apart, and then think it's going to be okay if you say you're sorry. You *moved out*. You moved out. Don't apologize; tell me how to fix it. Tell me we can sort it out. 'Cause right now I honestly don't get it at all."

Tai's still holding a surfboard. He plants it in the sand. His hands shake. He speaks so he can just be heard over the sound of the surf. "Of course you don't get it. It's not the same for you, Ollie."

Ollie says, "It is the same. This is the Blue House, Tai. It was the only thing that mattered to either of us. I thought you would give up anything for it."

"Almost anything, as it turns out." Tai says under his breath. He turns away. Then he says, "You're right. I'll fix things. It'll get better, I promise. It's just that—you can't understand how it's been impossible to be in the same room as you."

Ollie's eyes flicker to him, sharply, deeply hurt. "Don't say that—"

Tai interrupts. "No, not—that's not what I mean." He needs to make this better.

Ollie doesn't break his gaze.

Tai's been pushed into a corner. It takes a lot for Ollie to trust Tai with his friendship, to trust that Tai won't leave, and yet somehow the only way out of this conversation is breaking that trust. Or telling the truth. "It's hard to be in the same room as you because—" Tai lifts his eyes and speaks. If he's going to say this, he'll say it clearly. "The trouble is, Ollie, I'm in love with you."

The whole world is right there around them: the crashing waves, the crowds of surfers, the wind, and the rain. Still, it all narrows to one person. Ollie's breathing stops. Tai swallows, hard. There's no way for him to take the words back.

"It's okay," he says. "It's nothing. It's gonna be okay."

Ollie stammers. "No. It's not nothing, but—I don't even know. I can't—you don't want that stuff." Mostly, he looks horrified. "Tai. You've never wanted that."

"I know." Tai wipes a hand across his eyes angrily. "I know. Fuck. Sorry. I didn't mean to tell you." He takes a shaky breath. A tiny, secret part of him had hoped for a different response from Ollie. And that hope makes this hurt so much more. "Look, leave it with me. I'll fix this. I need to take a break for a little. But we get to keep our plans. I'm not letting them go just because—" He runs out of words.

"Okay," Ollie says slowly. "I'm not sure I know what this means."

Tai rushes to fix everything. "You're going on tour again in a week. You'll be in South Africa. I'll move back in to the house while you're there. And, hey. It's cool. I'll get over it. So don't worry."

"Okay." Ollie opens his mouth as though he has more to say, but nothing comes. They both stand there in the rain, stupid and lost. Tai runs his hands over his face.

"Want me to give your boards a run, too?" Ollie asks. Tai stops still. Ollie waves a hand at the boards lined up on the sand.

"No. You don't have to." Tai doesn't want Ollie's sympathy. He doesn't really want Ollie's company.

"I know I don't have to. But a second opinion's not a bad thing. I'd like to help."

Tai's miserable in a way he can't shake, but when he exhales it's half a laugh along with the sigh. He shakes his head. "Sure," he says. "Why not?"

"I'll take the one you already did." Ollie plants his own board in the sand. It's one of Tai's too, of course. He lifts the new board under his arm and lopes out toward the surf.

"Come on," he says, looking back.

Tai watches him and focuses. He can't change what he said. He can't change that it's true and he's somehow made such a fucking mess of everything with Ollie. But it's a relief to have it said. Now he has to figure out how to live with it.

CHAPTER TWENTY

THE SAME GUYS ARE HERE at Jeffrey's Bay in South Africa as were on the rest of the tour, so at least Ollie has a few people to nod and smile at. He avoids Ashton without deciding to, and sits with Brandon and some of the other rookies for breakfast or press conferences and the like. Most of the media attention goes to the couple of South African surfers, but Ollie gets a few questions, too.

Jeffrey's Bay is stunning: a long, perfect right point break. Ollie can read the waves from his hotel room window. There's a stand-out section, Supertubes, where everything links up together to form a long, consistent line of waves. It's one of the best surfing beaches in the world. But when Ollie looks out at the distance, at the waves from the south and the east, he feels off balance. This is not the Pacific.

He says that to Brandon over oatmeal and bacon the second morning.

"The Pacific's your ocean," Brandon says. "I get that." He yawns and leans his cheek on his hand. His hair flops comically to one side.

"You miss it too?" asks Ollie.

Brandon blinks at him. "Nah, mate. I'm from Perth. We're on the other coast of the ocean I grew up on."

"Right. Of course it is." Ollie shakes his head. "Sorry."

"No worries."

It's a reminder that Ollie's been on this ocean before, in the comp at the Margaret River. It wasn't his best surf by any means, but he hadn't spent his time worrying about the name of the ocean. He'd been distracted by other things.

"I reckon you miss Tai, too, though," says Brandon. Ollie peers at him closely, but he doesn't seem to mean anything by it. "How's he doing?"

"Good. Yeah. He's starting up his own shaping business. I'd get in early; I reckon his boards'll be popular."

"He shaped yours, didn't he? I've been eyeing them."

Ollie nods. "All of them."

"Thanks for the tip. I'd be keen to see what he's doing."

There's no plan for the day. Ollie was out on the surf early. Maybe he'll get out on it again this afternoon. After breakfast, he heads outside to the hotel courtyard to call home. It's nine a.m. in South Africa, so it's after dark in Hawaii. He calls on Jaime's phone.

"Ollie!" Jaime says. There's pop music in the background, but someone turns it down. "Ollie! How's it going?"

"Good, yeah, fine. No comp yet. There's a few days' lead."

"We know. I've been keeping an eye on the web updates. Maybe Wednesday, yeah?"

"Could be." Ollie can hear Sunny saying something in the background. Everyone sounds far away. "Painted any masterpieces today?"

Jaime laughs. Ollie's breath catches at the ease in it. "No, bro, I'm busy with algebra. I've got exams coming up." Ollie forces himself not to ask any more questions.

"Good for you, J."

Jaime sounds happy. "Yeah, it's coming together. Turns out I'm not bad at this stuff. Oh hey, here's Tai. Let me hand you over to him."

Ollie's heart thuds. He hadn't known Tai would be there. The phone clunks from hand to hand before Ollie gets a chance to say anything.

"Hey," comes Tai's voice.

Ollie presses the phone close to his ear. "You're home," he says as he walks toward the pool.

"I am."

"So you did it? You moved back?"

The background noise fades. Tai's obviously walked out to the deck. "I told you I would. I mean, Cerulean's kind of cute, but she doesn't sleep much. I prefer you guys." Tai's voice is comfortable in Ollie's ear. It's surprising that he can sound so relaxed after their last conversation. Ollie sits cross-legged in one of the deck chairs. It's not warm here. He wraps his free arm around his torso to hold his hoodie close. There's something deeply reassuring about knowing Tai's in the Blue House.

"So how's South Africa?" Tai asks.

Suddenly, Ollie has so much to say, as though he had been saving it all up for Tai. He wants to tell Tai everything he's seen and heard. He talks about the rides he's been getting. It's a longer break than anything they see at home. "I miss the Pacific," he says. "So much, Tai. But this is awesome. Supertubes, man. We need to get your boards out here and see if we can find that half-mile ride everyone's been promising me."

"Sounds good. I've always wanted to see J Bay."

Ollie tries not to sound awkward. "How's the uh—business. How's that all going?"

"It's cool. It's going well, thanks, man. But hey, about the Pacific."

"Yeah?" Ollie stands again. From here he can look out at the water. The sky's clear and the ocean stretches out beneath it in long, dark blue layers.

"You said you're missing it. You know they don't put a line in between, right?"

Ollie wrinkles his nose. "What?"

"You know what I mean. All the oceans are joined together. That bit you'll be surfing on was probably here at Pipeline a year ago. Some parts of it anyway."

Ollie huffs. "Yeah, yeah. I'm not an idiot. Of course I knew that." But he hadn't really thought about it.

"Of course you did," says Tai, and Ollie's more than glad to hear that laughing fondness in his tone again.

"Thanks," Ollie says. As he hangs up, he's happier than he was. He pulls up a search on his phone and types in a question about how ocean currents work.

He spends the next two days surfing as though he was born right here. Even in the most competitive heats, everything comes together. It's a dream run.

There's a press conference before the final. They've set it up in a room in the hotel, with a long table for the surfers and their crew. Ollie doesn't have much in the way of a crew, not here, but Carise sits beside him and it's better with her here. She's coached him on the answers to some of the questions he'll get. Somehow he's one of the big stories of the competition.

In the final he'll be facing an Australian, Josh Owens, a veteran who's been world champ twice. Ollie hasn't interacted with him much. The two of them stand and shake hands for the photographers. Josh's grip is firm. Ollie doesn't know whether to smile or look serious and competitive. Ultimately he simply looks uncomfortable. He sits down and tries not to let his feet tap or his knees shake as he faces the press. Most of the questions are forgettable.

"Did you expect to get so far in your first tour, Ollie?" asks a guy with worn, tanned skin and a worn surf T-shirt.

"Honestly, I didn't expect to be here at all," says Ollie. "I'm still waking up and pinching myself when I look out the window."

"And yet this is your third final out of six starts. You gotta be happy with that."

"Of course, of course, yeah. But I can't take it for granted. Like the quarters. I was up against guys I've watched my whole life, you know. I didn't want to be in a battle over waves with them. They're some of my heroes. But you have to surf what you get."

Another reporter speaks up. "And what about your board?"

Ollie sits back and grins. He was hoping for that question. He takes a breath to make sure his voice carries. "This one was made for me by my friend Tai Talagi. He's a shaper from the North Shore of Oahu. Home. He's been shaping amazing boards since we were grommets but now he's getting started commercially. Keep an eye out for his name."

After the conference, Ollie heads out to the beach alone. He takes off his flip-flops and walks past rocks and scrub with the sand between his toes. At length he sits and stretches his legs out in front of him. The wind is offshore and cool, the ocean choppy and inconsistent, but the sand is warm under his thighs. Ollie looks out to the curved line of the horizon.

Tai's in love with him. Tai said he was in love with him.

The truth is, Ollie couldn't say what love means. He wants to ask someone, wants to talk it through and pin it down, but the person he'd discuss it with is the same person who has him so confused.

He's heard Tai talking to Hannah, saying, "Do you love him?" or "Do you love her?" and Hannah humming as she considered her answer. He's never heard Hannah ask the same thing of Tai. Ollie had figured Hannah didn't bother because they all knew Tai didn't want that kind of love. But maybe she'd worked out something about Tai that neither boy had noticed. Ollie's heart thumps. He's known Tai for most of his life. He'd assumed there were no mysteries left.

Ollie doesn't have an easy language for what it would mean to be in love with Tai. His head doesn't work that way. But it's possible the words don't matter. Love. In love.

Tai's always been his best friend. Now he's the person whose skin Ollie wants to touch. Now Ollie wants to breath against Tai's lips. He's the first person Ollie wants to speak to, the first person he wants to see. Everything Tai does matters.

Maybe that's love already. There are surfing breaks all over the world, each with their own peculiarities and patterns. Ollie wants to see them all. And he wants to share them all with Tai.

IT'S MIDNIGHT IN HAWAII WHEN the finals get underway. Tai and Jaime and Hannah and Sunny pile onto the couch to watch Ollie compete. They've got a better television now that there's a bit of money, so they don't have to take turns standing beside the TV, holding the aerial at the right angle to get reception.

"This Josh guy Ollie's up against is pretty great," Jaime says.

"He is," says Tai. "He was world champ for a reason."

"But Ollie can take him?" Jaime asks.

"Ollie can take anyone." Tai's always believed it, and now it's coming true. If Ollie wins he'll be number one in the world.

The semifinals round was a hard-fought contest. Somehow this one seems easy by comparison. Josh is not quite in it. And Ollie, Ollie's perfect. Tai doesn't need to hold his breath because Ollie's taking each wave as though it's an exhibition. There's no tension in him. His fins snap out of the water. He lifts the board off the lip to take some gorgeous air. Tai quickly tamps down the pinprick wish that Ollie was only this good when he had Tai with him. That's not what he wants, not at all. He has his own life too, and he's not going to be that person. Ollie's surfing. It's a deep joy to watch.

Ollie wins. They all cheer and hug.

"Number one!" Jaime shouts in Tai's ear. Hannah lifts Jaime off the ground.

Tai figures he'll never stop smiling.

They watch as Brandon and a stranger raise Ollie to their shoulders. He stands on the podium and holds up the trophy and a ridiculous giant check. He looks proud and uncomfortable at once. Then someone opens a bottle of champagne and pours it over his head, and Ollie laughs that unexpected laugh. Tai's insides twist tight with a mixture of happiness and longing.

He almost misses it when Ollie shouts at the camera. "This is for you, Tai." Tai whips his head up to see the TV. Ollie's face is frozen for an instant, bright and so loved, before the camera pans to the ocean. They play some highlights of the day with a backing track. They show the upset of the South African champ, Ollie's quarters ride, some of the big air Ollie and a few others were getting. They show Ollie's final wave and his fist pump when he knew he'd won. Tai blinks away the brightness in his eyes. Hannah catches his gaze and raises her eyebrows.

"Talk to him," she mouths.

Tai shakes his head and squeezes back the tears. He can't be frustrated with Hannah. She doesn't know he already told Ollie everything. She doesn't know that Ollie already walked away from it.

"Stop," he mouths back. She narrows her eyes and her smile falters as she squeezes his shoulder.

Jaime's phone rings. Jaime puts it on speaker so they can all yell congratulations at Ollie at the same time.

Sunny and Jaime chant: "Number one, number one, number one."

Ollie's laugh is clear and welcome across the distance. "I can't believe it," he says.

"Believe it," Sunny yells. "You're the best surfer in the whole world. Told you."

Ollie laughs. "Some people might argue about that."

"They'd be wrong," says Sunny cheerfully.

"I really can't believe it," Ollie says, again.

"You were amazing," Jaime says.

At the same time Hannah says, "We never doubted you, babe." She's still squeezing Tai's shoulder.

Before Ollie hangs up, Tai adds his thanks. "It was great of you to mention my boards at the press conference. I really appreciate it."

He can hear Ollie's smile. "Oh, there you are. I was beginning to wonder. No problem. I love talking about them. It's the only time I enjoy the fucking media."

"And Ol, you were incredible out there. Best I've ever seen."

"Thank you," says Ollie, his voice focused and soft. "That means everything." The noise around him spills down the phone line. "Okay," he says self-consciously. "I'm sorry. I've gotta go. They're wanting to talk to me some more. Bye, guys. Bye. I'll talk to you soon."

"See you in two days," Jaime says.

"I can't wait," says Ollie. Tai's relieved to mostly feel the same.

Jaime's still dancing around the house with Sunny. Tai watches them and adores them and misses Ollie deep in his bones, in a way he always has and yet never thought he would.

CHAPTER TWENTY-ONE

EARLY THE NEXT AFTERNOON TAI'S at the factory space he and Tadashi have rented. After Ollie's win he was too wired to sleep. He stayed up talking, then cleaned the kitchen with Hannah, so he started the workday late. It's fine, he's his own boss and he can work late too.

He sets up the stands for planing, getting the levels right and checking that he's close enough to the outlets for the power tool cords. His phone buzzes in his pocket. It's Ollie.

Tai takes a breath before he answers. "Hey."

"Hey." Ollie's voice sounds heavy and soft, a late night voice, a dangerous voice Tai hasn't heard for a while. Tai walks out to the little parking lot outside and squints up at the sky.

"It's after two a.m. over there, dude. You should definitely be asleep."

"I'm in bed already," says Ollie. "Anyway, I don't need to sleep tonight. The comp's over, Tai." He hums a little into the phone. "Don't get your Mom tone on." His voice is a little messy on the consonants. He's tipsy.

Tai grins, rocking his feet forward and back on the crunchy gravel. "Sounds like you've been celebrating your win."

"Yeah. We went to this bar. You should have seen it. They let us in the VIP room; we were on the list. Some of the guys bought me drinks."

"I bet they did." It's hard not to be simply, inescapably fond of Ollie when he sounds like this: cheerful and eager and confused and sleepy at once. Tai closes his eyes but it doesn't stop images of Ollie flashing into his mind: Ollie facing him across hotel sheets; the two of them lying on their sides with only their knees and hands touching; Ollie's face, sweet and relaxed; his quick eyes glazed over with tiredness, and so steady on Tai.

"Have you had a glass of water?" Tai asks. He's distracting himself by caretaking, but he figures it might help Ollie in the morning.

"I did, when I got in. And I thought of you while I drank it," Ollie teases. "I'll be fine, Tai."

Tai rolls his eyes even though he's clear on the fact that Ollie can't see him. "Sorry, Ol. Old habits. Tell me about the win; the waves looked pristine."

Ollie's voice is dreamy. "They were. I didn't need to do a thing out there. The waves did it all. And your board was perfect. But Tai, I missed you tonight. Out on the water, and afterward." He takes a breath. "It's not even fifty degrees here, and I know how warm you are."

Tai gazes back up at the sky and doesn't say anything. He doesn't want to hang up, but this phone call is beginning to be enormously and achingly unfair.

Ollie's breath is soft along the line. "I'm really glad you're back at the Blue House. If you're not here with me at least you're there. It feels closer than other places. You know?"

"Yeah. I know." Tai swallows with difficulty. "I need to get back to work and I'm pretty sure it's time you got off the line and went to sleep, Ollie."

"We're okay?" Ollie asks.

"We're okay."

"Good," says Ollie. "I can't wait to see you. I have all this—stuff I need to say to you." Tai can hear him roll over in his bed, halfway across the planet. "I miss you so much."

Tai could laugh the words off, of course. He could simply not answer. Instead he exhales and tells the truth. "I miss you too, Ollie."

When they disconnect, Tai heads back into the factory space. He messes with the lighting in the shaping bay, angles the globes to consistently light the boards as he works. The factory setup's pulling together well. The shaping bay has racks and an air hose. There are slabs of foam, drums of resin, and rolls of fiberglass along one wall. There's an extra respirator mask for customers or visitors. Tai's happy with the quality boards he can produce here, which is lucky as they have a few orders already. At least one part of his life is working out the way he wants it to.

Tai turns on some music to distract himself.

It's probably lucky it's the middle of the night in South Africa. Ollie's certainly asleep now, snuffling gently into his pillow. There's no point calling and letting him know that it might be a nice idea to stop with the drunken telephone calls for a while. Saying something will make it into a big deal. Ollie only called because he's accustomed to talking with Tai last thing at night. And really, Tai wants to keep that option open. It seems more sensible not to pay too much attention to the way it hurts and to just let things rest. It's better this way.

JAIME'S WAITING IN THE AIRPORT when Ollie walks through the doors from the agriculture check. They're surrounded by happy families reuniting, parents and grown kids embracing, couples who should probably get a room, friends hugging as though it's been years. Jaime walks over and gives Ollie a quick, fierce hug, then grabs some of his stuff.

"Where are the others?" asks Ollie.

"No one's here. Just me. Tai went with me to get my license last week." Jaime glances across quickly, ready to be defensive. "But it's cool if you want to drive. I get it."

"No way. Nope, I'm not gonna get in the way when you are finally making yourself useful."

"Whatever, dude," says Jaime happily.

Jaime's mostly silent for the drive home, focused on the road as it winds into the mountains and then straight past the pineapple plantations. Ollie watches him navigate the road with an unexpected swell of pride. It's only driving, he tells himself. It's stupid to get all emotional about it. But tears prick his eyes. They're getting there, both of them, together.

At the lights near the turnoff to Haleiwa, Jaime says, abruptly, "There's this girl I like."

"Yeah?" It's good to have Jaime tell him stuff without Ollie needing to ask.

"Yeah. She's an artist and she's in this garage band." Jaime sighs and Ollie holds back a grin. "She's awesome, you just wait 'til you see her play."

"What's her name?"

"Mira. She's Hawaiian."

"Nice. Does she like you?" Ollie asks. He avoids telling Jaime to be careful. They've had that conversation before, and it went down better when Sunny did it.

Jaime blushes as he shrugs, but he answers directly. "Yeah. She says she does. And I like her a lot, Ollie. Like, more than anyone."

Soon enough they pull up; the wheels crunch over the ground. The Blue House is the same as ever, aqua paint peeling, familiar and tumbling down, as if the ocean wants to take it back. Ollie can't imagine life without it.

He swallows as he looks up at it. "So, is Tai here?" he asks.

He's aiming for casual, but Jaime peers at him. "Probably. He was here when I left." He pauses. "You guys going to be okay, bro?"

Ollie slowly undoes his seatbelt. "Yeah, don't worry. We'll be fine."

Jaime can see straight through him. "Which means you have no idea."

"Yeah." Ollie sighs. "No idea at all." He's spent the past week and a half missing Tai, wanting to tell him every single thing he thinks and sees and not sure how much to say over the phone. It's dizzying to think that he'll walk up the stairs and find Tai inside the house.

Jaime shakes his head. He climbs out of the car, then sticks his head back through the door. "You know what, Ollie? You're an idiot if you don't do something here. You're my brother so I have to love you. I've got no choice. But if you don't talk to Tai, you're an even bigger idiot than I thought you were." He closes the car door and walks toward the house.

Ollie gazes after him. His boards are here, his space, his room, his friends, his family. Everything he already loves and always will is in this house. That used to be more than enough for Ollie. But now, when he thinks of Tai, there's this sparking potential to the thought, a thrill like the early sun hitting the tiny crests of the waves, like lightning far away on the horizon. It's dangerous. It could tear apart all the things they've worked so hard to build. But the thought of Tai's skin on Ollie's skin, his eyes on Ollie's eyes—that's something altogether different from this other love that holds Ollie together.

Ollie's repeatedly asked himself what he wants from this. It's not as if he doesn't know.

He wants to reach for Tai before anything else. He wants to speak and know that Tai will listen. He wants to walk into the house, into any house really, and know that Tai will turn to him as though he's the only person in the room.

CHAPTER TWENTY-TWO

IT'S ALMOST DINNERTIME. TAI TOSSES more vegetables into a wok on the stovetop. Ollie's home. It's a sweet, sharp pain to know he's here, though he disappeared downstairs with his boards after an awkward welcome-back not-quite-hug. When he met Tai's glance, Tai had to steady his breathing.

In the living room, Jaime's convinced Sunny and Hannah to try origami with him. Hannah's attempts are a mess. She gives up and admires the others' pieces. Sunny and Jaime are pretty good. Across the room, Tai can see miniature cranes and frogs and flowers. He watches them now and then from the kitchen while he stirs the chicken fried rice.

"Dinner's up," Tai calls when it's ready. "Can someone get Ollie?"

"Ollie!!" Sunny raises her voice so Ollie can hear from the laundry where he's messing with the boards.

Ollie thuds up the stairs. Jaime puts all the leftover paper and the most successful origami onto the bookshelf before grabbing a plate of food. He sprawls in one big chair and Sunny sits cross-legged on the floor. Tai sits on the couch. He's surprised when Ollie sits beside him. He moves over to make space.

While Tai eats, Ollie's flickering gaze lands on him. Tai's heart twists traitorously in response. But when he glances at Ollie, Ollie's eyes shift away. Tai's skin simmers. The time apart has only made this whole thing clearer. Tai's in love. He honestly doesn't know how he's going to stop.

Toward the end of dinner, Ollie says, "Hey, is that a new tattoo?" He touches Tai's arm fleetingly. His voice is pitched low, but there are only five of them in the room. The other three look over.

"I figured you'd be pretty clear on the precise whereabouts of all of Tai's tats, Oliver," says Sunny. Hannah turns away and smiles at the wall.

Tai ignores them. "Yeah, it's new." He runs his fingers over the band of waves and heartbeats that trace around his wrist. It's recent enough that the tattoo is still slightly red and raised on his skin.

"I like it. It suits you." Ollie sounds so sincere it makes Tai uncomfortable.

"Thanks. Dude. Stop being weird." He scrunches up his napkin and throws it at Ollie. Ollie winces. It's the wrong thing to say and do, but Tai's not sure what would have been better.

Jaime looks at them both and rolls his eyes. He finishes his last mouthful and drops his fork to his plate with a clatter. "Okay," he says, "Who's ready to help me with my homework? Sunny? Hannah? It's math, you know you want to."

"Yeah, okay," says Hannah. She grabs her plate along with Jaime's and takes them to the kitchen.

"What kind of math?" Sunny asks. She takes a slow mouthful.

"Something complicated," says Jaime. "It's about derivation of logs." Sunny continues to relish her last few bites. Jaime presses a hand to his chest. "Help me, Sunny, you're my only hope."

She grins at him as she finishes her dinner. "Okay, okay. Though I don't get why our precious idiots can't talk somewhere else." She glares at Tai and Ollie. Something's going on. Hope hurts, sharp like a knife in Tai's chest.

Jaime sighs dramatically and drags her out before she says anything more.

Tai looks across the couch at Ollie beside him and doesn't say anything. Ollie twists his fork in his mouth. "Good dinner," he manages awkwardly around it.

"Ollie?" Tai asks.

Ollie's gaze flicks around the room. He runs a hand through his messy hair. "It's gotta be my turn to do the dishes. I've been gone almost two weeks."

"Oh," Tai says at last. "Yeah. Okay." Maybe he's imagined the tension and got his hopes up over nothing. "It probably is."

Ollie's shoulders drop as he heads into the kitchen, whether from relief or something sadder, Tai can't tell. Ollie stands at the sink and runs the water, his feet are bare, his hips are narrow, and his hair sticks up on his head in all directions. Tai wants to watch him do ordinary things forever.

"I'm heading out for a walk," Tai says to Ollie's back. He needs to take some time outside his head.

Ollie half turns. He looks as though he's about to speak, but just lifts a hand in farewell. Tai goes down the stairs and out onto the beach alone.

It's dark, of course, though bright moonlight breaks through the cloud cover. Tai walks a familiar path along the beach, around to a point where the rough sand juts out before sloping suddenly into the ocean. He stands still and wraps his arms around his body. The waves and the sand are a second home.

THE LAST PLATE IS IN the drying rack. Ollie is a fool and a coward. He turns off the hot tap and watches it drip once, twice. Outside, the surf is thunderous. A car drives past the house.

Ollie doesn't need to imagine the worst that could happen between him and Tai. That already happened, Tai moved out. Now Tai's back. It makes no sense for Ollie to stand here and do nothing.

Ollie heads to the beach. He knows where Tai is.

"Hey."

He can hear his own heartbeat over the sound of the surf. Tai turns. His eyes are red-rimmed. He doesn't try to hide it. If Ollie could, he'd go back in time and take it all away. "Hey."

"So hey," Ollie says at last. "I've known you for a really long time—"

"It's cool, Ollie, you don't need to tell me again. I get it. I got it last time." Tai's voice is flat, defeated.

"No. That's not—" Ollie takes Tai's hand in one of his. Tai looks down at their hands, then up to meet Ollie's eyes. "Let me say this," Ollie says.

"Okay." Tai sets his shoulders.

Tai is Ollie's best friend, his family. Ollie forces himself not to look away. "You've been part of my life for so long. I took that for granted. I thought that nothing would change. But." He wants to explain this perfectly but even now he hasn't found the words. His breath comes in a gust. "It's bigger now. What you are to me. It's big-big. Like you've woken me up and there's this part of me that I didn't know was there." He takes Tai's other hand.

Tai opens his mouth as though he might say something. But if Ollie doesn't finish now, he might never work out how to start again. He takes a breath and says everything. "I can't tell whether I've felt like this for a long time or if it just started. I've been turning all the words for how I feel over and over in my mind trying to figure out what it means and I still don't know what to say but—" He exhales. Tai's eyes are moonlit, dark and clear. "Not long ago you said you were in love with me. Tai. You know I'm an idiot. You've always known that. Give me another chance to answer?" He pauses, takes a breath. "Don't tell me I'm too late."

Tai is still. "You're not too late."

The mountains of Oahu fold up sharply toward the black sky. The waves stretch out forever. Unexpectedly, it's simple. Ollie doesn't rush the words. "I'm in love with you." He exhales. "I love you, Tai."

The ocean keeps its ageless beat around them.

"You can say something any time now," Ollie says.

Tai's face is vivid, all ease and amazement. His expression is really all the reply Ollie needs. "What do you want me to say?" Tai's teasing.

Ollie tackles him to the sand.

Tai laughs up at him. "I love you, Ollie. I love you."

"Yeah?" Ollie beams helplessly. Tai's covered in sand. This is ridiculous. "You do?"

"You already know how much I'm in love with you, asshole. I told you. It's not about to change."

Ollie leans down to kiss Tai. This is nothing new. They've kissed before, most of the time beside the Pacific Ocean. But this. This is huge and safe: on their beach, with a past and a future, with their stretch of water and waves to watch over them.

When they sit up, side by side, Tai is wide-eyed. He takes a slow breath.

"Did I surprise you?" Ollie asks, trying not to be smug.

"I'd convinced myself this would never happen."

Ollie kisses him again He might never stop. "It wasn't as complicated as I expected."

"What wasn't?"

"Telling you that I love you. Figuring it out."

"Fuck, I missed you," Tai breathes.

Ollie shakes himself internally and focuses. He's thought about this. He has to make it work this time. "But hey, I don't want to do all this and never communicate. You know. 'Cause we tried that once before. And I don't want to mess this up." He's embarrassed to be so earnest.

Tai nods. "Sure. Let's talk."

Ollie hasn't actually thought about what to say next, of course. It's usually Tai's job to get the words right. "What I wanted to say was— I'd like it if this isn't just about kissing. Not that I don't like kissing. Because I do." He stops. Starts again. "When I say I love you, I guess I'm wondering if we could maybe give this a try. This, you know, thing with us." The words are getting away from him.

Tai grins, radiant. He takes Ollie's hand. "Sure, let's do this thing with the thing."

"Fuck off, Tai. You know what I mean." Even through his irritation he can't help but move back to kiss Tai again.

Tai speaks against Ollie's lips. "I know what you mean. And yes, we should give this a go. I'm in. Anything. Everything."

Happiness simmers inside as Ollie leans back to look at him. "Really?" he asks.

"Yeah, really," says Tai, as though everything is easy.

"How can you do that?" Ollie asks.

"What?"

"How can you say that so easily, say 'everything' like it isn't the most terrifying thought in the world?" Ollie bites his lips and considers Tai in the almost-dark. He's the most beautiful thing Ollie's ever seen. He always has been.

"I don't know," Tai says. "It's easy to say because it's true. And there are some things that are just worth being terrified for."

"Yeah." Ollie nods. "But hey. I don't want you to be terrified."

"I'm less scared every second," says Tai against his hair.

They stay out on the beach for a while. But Ollie's only just back from South Africa. His eyes are drooping by the time they head back. He doesn't let go of Tai's hand the whole way home. When they get there everything's dark. The other kids' bedroom doors are closed.

"Will you come to my room?" asks Ollie in a whisper, and Tai hums a quiet, pleased yes.

They make their way through the house, unerringly avoiding the worst of the squeaking boards in the hallway.

Music comes from Hannah's room, but even so, the sound of Ollie's door closing echoes in the hall. They stand close together. The walls around them have been their walls forever. Ollie's shoes are lined up behind the door. His bed is rumpled. Hannah's next door. Jaime and Sunny are down the hall.

Ollie moves to drop the blinds over his window. When he turns back, Tai's closed his eyes.

"It's kind of strange to be here," Tai says when he opens them. "Good strange."

"I know."

Tai steps closer. It's not strange anymore. Ollie puts a hand on his waist. His fingers curl under the waistband of Tai's shorts. Tai pushes Ollie down onto the bed and tumbles on top of him, kissing up Ollie's neck and grinding against his upper thigh. The bed creaks a protest.

"Oof." Ollie muffles his laughter against Tai's shoulder. "Slow down babe, hey, easy. We've got so much time," Ollie says. "Promise." He rolls them over so that Tai is on his back and looks down. He's tired, but simply and gorgeously happy. "At least let me take off your shirt."

Tai arches his back and then lifts his hips so Ollie can struggle with his shirt and peel off his board shorts. He lies back, naked. Ollie kneels beside him, sits back on his heels, biting his lip. Everything has narrowed to this one person. Under Ollie's gaze, Tai's breathing hitches. When Ollie's hands trace a light path over Tai's body, Tai whines. He tries to push up and press against Ollie's hands, but Ollie just grins at him.

"Hold on, now," he says. "Patience."

He closes his eyes, takes Tai in by touch. Tai's skin is electric, his muscles taut. Ollie counts his abs, slips a hand down to skim over Tai's inner thigh and upward. Tai sucks in a shaky breath. Ollie wraps his hand around Tai's cock.

"Come down here with me." Tai's voice is a moan. He pulls Ollie's body over his own. Ollie huffs out a laugh and kisses Tai deeply. Their hips move relentlessly against one another. There's not quite enough lubrication, but Ollie knows what he's doing. He flicks his thumb over the head of Tai's cock to gather what moisture he can.

"Is this good?"

"Fuck," Tai mutters.

"Is that a yes?"

"Yes."

Tai reaches between them to where Ollie's cock rubs against his thigh. Ollie's body melts into him as they move together over and over, taking one another in a rhythm that's grown familiar and still reaches deep to Ollie's core.

Tai comes with a voiceless moan, shaking and breathless. His gaze is caught in Ollie's. The pleasure flares white in Ollie's chest and ripples over his skin, wave after wave, down his spine and into his toes. It leaves him soft-limbed. They breathe into the space between them, quiet and content. They've said everything already.

Ollie wakes to Tai's warm body. It's late, and the sun is already pooling warm on Tai's belly and chest. Ollie stretches, then bends his head to kiss Tai. Tai rolls to one side, facing away and reaching an arm back to pull Ollie close against his back. Ollie presses happily into him, sleepy and hard. He wants all of this.

Later, Ollie makes his way up the hall, leaving Tai to the bathroom. They're not hiding things, but he's not about to show up for breakfast clutching Tai's hand, either. Hannah and Sunny are out on the deck. Ollie pours a cup of coffee and joins them. When Tai shows up, stretching distractingly and scrubbing his face with his hands, Ollie can't help staring. Tai meets his gaze and smiles slowly. Ollie feels it to the soles of his feet.

A gull cries out in the wind. The waves keep up their usual rhythm.

Hannah says, "So hey, if you guys want to keep this whole thing quiet that's cool. But we kind of can't miss the way you're looking at one another right now." Her voice is warm.

Ollie blushes and studies the floor.

Sunny laughs. "Honestly, guys, if you think you're fooling anyone with your secret lovesick puppy looks and turning up five minutes apart, you're not. You might as well be making out in front of us. Plus, Hannah could fucking hear you last night."

Hannah waves a hand dismissively. "Not like that," she says to Ollie's startled glance. "Anyway, that's not what matters here. We want you to be happy."

"You're not worried?" asks Tai.

"Nah," says Hannah. She smiles at them both. "You got this."

Sunny adds, "Well, sure. I mean, you're both idiots. You're guaranteed to fuck everything up. But you've got our shoulders to cry on and you'll probably get through it. Especially if you listen to people who're smarter than you." She looks at them. "We're happy for you, babes."

Ollie meets Tai's gaze again and can't not grin.

When Jaime stumbles out of bed, half an hour later, Tai and Ollie are sitting together on the swing seat. Tai's fingers are tangled up with Ollie's. He drops Ollie's hand as Jaime approaches. Jaime considers them with blinking, just-awake eyes.

"About fucking time," he says, and grins.

THEY'RE OUT AT PIPELINE. THE crowds are out too. It's mostly tourists, and they leave Tai and Ollie alone, but that doesn't stop everyone from watching Ollie. Tai swells with pride at that. It's the way it should be.

They meet in the shallows and paddle out together.

"I've got a question for you," says Ollie as they slide down the back of a wave halfway to the lineup.

Tai eyes him, one eyebrow raised. "Yep?"

Ollie doesn't look at him as he paddles. "You told me you only wanted something casual."

"I never said that." Tai frowns. Things with Ollie could never be casual for him.

"Yeah you did, in Australia. You said you'd keep things easy and secret and wouldn't bring me poems or flowers."

"Oh." Tai thinks. "I said I wouldn't do that stuff. I never said I didn't want to." A wave moves under them. "Though the poems'd be a stretch." Ollie meets his gaze. "I was trying to convince you that we shouldn't stop having sex, Ollie. Because I hated the idea of giving up touching you but I didn't know what you wanted. It wasn't about casual; it was about making your decision simple."

"Huh." They've slowed down outside the zone. They watch the surf side by side. A set sweeps through the lineup with surfers scattered across its face. "But you're all about the casual thing. You weren't a tiny bit interested in something long-term with any of the boys before. I thought—" Ollie leaves it hanging.

There's a simple answer, of course. "None of them were you, Ollie."

"Oh." Ollie flushes. His smile is helpless and fond, the way it is only for Tai. "Well, that works out. I never wanted to touch anyone who wasn't you." He looks back at Tai as he paddles into the line-up. "Come on."

LATER, WHEN THE TIDE IS out, all five of them head onto the beach flats, standing barefoot in the low sheen of water that covers the sand. The ocean's dead here, nothing to surf. Tai is happy all the way to his bones.

"I'm thinking of making an offer to buy the house," says Ollie as he tosses a Frisbee for Hannah to snatch out of the air. Tai's not surprised; Ollie had talked about it this morning in bed.

Sunny has to pick up the Frisbee Hannah throws before a rippling wave grabs it. She looks stunned. "What?" she asks.

"I figure I could make an offer to the landlords," Ollie says. "See if they'd sell it to me."

Sunny whips her head toward Tai. "What?" she says again. "The Blue House?"

Ollie shrugs, "I wanted to talk to you guys first. I mean, it's not a big deal. Mostly I hate that they're telling us to move out. It's our home. This way we could all live there as long as we wanted."

"And *this* is not a big deal," says Sunny, echoing Ollie and amazed. "You're joking."

"It's not like you need to buy the place, Ollie," says Hannah. "That's huge. Something will come up."

"Yeah, maybe. But think of this, guys. This way you'll always have a place to live."

Jaime bounces closer. He says, "I'm in. At least until I head off for college." Sunny throws the Frisbee toward him. It's caught by the wind and veers wildly. It bounces against his chest. He wrinkles his nose as he brushes wet sand from his white T-shirt. "Careful, Sun."

Sunny ignores Jaime. "What are you thinking, Oliver?" she says. She tilts her head to one side as she steps toward him. Jaime throws the Frisbee to Tai, who catches it and holds still.

"You mean, practically?" asks Ollie. Tai watches Sunny. She's careful about financial stuff and accustomed to making decisions about money for all of them.

"Yeah," she says.

"I'm thinking that I buy it, we all live in it." He shifts closer to Tai but doesn't touch him.

"There's a lot to consider," says Sunny. "Financial stuff. Rent. Bills."

"Yeah. We'll talk it through. But I figure no one pays rent. We can split bills like we always have but it'll be easier to pay them."

"I'm—that's pretty huge. It's really what you want?"

Ollie glances at Tai then turns back to Sunny. "You all got me through for years before I pulled that prize money. The way I see it, the money isn't just mine. It's ours. The best use for it is making our family happy."

No one says anything. Tai's still got the Frisbee.

"Imagine," says Hannah. "The Blue House. Ours. Safe for all of us."

Sunny glances between them, then lets go of the tension in her shoulders. She beams. "Okay. Wow. Okay."

Hannah says, "Give my cousin Linda a call. The lawyer. She's your cousin too. Cousin-in-law." The meaning makes Ollie blush.

"What do you reckon, Tai?" asks Sunny. She raises her eyebrows at him. She's relaxed into the idea now.

He tosses the Frisbee to her and wraps his arm around Ollie. "I think it's an amazing plan," he says.

"Ugh," she says. "You're in love. Of course you fucking do."

He beams. "That doesn't mean I'm not right, though."

"THEY'RE NOT BUDGING ON THAT price, Ollie," comes cousin Linda's voice through his phone. "I know how much you kids love the Blue House, but I gotta say, it's totally not worth the kind of dollars they're talking about."

Ollie switches off the TV playing in the background and looks out the window.

"Damn," he says. "They won't negotiate?"

"Afraid not."

"Damn," he says again.

"You know I'm right," says Linda. "I can't recommend offering more. It'd make no financial sense. Sunny'd kill me."

"Yeah, I just hoped—" says Ollie.

"I know, bro. It was a nice idea."

Disappointment rests heavily in Ollie's chest. He wants to see Tai. He grabs his skateboard from the side of the house and goes up the headland to the factory.

At the gravel parking lot, he tucks the skateboard under his arm. The big doors of the warehouse are rolled up. Tai and Tadashi are at work, lining up a set of eight or ten boards. Tai runs careful hands over the one he's holding before putting it back on the stacking pins. He turns to talk to Tadashi. As he does so, he sees Ollie. His smile is as bright as the sun at the horizon. Despite his disappointment, Ollie beams back.

Tadashi turns and nods a greeting. "Afternoon, Ollie."

"Hi. Are these the boards you guys are taking to Europe?" Ollie asks.

"They are," says Tadashi.

Tai's still smiling. He comes close to Ollie. "I missed you," he says quietly.

"It's been a long six hours," Ollie says. It's part teasing and part sincere. He wants to touch Tai all the time. "I spoke with Linda about the house," he says. Tadashi looks at them, then turns back to check on the contents of the resin barrels.

"What'd she say?" Tai studies Ollie's face.

"Tai. It's not going to happen."

Saying it makes it real. It sinks like concrete in Ollie's stomach. He'd been so sure. The Blue House is their house, it's their forever, and yet they'll be out of it almost as soon as he and Tai are back from Europe.

"I'm so sorry, Ollie," says Tai. He moves toward Ollie and stops just in reach. Ollie's the one who reaches out with the arm not holding a skateboard. He wraps it around and rests his head against Tai's shoulder.

"I wanted to be able to fix everything," says Ollie. He breathes against Tai's shirt.

"I know," says Tai. "I know. Hey. We'll all be okay."

He doesn't sound as heartbroken as Ollie is. Ollie steps away. He pushes at Tai's chest and Tai steps back. Ollie says, "What do you mean, 'We'll be okay'. Are you psychic now? Tai, this is our house we're losing."

Tai exhales through his nose in an impatient half-laugh. "I'm upset too, Ol. You know I am. But we'll be okay." He glances around the factory and then back at Ollie. "Everything's already more than we thought to want. For all of us." He shrugs. "Especially me. I couldn't ask for anything else."

"Yeah," says Ollie, somewhat appeased. He considers the warehouse. The boards look good, lined up to go. "Have you and Tadashi booked your flights to France yet?"

"Yeah, we'll be there the day after you are. You can keep the bed warm for me." Tai takes Ollie's hand. It makes things easier. "I can't wait to try it out. A French bed has to be good."

Ollie laughs. "Are you almost finished here or will it be a while? No one else is gonna be home 'til late."

Tai turns to Tadashi. "Are we done here, Tadashi?"

Tadashi nods. "Yes, we have everything. I'll close up in a minute."

"Thanks, man."

They walk down from the headland, then along the beach just out of reach of the water. They don't touch much as they walk, but Ollie feels Tai's proximity. Now and then their arms brush. Every touch hums in

Ollie's blood. He watches the Pacific. The waves are coming in long, clean lines. Maybe later they'll get their boards and go out.

It's unexpected, the ease of all of this. Even with today's disappointment, Ollie can't be anything but happy. He walks closer to Tai, letting their shoulders touch.

"Hey," says Tai. "Check it out." Ollie looks. Tai's pointing at where the sand ends and the grass rises sharply to a line of houses.

One of the houses has a sign out the front. "FOR SALE."

Tai says, "Remember this place? Some kids lived here when we were growing up. Jade and Meri." He sounds thrown, a little puzzled.

Ollie shakes his head. He vaguely recalls some leggy girls living at this end of the beach.

They turn and walk up the sand. It's soft and sinks under their feet as they get close to the house. They stand side by side. "Are you thinking—could it be big enough for all of us?" Ollie asks.

"I don't know. It's been a long time since I've been inside."

The house faces the ocean. It's unimposing, wood, with wide steps leading up from the grass to a deck that stretches the full length of the building.

The sign has pictures: a view, a large kitchen, a backyard. It lists an agent. Ollie tries the number but there's no answer.

Tai approaches the sign. He looks as though he expects it to disappear. "The first open house is tomorrow," he says. "We can go and see it together. All of us."

Ollie exhales. "Fuck."

They're silent most of the way home. Tai takes Ollie's hand and squeezes. Before he can let go, Ollie tangles their fingers and holds tight. The connection isn't just between him and Tai; it stretches deep into the sand to the ocean at the center of the earth. Ollie doesn't let go until they reach the Blue House.

As they head up the stairs, Ollie runs his hand along the handrail. The peeling paint is rough under his skin. In front of him, Tai slides his key into the temperamental lock. It turns easily. Tai's always had that knack, ever since they moved in. He swings the door open and waits for Ollie to pass him into the empty living room.

Ollie's too excited to think but he can't stop. The place for sale may not have enough bedrooms for all five of them; it might not be what they want, at all, the asking price might be excessive. But there's a bubble of hope in his chest. His brain buzzes.

Tai says, "We don't need to talk about this. Not yet. We need more information."

Ollie's relieved. "I'm not sure I even want to think."

Tai nods, as though he knows what Ollie means. "I've got the solution for that," he says. He holds Ollie by the shoulders and pushes them both toward Ollie's room.

It's early in the morning. Tai reaches for Ollie without opening his eyes. He runs his hand over Ollie's chest and curls it around his taut waist. He lets his palms re-learn the muscles and bones beneath Ollie's skin. Ollie stirs.

"Morning, sweetheart," says Tai. When he opens his eyes, Ollie's gaze is the dreamy blue of summer.

"Morning."

Tai could watch Ollie all day, but the surf's up. They're out on the water in minutes. There's no one else here. Just the two of them, with the ocean stretching all the way to the horizon.

"We could have stayed in bed for another five," says Ollie. "It's not like we're fighting the crowds here today."

"Yeah, but what would we have done with five minutes?"

Tai's teasing. Ollie raises an eyebrow and doesn't answer. They could have filled the time.

The wind's offshore. The waves aren't forming tubes today, but they're not small. They're hard work; good training for messy, three- and four-foot swells. Tai tests his own board and takes his time watching Ollie. They don't say much. Tai knows what he's hoping for with the boards; Ollie knows what he's out here to practice.

Sometimes Tai looks back at the shore. He can make out the Blue House among the palms. Farther down the beach, fronting the ocean, is the place that's for sale. Tai keeps an eye on the angle of the sun. It's early. They're not going to miss the open house.

THE FIVE OF THEM STEP through the front door, one after the other. The real estate agent eyes them. She's dressed in a tidy skirt suit with a flower behind her ear.

"You're interested in buying?" She manages to hide most of her doubt.

"Yes," says Sunny. "You bet we are."

Tai refuses to be offended. He can't blame the agent. They'd walked up the road instead of along the beach, so they're not covered in sand, but he doubts they look like her usual buyers.

They stand in the living room. The windows look straight across the sand to their stretch of the ocean. From behind the house, the sun lights the water's surface. The waves glint. Tai takes a deep breath and looks around.

The kitchen's larger than what they're used to, and it has an island in the center with pots and pans hanging above. There are five bedrooms and a large, light studio. Even standing here is weird and maybe disloyal, but Tai can't help comparing. This place doesn't have the Blue House's quirky wooden charm, but the walls are more solid. The windows have real working blinds. The place isn't falling down.

Out in back, there's a huge shed. Tai suppresses a grin and catches Ollie watching him fondly.

They head onto the deck. All five of them lean on the sturdy white rail and look out to the ocean. Tai stands next to Ollie. Ollie lines his hand up against Tai's on the rail and loops a finger under the string around Tai's wrist. When he glances over, his eyes are soft and hopeful.

After a moment of silence, Sunny says, "Damn, guys, it's actually kind of perfect. This has everything we want."

Hannah nods in agreement, her mouth and brows thoughtful. "It's a good place."

"You okay, Jaime?" Tai asks. The kid was quiet while they looked around. More than anyone, the Blue House has the whole of Jaime's life in it.

Jaime falters. "I don't know. Yeah. It's not the same."

"No," says Hannah under the pounding of the surf. "Sometimes we don't get to keep things exactly the same. They can still be good."

"Maybe even better," says Sunny. "You'll have all of us. Plus, there's a lot of light in that back studio. Play your cards right and you can paint there. This could be an incredible thing, James."

Jaime's still silent.

"You don't like it?" asks Ollie. Tai places his hand over Ollie's.

"It's not blue," Jaime persists. He looks down, over the railing to the sandy ground below.

"Bro," says Ollie. When Jaime lifts his head, Ollie grins. "Fucking paint it then."

ACKNOWLEDGMENTS

FIRST AND MOST, MY WIFE and my children—finest creatures on the planet and my unfailing supporters, despite two of them not understanding why I'd write a book about love rather than football or zombies.

My friends who lent me apartments and cats and cocktails and kind words and snacks, who borrowed my children and remembered me fondly despite my absence from their social calendar.

Tania—the dearest all caps cheerleader; Jo—my gift, my curse and all my inside jokes.

And finally Interlude Press. Annie delivered clarity and vision so gently that I almost overlooked how exceptional an editor she is. Candy encouraged and energised me to bring this story to people who'll love it. Choi made the book more beautiful than I even imagined. Nicki and Zoe improved my writing with kindness, humour, and fearsome competence. Lex still makes me want to write for him. I owe you all this book.

ABOUT THE AUTHOR

PENE HENSON HAS BEEN MANY things—minister's wife, barefoot beach-town kid, New York City lawyer, British boarding school matron, baseball team manager, singer in a rock band, church choir member, queer party girl, and soccer mum. A resident of Sydney, Australia, and immersed in Sydney's LGBTQIA community, she spends her non-writing time playing and watching sports, camping and boating and gazing at the ocean. She's raising two unexpectedly exceptional boys with her gorgeous wife.

She has degrees in chemistry and in law, and works in intellectual property law, contemplating other people's inventions.

She is a published poet who has long been an active writer in online communities. *Into the Blue* is her first novel.

Portrait photo by Laura Simonsen (www.laurasimonsen.com).

One **story** can change **everything.**

@interlude**press**

Twitter | Facebook | Instagram | Pinterest

*For a reader's guide to **Into the Blue** and book club prompts, please visit interludepress.com.*

interlude press

you may also like...

What It Takes by Jude Sierra

Milo met Andrew moments after moving to Cape Cod—launching a lifelong friendship of deep bonds, secret forts and plans for the future. When Milo goes home for his father's funeral, he and Andrew finally act on their attraction—but doubtful of his worth, Milo severs ties. They meet again years later, and their long-held feelings will not be denied. Will they have what it takes to find lasting love?

ISBN (print) 978-1-941530-59-7 | (eBook) 978-1-941530-60-3

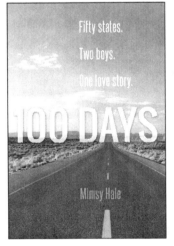

100 Days by Mimsy Hale

Jake and Aiden have been friends since childhood. Now 22-year-old college grads, they take a road trip across the United States, visiting all fifty states. A love story about two boys, an RV and a country full of highways, *100 Days* crisscrosses America as Jake and Aiden learn that their futures aren't as carefully mapped as they once thought, and that the road has a funny way of changing course.

ISBN (print) 978-1-941530-23-8 | (eBook) 978-1-941530-29-0

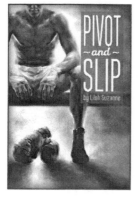

CPSIA information can be obtained at www.ICGtesting.com
Printed in the USA
LVOW11s2258140716

496351LV00001B/129/P